BURNT ECHO

A DCI EVAN WARLOW THRILLER

RHYS DYLAN

WYRMWOOD
BOOKS

COPYRIGHT

eBook ISBN 978-1-915185-12-9
Print ISBN 978-1-915185-13-6

Published by Wyrmwood Books.
An imprint of Wyrmwood Media.

EXCLUSIVE OFFER

Please look out for the link near the end of the book for your chance to sign up to the no-spam guaranteed VIP Reader's Club and receive a FREE DCI Warlow novella as well as news of upcoming releases.

Or you can go direct to my website: https://rhysdylan.com and sign up now.
Remember, you can unsubscribe at any time and I promise won't send you any spam. Ever.

BOOKS by RHYS DYLAN

The Engine House

Caution Death At Work

Ice Cold Malice

Suffer The Dead

Gravely Concerned

CHAPTER ONE

'WE COULDN'T HAVE PICKED A BETTER day.' Dennis Phillips inhaled a lungful of air and stared out across the empty grassy undulations leading up to Bryn Bras above the Rheidol Valley.

Gareth Walls looked up from adjusting his harness to follow Dennis's gaze. It wasn't the first time the older man had mentioned it and, Gareth suspected, it would not be the last. On the one hand, he was absolutely right. They could not have picked a better day for it if the weather, temperature, and situation were the only criteria.

But the prospect of clambering down a half-collapsed mineshaft, to find the root cause of the rotten smell reported to the Visitor Centre at Nant Yr Arian by a bevy of walkers over the last couple of days, raised another question altogether. No such thing as a "good day" for that, Gareth reasoned.

And yes, he realised that this provided a training opportunity, and if he wanted to be a part of the call-out team for Mid and South Wales Cave Rescue, he needed stuff like this under his belt.

When Dennis had called to say he and Arfon were

going to Ystumtuen and across to *Yr Het Fawr* on Wednesday evening, Gareth had needed a translation for the spot on the landscape: The Big Hat. An abandoned mineworks to the northwest of the village. The Visitor Centre at Nant Yr Arian, in tandem with the silver and lead Mining Museum close by, had done much to encourage people back to the area after Covid had done its worst. The establishment of the Silver-Miner's hiking trail to Devil's Bridge and beyond was proving popular with the more active visitors.

Less popular was the new and terrible stench emanating from one of the old shafts close to one trail at a lookout point. And so, Dennis, known to everyone locally as the go-to bloke for everything pothole related, had taken a call from the Centre the day before and immediately contacted Gareth to see if he was up for it.

He was.

Or, at least, in the bravado buzz following three pints of Brains SA, courtesy of the Black Lion pub, where he'd been when he took the call, he had been. But in the here and now, geared up with his two significantly more senior colleagues, second thoughts were intruding. He wasn't a complete novice, of course. He'd been down deep holes dozens of times and had even pitched up to offer his services at *Ffynnon Ogof Du* in the Beacons when a guy got trapped after falling and breaking his jaw. One of almost a hundred that turned up to offer support; a sentiment which had been applauded and admired as an example of how close knit a community cavers were.

But this… This was different. This was unglamorous, nitty-gritty stuff; just him at the bottom with the other two at the top as support.

Gareth glanced towards the raised square of dry stones marking the spot where the third member of the team, Arfon, had set up some ropes and equipment.

'Heat probably doesn't help,' Gareth said. 'With the smell, I mean.'

Arfon nodded. 'If it is a sheep or a fox that's fallen in there, it'll be cooking nicely. Mid-day the sun can get right in. Gas mark two, I reckon.'

Gareth nodded, not appreciating what Arfon's black humour was doing to his stomach after a bit too much fried breakfast that morning.

Arfon looked up and called across. 'Ready?'

'No time like the present, I suppose.' Gareth flicked the switch and checked his helmet light against the palm of his left hand, gave the harness around his shoulders a tweak, and walked to the edge.

'Funny, I can't see anything down there.' Arfon pointed his torch into the dark void one last time. 'Unless whatever fell in triggered a covering fall on top, of course. You'll know soon enough.'

He gave Gareth a lopsided grin to reveal a few missing teeth. In real life, Arfon worked for the council, fixing holes in the road. Gareth found it ironic that he would want to spend his leisure time clambering down the very things he spent his professional life filling in. But then, who was he to talk? He worked as an accountant for the university in Aberystwyth looking for holes of a sort himself. The only difference being they were financial as opposed to spatial. But, like Arfon, he, too, spent his working life trying to plug the gaps. As for Dennis, he ran a garage. Gareth sought in vain for a fitting hole analogy and could only come up with something vaguely vehicle related around holes in exhausts. But they weren't things Dennis's garage concerned itself with.

'You okay there, Gar?' Dennis asked as he walked over.

'Yeah, fine,' Gareth said, forcing a grin to shape his mouth.

'Whatever is in there, just get a rope looped around it. We'll do the lifting from up here, right?'

'Right.'

With a brief expulsive huff of air, Gareth took the offered rope from Arfon, clipped it on with a carabiner, and climbed into the shaft.

Mining for lead and silver in the Cwmystwyth area had been going on probably since the Bronze Age but had sped up in the eighteenth and nineteenth centuries. Some of the works had been big concerns. The Cwmystwyth mine itself and the area around Llywernog, where they'd created the museum, were spread over extensive areas. Here at *Yr Het Fawr*, as with other small enterprises, all that remained of mining operations were tiny scars on the landscape, laying like traps for unwary sheep or lambs.

Not much health and safety in the eighteen hundreds. Sod all a thousand years before. Though signs for the walkers, warning them to be wary, had been stuck on posts. But then Gareth didn't know any sheep who could read. Come to think of it, many of the students coming into the university these days barely had that skill. He shook his head. What was he doing thinking about illiterate students and sheep?

But he already knew the answer. These were classic distraction tactics on his mind's part. Avoiding the actual subject. The unpalatable knowledge that, at this time of year, putrefaction from dead animals set in early.

He adjusted the breather mask on his face. Yet, even through the respirator, the sweet butcher shop mix of mothballs and rotting cabbage got stronger as he descended. It wasn't a deep descent; seventy feet straight down before his boots dislodged some stones. He shifted his weight so that his feet splayed against the wall. There'd been no evidence of a fresh fall as he'd gone down, but some stones had fallen in, covering the source of the smell.

Still with his feet splayed, Gareth gave the rope one tug and felt it ease above him. He squatted on the stones and peered at the pile before slowly and methodically stacking them to one side, wondering if he'd need a bucket down here to shift some of them back up. But these crags, a mix of large and small, did not look like fresh fall. Some had spots of lichen and moss, one or two even smears of mud and grass, as if they'd been plucked from the ground above.

'Anything?' Dennis called down.

'I'm having to uncover,' Gareth called back up.

'Take your time.'

'No, thanks,' Gareth muttered. As he shifted the stones, fresh wafts of decay oozed up. 'Quicker, the better.'

He'd moved half a dozen when he saw it. Or rather, saw and felt it because as he brushed away dirt, the next stone he reached for looked, and felt, different. Firm but softer than stone. And ridged in a regular pattern. Something hand-crafted, then.

He got down closer and scrubbed harder with his gloved fingers to reveal a dark ribbed area between two lumps of granite, perhaps three inches long. As he rubbed it clean, his hand brushed against something else, dust-coated, soft, and protuberant. A jointed thing, darkly bruised, pointing at an unnatural angle down into the depths below.

The world suddenly shifted for Gareth. It felt as if the whole of his insides moved around clockwise for half a turn. Fresh sweat prickled his neck. This time cold, not hot. And suddenly, the stink of death made him gag.

Don't throw up. Do not throw up. If you throw up, you'll have to take off your mask. And if you take off your mask, the stench would be ten times worse.

Arfon's gravelly voice sang down, asking if he was okay, concern bouncing the words between his native Welsh and back again. 'Gareth? *Wyt ti'n iawn?* You haven't passed out on us, have you?'

'No.' Gareth's denial sounded more a croak than a word.

'Well, come on, *bachan*. There's money on this. Dennis says sheep, but my fiver's on fox. I got good odds for that one.'

Gareth looked up. The heads and shoulders of his two colleagues stood silhouetted against the flawless blue of the sky rendering their expressions unreadable. But later, in the pub over some fresh, cool pints in sweating glasses, Dennis would say that they had clearly seen the whites of their younger colleague's eyes all around his brown irises.

'Not a sheep,' Gareth called up. 'Unless they've grown fingers. And unless the foxes wear Adidas trainers, not one of them either. Now, can you pull me up, please? We're going to need a *much* bigger rope.'

CHAPTER TWO

DCI Evan Warlow sat on the other side of the desk from the consultant he was there to see. Sonia Emmerson, a woman in her late thirties – just a little bit older than his own surgeon son Tom – turned pages in her file, assimilating the information written there, information that might as well have been written in Sanskrit for all Warlow could make of the figures and letters. Trying to read them upside down didn't help much either.

'So, overall, looking at your bloods, things are going well. Really well.'

Warlow nodded.

'I'm not the biggest fan of an all-in-one pill. Sometimes the NNRTI's need their dosages juggling and that's difficult in a fixed combination, but in your case, the mix of emtricitabine, rilpivirine, and tenofovir are working well with minimal side effects. And this combo has come off licence, so it's cheap.'

Warlow felt the need to contribute something and so he quipped, 'Cheap is what my wife always said I was.'

Emmerson looked up, acknowledging Warlow's poor attempt at humour with a raised eyebrow and a curl of her lip. He winced, knowing he should shut up, but unable to pare back his default response to uncomfortable situations. They'd been here before, Warlow and Emmerson. Right from the beginning, in fact. When he'd been invited to attend the clinic after his screening for blood donation had thrown a spanner into the works.

Cerys Maclean, an aggressive junkie who hassled people for money, had seen fit to hide contaminated needles about her person. In an altercation he'd had no business being a part of, one of Maclean's poisoned arrows pierced Warlow's skin. He'd thought little about it. Only when Maclean OD'd in a squat six months later, did her proclivity for secreting needles in her clothes at her elbows and shoulders and headband become known to him. Even then he hadn't given it a second thought. Not even when someone muttered, 'Lucky no one got bloody AIDS from the nasty bitch.'

But the blood donor screening test picked it up. Emmerson ran tests on Warlow's liver to confirm Hepatitis and HIV, and twelve weeks of treatment followed. The combination was tricky and pharmaceutically unpleasant, but he got through it. The Hepatitis went away. The HIV didn't. Yet, it remained manageable, so she'd said, with suppression treatment. And Emmerson had done just that with Anti-Retroviral Therapy that they'd juggled between them so that now, Hepatitis free, he kept HIV at bay with just the one little pill.

'Your CD4 count is normal. And for the second time in succession, you have an undetectable viral load.'

'Does that mean truly undetectable?' Warlow asked. 'Something I'm curious about, being a detective, you know.'

Emmerson's curling lip curled a bit more. 'Most clinics classify anything under twenty copies per ml as undetectable.'

'Okay. So, not quite invisible, then, but almost?'

'It's the accepted science, Evan. It's important you understand that.'

'I do. We've got the bugger on the run.'

Emmerson sat back and placed her notes on the desk but kept hold of her pen, running the barrel through her index finger and thumb end over end on the table. A little tick that Warlow noticed. Something she did when she was gearing up to deliver something important.

'I know you will have researched this. Your son's a doctor, isn't he?'

'He is.'

'Then you'll have discussed it with him, no doubt.'

He resisted the urge to put her right on that one. Warlow knew full well where this was going. And yes, Tom knew he had HIV, but they'd never discussed the wrinkles this had regarding relationships. Besides, his family hang-ups had no role to play here with Emmerson.

'But it's important you understand the implications here on a personal level,' she continued. 'I know you gave up work because of worries over transmission, but I hope we convinced you that you pose little or no threat to others.'

Warlow nodded. Emmerson had played her part, so had some of his colleagues. A mixture of reassurance and a hope that he still had something to contribute, combined with the alternative of gardening and long walks alone as his only early retirement options, had spurred him back to work. All catalysed by a superintendent called Sion Buchannan who was short of experienced staff.

'But I also know that work is one thing and personal life is another,' Emmerson added.

Warlow waited. He was old enough to be this woman's father, but she was being a lot more grown-up about things than he was. He realised it was her job, even so, this part of the consultation was never the bit he enjoyed.

'There have been studies. Extensive studies of couples, both heterosexual and homosexual, where one partner has HIV and an undetectable viral load. No cases of HIV transmission were found in thousands of episodes of unprotected sex. You're safe, Evan.'

'There are outliers, though, right?' Warlow asked.

'Outliers? Such as?'

'Such as the chance of getting HIV from a needle stick is, according to my reading, pretty slim. And yet, I hit the jackpot.'

'Agreed.'

'What if I'm the outlier in transmissibility?'

'It's an even tinier risk,' Emmerson protested.

'That someone else has to take.'

She sighed with tempered frustration and asked a question that bordered on pitying. 'Is your glass always half empty, Evan?'

Warlow's turn to bring up the shadow of a smile. 'Depends on what I'm drinking.'

Emmerson snorted. Genuinely amused this time. 'I get it. And yes, your personal life is none of my business. But sometimes I feel patients need reminding of the facts. So, we'll see you in six months' time. You have Jenny's number?'

Warlow nodded. Jenny was a no-nonsense nurse practitioner who rang him once every couple of months.

'She's still your point of contact for anything untoward. Any issues, physical or psychological, call her.'

'I will,' Warlow said.

The look on Emmerson's face told him she didn't believe him for one minute. Not on the psychological point anyway. So much so that she added, 'You're doing brilliantly, Evan. It's safe for you to share. And I mean everything.'

Everything?

What was this? Marxist medicine 101? Warlow barely suppressed a quasi-political comment along the lines of 'up the revolution' and instead stood up, shook Emmerson's hand, and said, 'Thank you. I appreciate it.'

He walked outside into the fresh air, mulling over Emmerson's words. He'd tell the boys – his boys – the good news. He was fit and well. Yes, he creaked when he got up from a chair and had made a noise in the back of his throat when he bent to pick up his black lab's bowl. But all that was normal. A youth misspent throwing himself around a rugby field and the passage of time accounted for all that stuff.

Even so, he still had the virus. And HIV could still stick its head up out of the little hole his immune system had it trapped in. Couldn't it?

'Not if you stay on the drugs.' Emmerson's voice echoed in his head.

'Keep taking the bloody tablets it is, then, Evan,' he muttered out loud as he got into his Jeep Renegade and fired her up.

Singleton Hospital in Swansea, where Emmerson held her clinics, sat on the edge of a sweeping bay, a stone's throw from the Mumbles. On a fine August afternoon like this, and with an hour or two to spare with no pressing cases on his desk, no one would have blamed Warlow for heading down for a stroll along the coast to Langland. A celebratory jaunt after such good news. Maybe even stopping off for a Joe's ice cream on the way. If he'd had the dog, he would have done exactly that.

But she was being looked after by Molly Allanby, a colleague's daughter. She'd more or less adopted the black Labrador over the long summer holidays. He could not use her as an excuse. He needed to head back to his Pembrokeshire cottage in Nevern where he'd meet Molly and her boyfriend for a dog hand-over at six. He was looking forward to a long evening walk with Cadi after that.

So, no walk now. Instead, Warlow pointed the car north and headed through the ugly old town and up the valley. It was only eight miles to the Ynystawe intersection with the M4 that would take him quickly west. But at the lights, he continued north along the valley floor, to where his last case had taken him. To his old stomping ground at the very head of the Swansea Valley, the borderland between South Wales police's patch and Dyfed Powys's eastern fringes.

His visit to Emmerson was one reminder of his mortality. A house on the edge of waste ground near the mining village of Cwmtwrch was another.

The trial of Iwan Meredith for the murder of DI Kelvin Caldwell was yet to take place. He'd plead diminished responsibility, no doubt. He'd need some way of mitigating the fact that he'd killed three people. A fact that Warlow knew only too well since he'd narrowly avoided being number four.

Erw Foel was more a shack than a house. It stood in an isolated spot on the edge of the Patches. An area of despoiled land; the un-eco-friendly consequence of the Industrial revolution's demand for iron and coal.

Warlow hadn't been back since the incident that led to Caldwell's death. He'd seen crime scene photos of course. Pored over all the brightly lit images of where he'd lain in darkness, poleaxed from Caldwell's taser. All the while pretending to his colleagues he was seeing those images with professional detachment, whereas in truth, they were more like forbidden fruit.

The crime scene techs were long gone by now. And

though police tape still fluttered across the entrance to the pitted drive, it was more an emblem than a warning. No one had cleared the cluttered yard. The Berlingo that the killer, Meredith, used to transport other victims to a charnel house and then on to a desolate spot on the Black Mountains was gone. To the left of the front door, they'd boarded the window up with marine ply. That same window was the one Warlow's colleagues had smashed in and dragged him through and out to safety.

He sat in the car, staring at the property, wondering why he was here. On the drive up, he'd considered going in and confronting the very place Meredith did his butchery on Caldwell. The DI had been a far from innocent victim and intended Warlow harm as well. In that sense, Meredith had ironically been his saviour.

But that had not been his intention.

Warlow thought about the long dark passage in the middle of the house that led to an old slaughterhouse where the DI fell. He thought about the parlour adorned with samplers of embossed proverbs and quotes where he'd struck out with his waning strength and injured Meredith just enough to buy time for his rescuers to arrive.

But suddenly, it was enough to be outside and seeing it again. A broken-down shell of a property soaked in tragedy and horror. There would be no need to drown or wallow in it. No need to relive what he'd already relived a dozen times in the darkest stretches of the long night. He wound down the window and listened to the distant hum of cars and heard the wind gusting its regret at having to brush against this decayed corner of a once-green land.

A couple of miles away was another village. Ystradgyn-lais was in the southwestern corner of Powys with a station where they'd set up an Incident Room for the Meredith case. There was a café in that village where an old flame of Warlow's worked. She'd been kind enough to supply the team with refreshments during the investigation. He ought to go back and thank her. Especially since his departure from the case, courtesy of the taser and an emergency admission to hospital as a result had been abrupt, to say the least. Saying thanks properly would be a better use of his time than sitting here rehashing a near-death experience.

He reversed the Jeep and drove out, promising himself that he would not return, content that, like some squeezed-out festering splinter, this visit had managed to finally remove the cause of a nagging pain. He drove out and down to the river bridge across the Twrch, the winding river named after a snouting boar, and a driver paused to let him out to join the stream of traffic. A tiny act of kindness that confirmed to him he was better off among the living than revisiting the dead.

CHAPTER THREE

DI JESS ALLANBY watched her officially soon-to-be ex-husband bring the drinks across the lawn. A pint of something pale for him, lime and soda with lots of ice for her. They had umbrellas up over the tables and she welcomed the shade. It had taken just shy of an hour to get to *Pant Yr Ochain* in Gresford, on the outskirts of Wrexham, from Welshpool; delays that had more to do with summer traffic than distance. And since it took about the same time to get to the pub from Manchester, her visit north to help interview some fast-track candidates to the Dyfed Powys Force had seemed an opportune moment to deal with Rick Allanby's "we have to talk" request.

At first, Rick had said it would not be convenient. He'd agreed only after she'd pointed out that this would be his one and only chance for a one-on-one unless he wanted to drive to Cold Blow in Pembrokeshire where she rented a property.

'Not a bad little spot,' Rick said, putting the drinks on the table and looking around at the families enjoying the sunshine.

'We ate at this pub once if you remember,' Jess said.

'On the way back from a weekend in Wales. That's why I suggested it. Molly must have been about ten.'

'Oh yeah.' He nodded but without any real conviction.

He didn't remember. She could tell. They were on the terrace. Square tables with individual wooden seats under the umbrellas, picnic-style benches and tables on the lawn.

Rick pulled out a chair and folded his long legs under him. 'How'd your interviews go?'

'Okay. One good one. The rest… Not so hot.'

Rick nodded. 'Last lot we had in were rubbish.'

'The old lags that were there when we joined probably thought the same of us.' She sipped the drink. It tasted bubbly and tart. She almost said it out loud but knew it would give Rick ammunition. She could almost hear him say, 'Like you, eh, Jess?'

'Mol okay?' Rick asked and swallowed an inch of ale before he got an answer.

'She's fine. Enjoying the summer.'

'All she ever sends me are selfies of her and your DCI's dog. Or her and her boyfriend and the dog.'

Jess nodded. 'She and Cadi have bonded.'

'Doesn't he ever look after her, Warlow?'

'He does. But he's busy…' She paused before adding, 'Like me.'

'Like we all are, Jess.'

She smiled. It didn't take much for the real Rick to break through the veneer. These days, with the benefit of distance, she wondered how she put up with all his passive-aggressive bullshit. You became inured to it, she supposed. Marriage and familiarity had a lot to answer for, sometimes. 'Exactly. So, let's not mess about pretending we're here for a cosy chat and peanuts.'

Rick's brows curled down. A tick she recognised as a mark of belligerence. In times past, he would have protested, accused her of being uncharitable, but those days were long gone. He sat forward. 'I tried to talk to you when I came down to see Molly.'

'The day you argued with her, and she lost Cadi, you mean?'

'You can't blame me for a dog running off.'

'Molly does. She said you were helicoptering her. Interfering.'

'She's still my daughter, Jess.'

'She is. But she's all *growed* up, Rick.' Jess affected a terrible American accent for that one. 'Time you accepted that.'

'It's hard, as a dad.'

No denying that. Her own father had struggled with the same thing. But there was no stopping it and she didn't feel like giving any ground. Instead, she brought the conversation back to the present. 'But Molly's not here. I am, and I'm all ears. And please don't let this be you asking me for understanding or forgiveness. Because if it is, I'm leaving now.'

Rick's face fell. 'We've signed the papers, haven't we?'

'We have. And my solicitor says it's all going through, swimmingly.'

'I still don't know why we need that extra expense. I'm not contesting anything.'

'Yeah. Big of you.'

He sighed. 'I am sorry, though. Genuinely.' He kept his eyes down mostly, flicking them up from his pint occasionally to gauge Jess's reaction.

'So am I. But only for what we've put Molly through. Nothing else.'

Rick nodded. 'That's why I wanted to speak to you. I've got into a bit of trouble and…' He stopped, searching for the words.

Jess waited, but Rick seemed to fold in on himself.

'What kind of trouble?' she prompted, unable to suppress the irritation in her voice.

He wouldn't look at her now. Saying what he had to say instead with his eyes on the drink in front of him. 'I did someone a favour. A friend of a friend. Lost some paperwork on a speeding fine and made a stupid charge disappear. It was nothing, honestly. He was grateful, this friend of a friend. Got me some freebies to a United game. Only, when I went, it wasn't just a seat. It was the full soddin' Monty. Box. Booze. Food. The works. Only thing missing was the dancing girls. People were nice. I didn't know anyone. Neither did Helen.'

'Was the friend of a friend anything to do with her, by any chance?' Jess tried and failed to keep the accusatory tone at bay.

'As is happens, yeah, it was. So, a couple of weeks later, someone delivers an envelope addressed to me. Inside is a phone. I get a call asking me to eyeball some information. Progress of a charge. I didn't. I thought they'd delivered the phone to the wrong person. A snitch playing silly beggars. But then I got some more messages telling me they knew I'd accepted a bribe for losing that paperwork on the friend of a friend's case. Photos of me in the box. Photos of the charge sheet I thought I'd lost.'

Jess shook her head. 'Doesn't sound like much of a friend,' she muttered.

'Not anymore. Point is, I found out that the box is leased by a big cheese. Someone who doesn't get his hands dirty. You know the type. Squeaky clean on the outside. Kosher business, recycling plant and some restaurants. But dirty as a sack of dogshit on the inside. Money laundering, cocaine deals, you name it. And now I'm linked to him.'

'Jesus, Rick.' Jess squeezed her eyes shut.

'I know, I've been stupid, right? But I turned it into an opportunity. I talked to the higher ups. They want me to play Big Cheese's game. Tag along and let him think I'm hooked.'

'So, swimming with piranhas, then?'

'Kind of. And if the shit hits the fan, I'll have to disappear. Me and Helen. Witness protection. The works.'

'So, if Molly hears nothing from you, you'll be someone else? Somewhere else?'

'There's a chance that might happen.' This time, he held Jess's gaze. She read fear and a pleading for understanding there.

'But I can't tell her that, can I?' she asked, confused.

Rick shook his head and let his eyes drop again.

'What is it you're not telling me?' she pressed him.

'This guy… The big cheese. He's ruthless, Jess. He's had people knee-capped and worse. He warns people that if they cross him, he takes it out on their families.'

'Oh my God. Are you serious?' Jess was helpless to stop her voice from rising. 'First of all, you throw away every soddin' thing we had, and now… Now you're in an episode of the soddin' Sopranos?'

'He only knows me as a cop with a girlfriend. I'm hoping—'

'If anything ever happens to Molly, I swear I will find you and rip off your testicles. The ones that got us into all this bloody trouble to start with.'

Rick reached for his drink but didn't pick it up because his hand shook too much. 'I've been dreading telling you.' He wiped sweat from his brow with trembling fingers. 'And don't worry. If anything ever happened to Molly because of me, I'll save you the trouble of finding me. I'll cut my balls off myself.'

'You're such a—' Jess's phone ringing saved her from breaking one of her rules of never using a word she wouldn't call herself. 'Rhys? What can I do?'

The DC's voice sounded distant and on the move.

'We've been summoned, ma'am. Body down an old mine-shaft up near Aberystwyth.'

She glared at Rick. She could have found an excuse not to go, but a body down a mineshaft sounded a great deal better than sitting here with Tricky Ricky one moment longer.

'Does Warlow know?' Jess spoke into the phone, her eyes still on her ex.

'I'm about to, ma'am.'

'Okay. Text me the location. I'll see you there.'

She put the phone face down on the table. 'I have to go.'

'Really?'

'Yes. Really. Work. And anyway, what is there left to say?'

Rick took on a pained expression. 'I thought I was doing the right thing here, Jess.'

'You wouldn't know the right thing if it fell on you from a passing 777.'

'That's bloody harsh.'

'Yes, it is.' She stood and glowered down at him. 'I can look after myself, Rick. But if any of this comes back on Molly...' She shook her head and made a scissoring movement with her fingers. 'I'll keep those secateurs bloody sharp.'

————

WARLOW APPROACHED A ROUNDABOUT. Ystradgynlais and the café was a left, the road back to Pembrokeshire was a right. Two options. Picturesque across the hills, or a faster route back to the M4. It should have been a simple decision. He and the woman who ran the café had history. A good history. One where indiscretions had been forgiven and, for once, he'd done nothing he regretted. And hadn't he just had the all-clear from Emmerson to... Explore his options?

He'd thought about Betsy a lot since they'd met by chance while he'd been investigating the Meredith case. She'd been his first genuine love. And no matter how clichéd it sounded, the first love was always the sweetest, and, when it ended, left the deepest wound and a bitter scar. From syrup to sour in one rollercoaster teenage ride. He'd been surprised at how regretful she'd seemed, even after all these long and winding years.

The noise of Led Zeppelin's opening chords to *Heart-breaker* broke his reverie. The contact's name was a familiar one, and he pressed a button on the dashboard screen to accept the call.

'Rhys, what's up? Where are you?'

'On the way to Nant Yr Arian, sir. Fifteen miles east of Aberystwyth. We've had a shout. There's a body down a mineshaft.' The DC's voice came through a rumble and hiss of background engine noise. But his words released a memory from Warlow's childhood that, despite the flashing red light in his brain warning him he'd regret it, he felt suddenly inclined to explore with an amusing little comment.

'You never auditioned for *Lassie*, did you, Rhys?'

'*Lassie*, sir? Was that the one about the Scottish drug-addict prostitute who turned a corner and almost became First Minister?'

'No,' Warlow's reply was slow and low. 'It was a TV show from my youth about a Collie dog who was always finding people who'd fallen down wells and was able, despite being a dog, to somehow miraculously impart that information to its owner.'

For several long seconds, only the murmuring growl of the engine came back to Warlow through the speaker until some whispering and a stifled laugh broke through.

'Who is with you in that car, Detective Constable?'

'Sergeant Richards, sir.'

'Right, forget I ever mentioned *Lassie*, but make sure the sergeant gives you a bowl of water when you arrive.'

A muted giggle followed.

'You've contacted DI Allanby?'

'Just did, sir.'

'Good. Get up there and keep me informed.'

Warlow pulled up at the roundabout. Still thinking about the café and the woman there. She was married; he knew that. But he remained ignorant regarding the state of the arrangement. From their last meeting, he'd discerned hints it might not be altogether rosy. But frankly, that should not be his concern either way. He was lying to himself by suggesting a visit to her was anything other than an exploration of buried feelings from long ago. And whereas he might have a badge of office, and even a certificate of validation – no detectable virus, yay – it wasn't the right thing to do.

He could text his thanks for the cakes.

As for anything else, he already had someone to spend his days and nights with. She was black and furry and loved him even when he burped too loudly. She didn't care if he had the virus or not.

And when it came down to it regarding the woman in the café, or women in general, there was always that one in a million chance buzzing around his conscience like an irritating mozzie. And he simply couldn't ignore that. Not yet.

A car pulled up behind him. Decision time. Rhys's call meant that decision was already made.

He indicated, pulled out into traffic, and went around the roundabout to head back up towards the hills.

CHAPTER FOUR

ALMOST EIGHT-YEAR-OLD HELEDD RAMPLEY sat next to her
father on a sofa that had seen better days, and with more
than one family, according to the charity shop Joel
Rampley bought it from. Heledd, untroubled at her age by
the trappings of wealth, spared no thought for the sofa,
other than noticing a few saggy bits which she sometimes
sank into and had learned to avoid. But where she sat now,
cwtched up to her dad with the telly on, seemed totally fine.
They were watching *Malory Towers* on iPlayer. Though it
fascinated her and made her laugh and sometimes cry,
Heledd wasn't sure she'd want to be away in a school all on
her own. Even if the girls of the second form seemed not
to mind too much and always made the best of it.

To begin with, her father had not been too keen for her
to watch a programme about privileged kids in a boarding
school. But, as *Tadcu* – the Welsh name she gave to her
grandfather – pointed out, the kids had the same problems
everyone else had in making friends, making mistakes, and
dysfunctional family backgrounds. Ms Blyton understood
that, even if the stories were of their time and not a reflec-
tion of today's society. And of course, the BBC put its very

inclusive stripe upon the modern reworking to take care of all that. But you could not take away the fact that it was a private school and so, yes, the girls all had a cushion of money that enabled them to play out the drama of their issues in an exclusive setting and away from the meddling voices of adults. But it didn't change what the kids were going through daily. Heledd's dad listened and, after sitting through an episode, and seeing the lights go on in his daughter's eyes, he'd grudgingly agreed.

'Victims come in all shapes, colours, genders, and backgrounds, Joel,' Carwyn Hughes had said. 'Though some of them shout a lot louder than the others. The sooner Heledd understands that, the better, because the truth can sometimes get lost in all the noise.'

Heledd had not understood what *Tadcu* meant, but she didn't care. She liked *Malory Towers*. And, just like her heroine Daryl, Heledd had a great deal to look forward to. A birthday loomed. Dad was taking her to McDonald's and then to the pictures to see *Dogtown*. And on Sunday, *Tadcu* had booked them in to Kartwheels where she was going to drive her own Go Kart around the track.

What Heledd didn't know was if her mother would be there for the big day. Since she'd gone away this time, her dad had been a bit weird when she'd asked him questions about it. Not the first time Mirain Hughes had left, and it would not be the last, she knew. Heledd's dad called them "Mam's away days". Sometimes he waved his finger around in a circle at the side of his head when he said the word "away", but never when *Tadcu* was around, and only ever after he'd swigged two or more of his cans from the fridge. Mostly, he'd say things like, 'she'll be back before you can say superdocious.'

Heledd knew he meant a much longer word, but he could never remember it, so he shortened it instead. Dad always got things wrong. Not like Mam. She never got things wrong unless she got a bit airy-fairy, as Dad said, again with the rotating finger after a couple of lagers. It was when she got airy-fairy that she sometimes went on away days.

Tadcu never used words like airy-fairy. He'd simply said that Mirain sometimes got a bit confused and forgot to take her tablets. That was when she went away. Once even for an entire month. But she'd come back when she woke up from the dreams that made her confused, he explained.

Alistair used much bigger words when he tried to explain the absences to Heledd. He'd told her that her mum was a pipe-poler. Alistair, the man that Mirain lived with, and whose nice new house she stayed at with Heledd could be a bit serious like that. Mirain moved in with Alistair nearly a year ago, sharing Heledd with her real dad. Alistair was always trying to make friends with Heledd by giving her things. But she couldn't *cwtch* up on the sofa with him because he wasn't her dad. What Alistair had instead was a gigantic TV in his living room stuck to the wall like a painting and a smaller one in Heledd's bedroom. Alistair quite liked it when Heledd stayed in her bedroom and watched TV, whereas her mam kept telling her to read instead. That was why Heledd liked *Malory Towers*. Watching it seemed like reading and seeing at the same time. *Tadcu* told her that *Malory Towers* was a book before it landed on TV. He'd even given her a copy.

But Alistair had never heard of *Malory Towers*. It shocked him when Mam went away this time. But after Mirain had left, and before she'd moved back to be with her father, he'd shown Heledd the notes she'd sent them both on WhatsApp and Facebook. Mirain posted messages saying she'd gone to find the Enlightener who would tell her where she needed to be. Once she was there, she'd send for Heledd and they could be all together again. Heledd did not know who the Enlightener was. Her granddad used the Welsh word, *Goleuwr.* Someone who sometimes appeared in Mirain's dreams.

Her father, Joel, let Heledd look at Mirain's Facebook page, too.

'She's off on a good one this time,' he'd said when he'd read the messages about the Enlightener.

'Will she find the Enlightener soon?' Heledd asked.

'I bloody well hope so, darling.'

When the episode of *Malory Towers* finished, Heledd asked her dad to switch on the iPad and look at Mirain's Facebook page. But today, there was no message. And nothing on WhatsApp either. No silly emojis or xxxs.

'She's probably out looking for mushrooms.'

'Mushrooms?'

Joel Rampley smiled at his daughter. 'I'm being silly, Hel. Come on, time to get you to bed. School tomorrow. And remember, *Tadcu* will pick you up and give you your tea, right?'

Joel hugged her, and she gave him a smile that was going to break a hundred hearts when she was older. He always said she smiled exactly like Mirain. In fact, everyone said she was a mini version of her mam. But Joel would look at her sadly whenever she reminded him of that and say, 'You do. But let's hope you're a bit different, too. You don't want to end up having all those away days, do you?'

She'd thought about that and shaken her head. She wouldn't want to miss anyone's birthday.

———

WARLOW MADE good time on bad roads the following morning. By bad, he meant nothing straight for more than a third of a mile, with minimal passing points, even though the traffic was light. Par for the course in this patch of West

Wales. Something he factored in on his journeys, so that when he turned up earlier than expected, it gave him a little ripple of satisfaction. What did that voice from the Sat Nav world know, anyway?

Though the crime scene was only fifteen miles from the university seaside town of Aberystwyth, it might as well have been a hundred and fifty, given the barren nature of the landscape. Warlow had made his approach cross-country from the South, avoiding the busy coast road, and the way became emptier and wilder as the miles ticked by.

They flagged him through to a marked-off parking area next to some stacked logs on the edge of a woodland outside the village of Ystumtuen. Though village would be stretching things a bit in the descriptive sense. Hamlet would have been nearer the mark, with a few houses in the little hollows accessed only by single-track roads and the only street a line of three or four houses next to a chapel and an old school.

Rhys Harries waved a greeting and handed Warlow an enamel mug full of steaming tea as the DCI got out of his car and stretched.

'Thought you might need it after the winding roads, sir.'

Warlow took the mug, unable to hide his surprise. 'Tea? Did I miss the sign to the café?'

Rhys grinned. 'The Visitor Centre sent us a van with hot water, tea, and coffee. The find is on one of their walking routes, and they called it in. Or at least one of their punters picked up on the foul smell coming from a hole in the ground.'

'Misplaced guilt, you think?'

The young DC shrugged.

Warlow studied the steam coiling up from the mug with suspicion. 'I expect you asked Povey's forensic lot to do a quick check for toxic substances in this?'

'Good one, sir.' Rhys's chortle fizzled out when he saw the look Warlow threw him.

'Did it not occur to you that whoever put that body in a mineshaft might be just as capable of lacing a couple of urns with strychnine in order to derail the whole investigative team?'

Rhys's face fell in horror. 'Not really, sir, I—'

'In order that they might buy some time to sod off to the costa del come and find me?'

Rhys swallowed loudly, no doubt reconsidering his own already consumed mug of tea in a new and altogether less favourable light. 'It was just a mug of tea. I didn't think anything of it—'

'Good. Delighted to hear it. If you had, I'd have had you certified.' Warlow took a sip and smacked his lips. 'Good brew. What sort of world would we be living in if that kind of thinking occurred to you whenever we were offered refreshments by some kind soul with a soft spot for the police?'

Rhys closed a mouth that had dropped open.

Warlow enjoyed the younger man's momentary confusion. Keeping him on his toes enough to recognise a Mickey-take when one was being dropped upon him was Warlow's constant goal in life. Let him ponder that one. Worse would undoubtedly ambush him during his police career. The DCI turned away to look at the surrounding landscape. They were on higher ground with little or no horizon to view, but with the land rising to the North and a single farmhouse way in the distance. Back along the lane, the rural idyll was blighted by someone deciding to use a field as a breaker's yard for old farm machinery, tractors, various bits of equipment with jutting arms and tubes, some old fridges, and a couple of decrepit caravans. A jumble of police vehicles stood untidily clustered around the field entrance. This was wild country. Open and windswept. Warlow had done a bit of reading up the night before. The Romans had mined here. He did not envy them the occupation. No doubt regretting it from day one, battered by the woad-streaked Celts on the one hand, and the unremitting weather on the other.

'Catrin and Jess made it yet?' Warlow asked.

'They're over at the Visitor Centre, a couple of miles up the road, sir. Getting background info on the people who called it in.'

'The body?'

'Just out, sir.'

That was a pleasant surprise. 'Really? Then why the hell are we wasting time here rabbiting on about tea and the one in a million chance it's poisoned? You need to get a grip, Rhys. Now, lead on, MacDuck.'

Rhys hesitated. 'Is that Shakespeare, sir?'

'A bastardised bit of it, yes. It should be "lay on, MacDuff", but that variation is the phrase Emlyn the Impaler, an old rugby coach of mine with a penchant for forgetting people's names, used as a generic. At least what he used for the players he liked. He was the kind of coach no one dared correct, unless you wanted to spend a lot of time doing press-ups. So, lead on, MacDuck, is what he used when he wanted someone to get on with it.'

'Thank you, sir.' Rhys's slightly crestfallen response was not lost on Warlow.

'Don't take it personally, Detective Constable. Lucky I didn't use the phrase he reserved for the players he didn't like. That one's a beauty. Suffice to say the adulterated name rhymes with duck. I don't think I need to draw a diagram, do I?'

Rhys shook his head.

'Good. Now, if you're done with the Q and A, let's go. Time's a wasting.'

CHAPTER FIVE

DI JESS ALLANBY and DS Catrin Richards stood in the office next to the shop at the Visitor's Centre at Nant Yr Arian. Though calling it an office would be a stretch which was something Jess had been tempted to do, to see if she might be able to actually touch the walls on either side of the space they stood in. There was no room to sit, even if they'd wanted to.

Lorna Dickson, the deputy manager, sat hunched over behind a cheap desk next to a bank of battered filing cabinets. A nervous woman in a baggy sweatshirt with the Red Kite logo emblazoned on the chest, she'd taken off her glasses and, with her pale face only six inches from an exercise book, riffled through it searching the entries.

'Ah, yes, here it is.' She looked up with a triumphant smile on a flat face. 'Knew I'd seen it. Wasn't me who took the call, but I'd noticed the report.' She laughed nervously. 'I mean, someone has to, otherwise the world would descend into chaos, right?'

The two detectives waited. When, after several seconds of Dickson's grin, nothing else seemed to be forthcoming,

Catrin patiently repeated the question they'd asked five minutes before.

'You have the date and time of that entry?'

Dickson blinked and swallowed, grimaced, and let out a what-am-I-like guffaw. 'Oh my God, my head is well and truly in the shed today. I don't know what's wrong with me.'

Catrin nodded. She did. Even the most upstanding citizen could lose their composure when confronted by two officers investigating a suspicious death. It was as if behind the perfectly innocent question of how and when the Centre first got a report of a terrible smell emanating from the ground on one of their trails, lurked something altogether more insidious. Something designed to crowbar out of the person being questioned a confession about the day they got on and off the train to Bangor without paying the full fare.

Dickson's eyes fell to the notebook again. 'Umm, yes, let's see… Right… 11.20am, the 22nd of August.'

Catrin wrote it down in her notebook.

'Were there any more complaints?' Jess asked.

Once again, the question seemed to floor Dickson, until meaning seeped in.

'Oh, yes. Two more. I know because I took one of them.' She turned a page in the book and let out a zippy, 'Yep, this time it's my handwriting. One call at 10.17am, the other at 2.30pm, though the second time wasn't a call. The hiker came back to the Centre and reported it. It's a circular walk.'

'Did they give a name, by any chance?'

Dickson blinked and froze again. 'No. The woman who complained, she said the smell was really bad. Rotting was the word she used. I mean, we had no idea it could be a person… I am so sorry.'

'No need to be,' Catrin said. 'You weren't to know how this would turn out.'

'I suppose.'

Jess gave her a reassuring smile. 'Thanks for this, though. Always helpful in establishing a timeline.'

Dickson had the sort of demonstrative face that, when unhappy, constantly looked on the verge of tears. 'Have you... I mean, is it... Has someone fallen in? I haven't been able to sleep. We had no idea the shaft was so dangerous.'

'I don't think you need to worry about that, Lorna.' Jess chose her words carefully. They'd released no information about the find and the removal team who'd found the body were, as yet, sworn to secrecy until they established the dead man's identity. 'I doubt any of this will come back on you.'

'Really?' Dickson's delight was almost childlike.

Jess sent Catrin a side-eyed glance and Catrin shut her notebook. 'Do you have maps, by any chance?'

'Of course.' This was solid ground for the deputy manager at last. 'We have half a dozen trails, all carefully mapped out. The Miner's Trail, the Silver Tramway, the Lead Road—'

'Could we have some?' Catrin cut her off.

'They're on the wall outside, next to the shop.' Lorna got out from behind the desk. Even though she was stick-thin, she had to squeeze past the detectives to the door. Catrin and Jess followed into the bigger space of the atrium, where a sizeable café catered for visitors. Dickson hovered next to a wall containing shelving units stuffed with pamphlets. As they reached the shelves, a man with a dirt-smudged face dressed in a smock and scruffy trousers walked towards them.

'Ah, Lorna. We're off to sort out that fallen tree up on

the Ridge Walk. The path is clear, but it needs tidying. I'll be back in time for feeding.'

'Thanks, Simon,' Lorna sang back. On seeing Jess's inquisitive expression, she explained. 'We feed the Kites,' she pointed to her badge, 'they're carrion feeders. They're trained to be around at three when we throw out the food.'

'Do many people come for that?'

Dickson's eyebrows shot up. 'It'll be packed. All year round.'

'So, families and kids?'

Dickson nodded. 'We get three sorts of visitors. Families, often with small children, who come to see the Kites being fed. They may walk around the lake if the weather is good, or they'll have a cup of tea in the café and visit the shop.'

Jess glanced outside at the little groups sitting at picnic tables.

'Then there are the mountain bikers. You'll spot them. They'll be the ones covered in mud and wearing T-shirts over their long-sleeved shirts. And then there are the walkers.'

'We've had a look around. You have running routes and walking routes?' Catrin had spotted the maps dotted all over the car park.

'Yep. They would be the Miner's Walk and the Ridge Walk. Not too far, either. You could do them all in under three hours. They're all marked with information boards and sculptures highlighting the mining heritage.'

Jess picked up a brochure. This one for the Mining Museum further down the road. 'Are you linked to the museum?'

'No. It's a private concern. They do interactive tours in costume, that sort of thing. They like to give people a flavour of what it was truly like.'

'Damp, cold, dark, and dirty,' Catrin said.

'Oh, have you done a tour?' Dickson asked.

'No, but a mine is a mine.'

Dickson's smile faltered, but she recovered enough to turn to the shelves and pick out a couple of brochures.

'What's the entry fee?' Jess asked.

'Ten pounds. Fifteen if you want the tour. There's the Pig's Trotter Café, too, and a very interactive display of old tools and methods, as well as the Sow Hall.'

Jess nodded. 'I have a daughter. She's seventeen, but she'd love all this with the Red Kites.' She tapped the museum brochure. 'And this might just be quirky enough to be up her street, oddly enough.'

'I'm sure we could arrange a discount—'

The look from Jess stopped her dead. 'That won't be necessary, Ms Dickson.' Jess turned again to the maps on the wall. 'I see that there are paths across the road, too. Leading back towards… What's it called, Istimteen?'

'Ystumtuen, ma'am,' Catrin corrected her. '"Y" as in "huh", "stum" as in "dim" and "tuen" as in… "Brien".'

'What she said.' Jess grinned.

Dickson joined her at the map. 'Yes, well, the keen walkers finish the routes here quickly and, as you will see, there are cairns and more evidence of mining activity all over the place. You can indeed walk from here back towards Ystumtuen and all the way to the river at Cwmrheidol. Not many people use them, but it's on those paths that the report of the awful smell came to us. I mean, we're not responsible for them. They're rights of way on private land.'

The detectives took their leave and walked back to the parked pool Focus. 'What's with all the pig references?' Catrin asked.

'Pig was what they called the heavy ingots of lead and silver ore that were shipped back to Rome after being dug out of the British earth,' Jess said.

Catrin tilted her head. 'Every day's a school day with you, ma'am.'

Jess shrugged. 'I'm no expert, but I helped my daughter through her GCSE's, don't forget. In other words, I've done a refresher course. I expect Rhys might have more to say if you asked him.'

Catrin rolled her eyes. 'Oh, God, that would be a long half hour I'd never get back.'

Jess grinned. She imagined the young DC waxing lyrical about Roman Wales. On the road, they passed a sign for an alternative route to Aberystwyth, prompting Jess to ask, 'Didn't you go to university up here?'

Catrin nodded and two little red spots appeared on her cheeks. 'You have a good memory, ma'am. I did. But only for a year. I changed tack and transferred out to Swansea. It's one of the top ten in the country anyway for criminology. Plus, I lived at home for the first year after wasting twelve months at the seaside.'

'Did you enjoy your year up here?'

The reply, when it came, seemed to groan under the weight of unspoken baggage. 'Honest truth? Not in the slightest. Wrong course, wrong people.'

Jess waited, but the DS did not elaborate, and she did not probe. Catrin Richards was an outstanding officer. A terrier when it came to work, and Jess had worked with her long enough to appreciate when to give her space. These questions about her past had nothing to do with why they were here and if she decided to open up about it, she no doubt would.

Changing the subject, Jess unfolded the brochures Dickson had provided and studied the map of the extended Miner's Trail, using her finger to trace it to a point known as *Yr Het Fawr.*

CHAPTER SIX

WARLOW AND RHYS walked up towards the "Apache Village" – the irreverent name DS Gil Jones used to refer to the CSI Tyvek tents whenever they were called to a crime scene. They were north of the hamlet of Ystumtuen on the fringes of the Rheidol Valley. This was hill country, with rolling green pastures dotted with sheep and conifer plantations. Very much the norm for rural Ceredigion in this part of Wales. But the Apache Village stood out like a sore white thumb on a reed-strewn patch which, given that it was August, looked reasonably dry. Warlow had hiked enough of this land to know that it would be treacherous and boggy come October and would stay like that for six months or more.

Above, sluggish cottonwool clouds failed to blot out the sun and, under their white jumpsuits, Warlow wondered if the techs were down to their underwear on a warm day like today. As they climbed the slope, the DCI and Rhys quickly shed their jackets and ties. They reached the path and a signpost showing distance and direction to Devil's Bridge and Nant Yr Arian.

Warlow spotted Alison Povey, the senior crime scene

investigator, suited and booted in her usual white onesie, waving to them from outside one of the tents. Unusually, her hood was down, and her round face looked red from the heat of the day.

'Glad you made it,' she said. Povey was a straight talker. 'Once you've had a shufti, we'll get him off to be sliced and diced.'

'HOP been?'

'Yes. Tiernon turned up, as happy-go-lucky as usual.' Povey's wry smile told Warlow that Tiernon had been his curmudgeonly self. Though he wasn't the worst Home Office Pathologist in the Cardiff-based Forensic Pathology department, he languished at the bottom of the league table for comedic prowess and bonhomie. And none of the others were on the stand-up circuit either. Not that any of those things were a requisite in this line of work, but a little dark humour went a long way, Warlow had found.

'He wanted to get the PM done this afternoon, if poss,' Povey added.

'Understandable. This sort of weather isn't kind to the dead.'

'Agreed. No time like the present.' Povey pulled back the tent flap. Two white-suited and masked techs were attending to the body, photographing, and teasing aside folds of clothing to allow better views. Where material adhered to the flesh from the glue of seeping fluids, they'd left it well alone.

A good few days' growth of designer stubble on the side of the visible part of the face immediately gave the corpse a gender, which was just as well because whoever this was had gone headfirst into the shaft. The flattened skull and distorted features would not make ID easy, even for someone who had known this man in life.

'There's not much blood in the shaft itself. What there is may have come from oozing,' Povey said.

'So, he was dead before he ended up here?' Warlow asked sharply.

Povey nodded. 'Tiernon thought so, too.'

Already putrefaction had caused the corpse to swell and bloat. The exposed parts of the torso where the shirt had ridden up were stained a dark purple from lividity.

'Any clue as to the cause of death?' Warlow asked.

Povey shook her head. 'Too early to say. The skull is smashed, as is the left side of the face. That could be from the fall. Could be from a blunt instrument. Tiernon will be better placed to tell. But there is something you ought to see. He was doubled over in the shaft and we've straightened him out a bit. But when they found him, his right hand reached back up to where his right foot was.' Povey walked around the body and indicated the fingers of the right hand. 'See them?'

Warlow did and couldn't help but grimace. The tips of the index, middle, and ring fingers were all bent, broken at the terminal joint to point backwards unnaturally. 'From the fall?' he asked.

'No. They're all too regular. And, close up, there are ridges in the skin.'

'What does that mean?' Rhys asked, his eyes alight with genuine interest.

'My best guess is that the fingers were clamped in a vice and a weight brought down on the outstretched back of the hand, causing the joints to snap. I've seen it once or twice before.'

Warlow sighed. 'Lucky you love your job, eh, Alison?'

'Does that mean an accident?' Rhys asked.

'No accident,' Povey said.

'Torture, Rhys,' Warlow explained. 'Someone has had their way with this chap before throwing him down the mineshaft. Speaking of which…' Warlow stood up.

Povey led the way back out and walked a dozen steps

to the spot where Arfon had fed Gareth Walls his rope before he'd clambered into the shaft of *Yr Het Fawr*. The three of them peered into the ragged hole in the ground and Povey shone her torch in. Warlow was struck by its narrowness.

'No way he would have fallen headfirst into this,' he said.

'No,' Povey agreed. A strapped-up tech looked ready to descend the shaft once more. 'We're removing layers of debris as we go. There's a lot of it. My guess is someone threw most of it down on top of the body.'

'So, definitely not an accident,' Rhys summed up.

'Most definitely not an accident,' Povey replied.

Warlow stood up and peered around. From where he stood, he could look back and east towards the empty hills and isolated spinneys. This was another desolate spot. Not overlooked, which made hiding a corpse easier, but difficult to get to, which made it harder to get a body up here. But one thing was obvious. 'I suspect it's safe to say that we are at the site of a very unlawful death.'

———

RHYS STAYED BEHIND with Povey while Warlow went back to his car. Jess had texted to say they were on the way and the DCI was waiting for them when they pulled up.

'You've seen the body?' Jess asked when she and Catrin got out of the Focus.

Warlow nodded. 'Just. You?'

'We watched it being lifted out. Luckily, I'd avoided breakfast.'

'Any joy at the Visitor Centre?'

Catrin consulted her notebook. 'First report of the unpleasant aroma was the twenty-second. A few more followed. Then they sent a team out to verify the shaft.'

'Right, so this man, whoever he is, has been missing for days. Get Gil to check for any missing persons reports.'

Catrin nodded. 'Where's Rhys?'

'Still with Povey.'

'I'll catch up with him. We need to brief the Uniforms on getting a proper search of the area set up.'

Warlow watched her go before turning to Jess. 'You okay?'

'As okay as anyone who's seen a body come up from a mineshaft.'

'I meant after your meeting with Rick.'

Jess lifted her chin and sucked in some good air before letting it out with a sigh. 'Hunky-dory. Rick wanted to see me because he's been a naughty boy.'

'I thought you knew that.'

'Nothing to do with trying to keep his fly zipped shut. This time it's work related. An organised crime syndicate has set him up.' Jess let out a mirthless laugh of disbelief. 'Asked him to find something out and then offered some tickets to a match in gratitude. Bribery, in other words.'

'Oh, Christ.'

'That's not the worst part. Ricky always fancied himself as a bit of an action man. So, he went to his bosses and IA and they want him to assume the charade and gather intel.'

'Not a good game to play,' Warlow said.

'No. And the gang boss is a nasty piece of work that has already threatened Rick and anyone he knows.'

Warlow couldn't hide his shock. 'What the hell is he doing that for?'

'Himself. As always. He has a macho streak as big as a skunk's stripe.'

'But if he's putting you or Molly in danger—'

'He assures me that the OC boss only knows about him and his girlfriend.'

'Still, it's—'

'Crap. Agreed.' Jess inhaled through a couple of flared nostrils. 'Don't worry. He knows where I stand.'

'Is there anything I can do?'

'You can take my mind off my ex by telling me what the hell is going on here.'

Warlow hesitated, but then shrugged. 'Let's go up to the path. To where the walkers noticed the smell.'

They walked across the tussocks and climbed back up to a point just east of the Apache Village while Warlow explained about the torture and the assumption that the body hadn't died from the fall into the shaft until they got to a point just north of the opening.

'Weather's been like this for the last week. The Met Office has the prevailing winds from the Southwest. At about this point, the wind would come over the open mouth of the shaft.'

Jess stood with hands on hips, looking around. The path roughly descended to the Southeast and ascended to the Northwest. A quad bike track led off across the fields to the left. Not the muddy tracks of something well used, merely a paucity of grass where the tyre had been. 'If the body was brought here, it would either have been carried or transported.' She nodded at the tracks. 'I'll text Catrin. Get some bodies out to follow where those lead.'

'Good idea.'

But such tracks were commonplace. Quad bikes were, these days, many farmers' chosen mode of transport across these hills.

'Have you been to this neck of the woods before?' Warlow asked.

Jess shook her head.

'Nor me. It's an extensive area. I know we're near to the hydroelectric power plant at Rheidol Reservoir, and I've been to Devil's Bridge.'

Jess cocked her eye.

'What?' Warlow asked.

'Oh, come on. You're the font of all knowledge in this stuff. There must be a legend attached to a name like Devil's Bridge.'

Warlow grinned. 'Something to do with a cow getting lost across a river and the old woman who owned old Daisy making a deal with the devil to build a bridge in return for the soul of the first living thing to cross it. The old woman sent her dog over and cheated the devil. I think I'd have preferred it if she'd gone over instead.'

'That's because you're a dog softie. How is she, by the way?'

'Cadi? Ask your daughter. She's going to forget what I look like. Cadi, I mean, not Molly. That girl's got a memory like a pachyderm.'

'We realise she's a bit of an eidetic.'

'Is she on tablets or the injections?'

Jess's side-eyed look was long suffering. 'Careful you don't cut yourself on that wit of yours, Detective Chief Inspector.'

Warlow grinned. 'Explains a lot, though. We had one of those in school. Did bugger all work and looked at the books the night before the exams. Not quite a photographic memory, but as near as damn it.' Warlow contemplated the path some more. 'I think I'd like to walk this trail. Get a feel for it.'

'Now?'

'No. We need to set up an Incident Room and—'

He was cut off by a shout from Rhys, who was hurrying across the moor towards them. The DC looked pleased with himself when he arrived. He blurted out the words breathlessly. 'Bit of luck, sir. They've just found a wallet in the shaft. Povey thinks it could have fallen out when he fell.'

'ID?'

'There is a driver's licence. And the right age. Obviously, we can't tell yet if it's a match because of the facial damage.'

'Who is it?' Jess asked.

'The name on the licence is Alistair Lyndon, thirty-one.'

Warlow looked again at the path leading away in two directions and made his mind up. 'Right, let's get moving on this Lyndon. You've found an address, I take it?'

'Yes, sir.'

'Then what are we standing around here for?'

CHAPTER SEVEN

AVA FARLEY PLACED the T-shirt dress in a bag and handed it over to the customer with a smile. She didn't feel like smiling, but this was work, and her smile was something people visiting the Dressy Fox remembered. Someone commented on it at least once a day. And not only the men who came in. Women did too. Just as they commented on her clothes, all of which were on sale in the shop. Ava and her boss, Tessa, agreed on that, and Ava got a hefty discount on the clothes, so long as she remained on Dressy Fox trend.

She'd dressed today in a "Crumpet" cardigan and "Palazzo" wide-legged pants, both by Queen Loys, an ever-popular brand in the shop with the young set that came in. Including the students when they could afford them.

Ava didn't mind even dressing in some of the vintage or repurposed stuff in the collection, too. But that meant what she wore was not on sale. More than once she'd changed clothes for a customer to try on. And that was a faff.

But it wasn't her choice of clothes that clouded her

sunny disposition today. Something else had pierced her little balloon. Ali hadn't phoned or messaged her for five days.

To say that she'd been unlucky in the romance lottery would be an understatement. Before Ali, there'd been Mosh. He of the flawless mocha skin and long eyelashes who'd proved to be a manipulative green-eyed monster. He'd been difficult to shake off. Luckily, he'd moved to London, and her refusal to go with him had been the opportunity to break it off. He still messaged her, though. Usually when he was drunk or randy. So, at least twice a day.

Which was more than could be said for Alistair. And she was upset because with him it seemed different. A chance encounter in the shop while he'd sourced a present for someone led to a chat and a smile. Her smile. His direct approach and easy manner were exactly what she'd wanted then. He'd been kind, measured, and being five years older than her, knew how to woo.

She'd laughed when he'd used the word "woo". Never thought of herself as a girl that ever needed wooing. And his maturity attracted her. She'd grown bored with the pub, club, shots scene by then anyway, having been on that roundabout since she was fifteen. So, a man with a car, and a job, and a house, for Christ's sake, was a novelty in itself.

He'd taken her for drinks and meals and, finally, last weekend, to his house.

She'd stayed the night in his bed. It had been fun and more tender than she'd experienced before. He had tricks and so did she. But there'd been Sunday commitments for each of them. For her, lunch with her mother and grandma. He'd got some unfinished thing that needed doing before the college he taught at came back for a new term. But he promised to ring her on Sunday night.

He hadn't.

Nor Monday, Tuesday… Today was Thursday.

The customer left, the bell above the door announcing her exit. That left the shop empty. Ava walked over to the T-shirts and started tidying the display.

Tessa appeared at her shoulder.

'I'm popping across to Pippa's. Flat white with almond milk?'

'There's instant out the back,' Ava said, sounding flat.

'My treat.'

Ava forced a smile.

Tessa read it. 'Still nothing?'

Ava shook her head. 'I think he's turned his phone off because my messages aren't getting through now.' She didn't stop her tidying. 'One tick on WhatsApp. I bet he's blocking me.'

Tessa raised one laminated eyebrow. 'Who in their right mind and a pulse is going to block you?'

'Someone who tried before they bought and didn't like what they found?'

'I don't believe that for one minute.' Tessa sighed. 'I hate to say this, but have you considered… That he's been in an accident or something?'

'Really?' Ava swung her pretty face around, her expression crumpling with doubt.

Tessa, at thirty-eight, saw Ava as a protégé as much as an employee and hated to see her mope. Doing nothing was eating at her. And Tessa had done her share of waiting for someone to phone or text. Before Mike and the twins came along a million years ago, she had, anyway. 'All I'm saying is it's worth giving Bronglais a ring. See if anyone's been brought into A&E. It's a shitty thing to think about, but at least it's worth a try. You never know.'

No smile on Ava's face now. 'And if they haven't? If he's just changed his mind?'

'Then he's a complete idiot and you're better off without him.'

'But I like him. He was… is, different.'

'They're all different, Ava. But some parts of them are all the same. I'm getting us a muffin to share.'

'I don't—'

Tessa waved away Ava's objection. 'No argument. This calls for baked goods with chocolate chips. If you like, I can make the calls when I come back.'

'Okay,' Ava said, and this time, her toothless smile bore a sprinkling of gratitude about it.

———

DETECTIVE SERGEANT GIL JONES stood in front of a board in one of the designated spaces that doubled as an Incident Room at Dyfed Powys's Police HQ on the outskirts of the market town of Carmarthen. He'd commandeered it, dismissing a seminar on Recruitment of Specials and Volunteers to a pokey room on the ground floor.

'Tough testicles,' he'd muttered to the disappointed HR bod, before adding, in an appalling Scots accent, 'There's been a murder.'

It earned him a look of strained pity from the admin clerk. But she got the message and scurried off to find a new venue.

The whiteboard would double as a photo gallery once they had something to pin up. But so far, all the board contained was a name written in Gil's best non-cursive hand.

ALISTAIR LYNDON

Above that, he'd begun a timeline with sticky notes, based on the information Catrin had given him on the bad smell reports. There were gaps, and the stuck-up paper looked uneven. With his usual inability to resist humour, he'd drawn, as he always did on the first note, a feathery fletching. At the other end on the opposite side of the board, an arrowhead.

'*Tempus fugit sicut Sagitta*,' he'd said when she asked what they were. 'Time flies like an arrow.'

'Tempus fudge-it more like,' Catrin muttered in response.

Beneath Lyndon's name, he'd written a date of birth and a comment – NO POLICE RECORD. Something he'd been able to check quickly on the PNC.

White space stared back at him. Space that needed to be filled with Lyndon's workplace records, family connections, next of kin. But these mundane tasks, essential for the beginning of any investigation, were hampered by Gil's ability to concentrate. The source of that distraction lay squarely behind his pubis bone. And given the degree to which his bladder had expanded with two mugs of tea, it probably, by now, stretched a good couple of inches above.

And the bladder was a wondrous thing. Or so he'd learned after looking it up online. A squeeze bag that complained when it was full and, just like any other organ, could become inflamed. Worse was that it sat on top of the old prostate. A piece of anatomy a man of Gil's age never quite escaped hearing about. Not only was it, like it's near neighbour, the bladder, flouted as a cause of all kinds of ageist issues, like poor stream, hesitancy, the need to get up at night to pee, etcetera, it also, or so the posters at the surgery said, could be a common host for the big "C".

So, like the bladder, not a laughing matter, the prostate. Not even when half the men he knew, even the ones who were not illiterate oafs, referred to the gland as their prostrate. A fact which gave rise to a whole extra imaginative dimension when people said they had "Prostrate trouble". No doubt some people did indeed have difficulty lying face down. But overall, that common slip of the tongue meant something else altogether.

Wincing, Gil did a little dance in front of the Gallery. He needed to pee with some urgency. But he was putting it off in the same way as someone with a toothache put off going to the dentist. He had relief at hand, but it came at a price.

And in Gil's case, the price was having to look in the pan.

He'd done it this morning as he had a thousand times before. Sometimes, like all men, he'd manipulate the stream to reduce splashing by directing it away from the water reservoir, and power-wash the porcelain. Whoever had thought of designing bowls with an image of a fly baked into the urinal deserved a medal. Giving a man a target to aim for suggested a deep and meaningful understanding of the male psyche.

But there were no flies in the porcelain of the Dyfed Powys toilets.

Only water.

And that morning, when Gil had peed, the toilet bowl water transformed into pale yellow tinged with pink. Something that had never happened before. Something he'd kept to himself until he'd looked up online. It hadn't hurt, but nonetheless, the list of potential causes was as unedifying as it was long.

Urinary Tract Infection.

Kidney Stones.

Enlarged prostate.

Bladder tumours.

It went on.

Gil's bladder twinged. No point putting it off. Not the immediate need for relief, nor the long-term strategy. He'd need to talk to someone about this. On the rare occasions he visited his local surgery, he'd got on okay with his GP.

And thanks to rude good health, he hardly knew any at the practice well. He did know it would be potluck who you got. No doubt they'd want to put a finger into an orifice designed for exit rather than entry – recherche tastes not withstanding – and at the last count, he'd noted four of the six GPs were now female. Sexist, he was not when it came to doctors. But his wife always preferred talking to a female GP when it came to downstairs matters.

On balance, Gil thought that maybe he'd prefer to do the same; that is, talk to a male GP about a problem that might be uniquely male. But one of the XY GPs was a six-five giant with hands like those promotional foam jobs you saw at football matches and the like. It didn't help that said giant GP was also known as Coldfinger, with a nod to the Bond film of a similar name.

Another bladder pang made him bite his lip. No good. He'd have to go. Perhaps he'd do it with his eyes shut. He rewound that one. He obviously could do it with his eyes shut. In fact, he could do it by ear only, listening for the reassuring splash. But that made the final shake-to-clear manoeuvre a lot more dangerous, especially if your trousers were light coloured and showed up fluid of any kind.

A fresh urgency gripped him, and this time he actually whimpered.

This was hopeless. Gil put down the marker pen he held and quick-stepped out towards the loos, whistling, his customary walking-to-the-men's tune – Police's *'Don't Stand So Close To Me'* – as he hurried along.

CHAPTER EIGHT

ALISTAIR LYNDON LIVED on the edge of the town in the Crugiau Estate, southeast of Aberystwyth. It meant that the detectives didn't need to go into town to get to it. From what Warlow remembered, that was a blessing because the one-way system was a time-sucking labyrinth. Instead, they used the A44 and cut south through Llanbadarn. *Lon Las* was a cul-de-sac dotted with a dozen identical, half-rendered, semi-detached houses.

Number 7 looked unprepossessing. A box with dark-brown window frames and a few shrubs in a bark-mulched border next to the pavement. No garage in this design, but off-road parking on a tarmac drive. They approached the front door and stood underneath a hipped canopy. At their feet, a couple of pots containing Hebes next to a couple of stone Buddhas broke up the mixed gravel that formed an edge beyond the flagstones.

Jess rang the bell.

No one answered. Warlow stepped across to peer through the front window. Vertical blinds did a good job of obscuring the view. A wooden, creosoted picket gate blocked the way along the side of the house to a garden at the rear.

Jess rang the bell again.

'No one home.' She shrugged.

'Well, we know Lyndon isn't.'

'Worth a look round the back?'

They pushed through the picket gate and walked around to a rear garden with a lawn and some shrubs and a small wooden shed against a shiplap fence at the bottom. The back end of the houses on the street beyond faced them above the fence.

Another brown UPVC back door barred entry to the house. This time, Warlow knocked. No reply.

He studied the little patio at the rear. More pots and a couple of odd-looking pebbles in a vague attempt at alleviating the dull grey flagstones. He knelt and picked up the pots in turn. But the key, when he found it, was under one of the pebbles. A false one. Light as a feather with a little concavity to house the key.

'Bingo,' he said. 'Lyndon should have had some security advice.'

'You ever thought of doing this professionally?' Jess stood, arms folded.

Warlow tried the key. It slid home, and he unlocked the door. 'Hello? Anyone home. It's the police?'

No reply.

He turned to Jess. 'I see no alarm. Shall we?'

They fetched overshoes and gloves, slid them on and walked in. This wasn't breaking and entering. They had a key. And there was good reason to believe that a crime had been committed, judging from the state of Lyndon's corpse. Both officers donned gloves as they walked through.

The back door opened onto a modern kitchen.

A modern, immaculate kitchen.

No unwashed dishes. No pizza boxes. Alistair Lyndon was a tidy man.

The dishwasher was empty, the sink clear.

The same neatness applied to the living room, whose windows Warlow had tried to peer through from outside. A TV, sound bar, set-top satellite receiver, the remotes neatly stacked under a coffee table, out of sight. A cream three-piece suite and an unblemished laminate floor. All the walls were unadorned, the surfaces free of any photographs or knick-knacks. But on a dresser next to the TV was a family photo of a man in cap and gown flanked by two beaming older people.

'That him, you reckon?' Warlow asked.

'Probably. I'd say he lived alone, wouldn't you?' Jess said.

Warlow went upstairs, three bedrooms and a bathroom. He entered the master bedroom. On a bedside table was a propped-up card with a shiny image of golden lips over the words; Thank You For The Invitation. Inside, it had been signed simply "A" with a large X.

'Lives alone but obviously entertains.' Warlow put the card back down.

The bed was a king double. Plain wooden frame, unpatterned off-white and grey sheets and covers. A cupboard nearby held men's clothes. Trousers and suits hung up, shirts folded, underwear and socks in separate drawers.

Warlow knelt. Under the bed was a storage box on wheels. He slid it out and lifted the lid to reveal an array of women's clothes. Colourful, neatly folded, but definitely female.

'His?' Warlow asked, having learned never to be surprised by anything he ever found in a bedroom.

'Or A's?' Jess replied.

Warlow pulled out a skimpy T-shirt. 'Too small for him, I reckon.'

'Could be.'

Jess left the room, and a couple of seconds later, called to him. 'There's a cupboard here on the landing, but it's locked.'

'See any keys in the kitchen?'

'No, but I wasn't looking.'

A loud and forceful knock on the front door startled them both. Warlow took the stairs. Jess went into a second bedroom.

The knock came again.

Warlow opened the door to find a woman and a man standing there with looks of unbridled suspicion all over their faces.

'Who are you?' demanded the man.

Warlow produced his warrant card. 'DCI Evan Warlow. And you are?'

Surprise washed away the belligerence at a stroke. 'Oh, the police. What are you—'

'Do you know Mr Lyndon?'

The woman answered, 'We're Alistair's neighbours. We live across the street. Sometimes, when Alistair goes away, Hubert cuts his lawns, takes out the rubbish. You know?'

Warlow waited.

'Sorry,' said the man. 'Hubert Marks. And this is Glenda.'

Warlow put them at around seventy. Glenda looked fit, but a little scruffy in worn corduroy trousers and crocs under a stained sweatshirt. Hubert was overweight, with a bulbous nose and flyaway hair.

'We didn't mean to—'

'No, no, you're alright,' Warlow intervened. 'You're being good neighbours. Commendable.'

'Is there anything wrong?' Glenda asked.

'We're following up on some inquiries about Mr Lyndon. When was the last time you saw him?'

'Last weekend,' Glenda said. 'He was out and about.'

'Not since?'

'No. When we saw you go around the back, we thought something might be up,' Hubert explained.

Jess appeared in the passage behind Warlow. He made the introductions before half turning to Jess and looking at his watch. 'I probably need to set off if I'm to get to Cardiff by two. Said I'd pick Rhys up.'

Jess nodded and turned on her smile for the Markses. 'Where is it you live, Mr and Mrs Marks?'

Glenda turned and pointed to a bigger semi with an attached garage across the street. 'Number 14.'

'Great. Do you mind if I come over and ask you some questions?'

'Nothing's happened to Alistair, has it?' Glenda asked, her voice suddenly shrill.

'Well, we can't answer that because as yet we aren't sure.' No lie in that. They still couldn't identify the dead man from the photograph. They may even need to go the dental records route. There'd likely be some DNA traces in the house for Povey to play with, too. However, all that took time. 'That's why it's important I talk to you,' Jess added. She turned back to Warlow. 'I've texted Catrin. She's on the way. She can help me here while you two get off to Cardiff.'

'Sounds like a plan.'

Warlow left Jess with the Markses outside Lyndon's house as he headed for the Jeep, wondering about a set of women's clothes in that under-bed storage.

———

THE QUICKEST WAY TO get to Cardiff from Ysumtuen was to cut directly cross-country in a diagonal through Builth Wells, bypassing Brecon, and skirting Merthyr Tydfil. A good two-and-a-half-hour drive, even on a good day. And so far, today wasn't turning out so great. Not if you were Alistair Lyndon. And not if you were DC Rhys Harries, either, since two and a half hours in the car non-stop meant missing at least one meal.

Warlow had spent a great deal of time in vehicles with the young detective and knew his foibles by now. Most of this involved food. Whereas Warlow did not mind missing the odd meal, Rhys, now punishing himself with three sessions of cross-fit a week in the rugby off-season, needed fuel.

Some officers, knowing they were on the way to a slice and dice at the mortuary, shunned food until afterwards. But Rhys, much to everyone's surprise, was made of much sterner stuff and had shown a keen interest in this gory aspect of murder investigation. So much so that he'd been given, and accepted, the role of "resident ghoul". Rhys was their man when it came to visiting the Path department at the University Hospital of Wales and was fast becoming good at distilling the findings into an acceptable, if not easily digestible, précis.

But that didn't excuse the SIO from being there at the death, so to speak. Warlow was going along to see if Tiernon had anything useful to add, though, in all honesty, he might as well sit in the car and let Rhys do the whole thing. But Warlow was a pro. Unlike Rhys, though, he would not fill his stomach up beforehand.

Still, he was not a cruel man.

And so, they stopped just outside Brecon in an Esso garage with an attached SPAR convenience store. This one had hot food and, while Rhys headed for the shop, Warlow filled up with fuel.

'Want anything, sir?'

'A coffee.'

'Anything else?'

'Surprise me. See if Gil's training has paid off.'

Warlow paid at the pump and sat in the car until Rhys returned, coffee in one hand, carrier bag and a hot dog in the other.

Seeing Warlow's eyes narrow as he opened the car door, Rhys said, 'No onions, sir. I'm not a barbarian.' He handed over the coffee and Warlow drove back out onto the road.

Doing his best not to sound too much like a cow in a field full of lush grass, Rhys slowly demolished his hot dog with exaggeratedly damped-down chews, carefully mopping up the ketchup and mustard as it oozed out onto his fingers and using a wet wipe to finish the job. Warlow sipped at his coffee and waited, eyes on the road.

'Good?' he asked when Rhys finally finished.

'Brilliant. When you're hungry, nothing can beat a hot frankfurter.'

'You might want to rephrase that in polite company, Rhys.'

'Ha, ha, good one, sir.'

Rhys settled back in his seat, for the moment content, if not completely satiated.

Warlow threw him a couple of glances, hoping he'd take the hint.

After the third pointed look, Rhys finally said, 'What, sir? Is there something on my shirt?'

'No, but there might be in a minute if you don't tell me what you got for me.'

Rhys's pop-eyed look of apologetic horror induced nothing more than an inevitable shake of Warlow's head. The DC reached for the thin plastic bag between his legs and carefully extracted a small brown paper bag. 'I didn't think you'd want a biscuit, so I spotted these in the fresh food section. Local produce, it said.' He carefully removed three bite-sized pastries, white on top with a golden yellow layer sandwiched between rough pastry. 'Bite-sized custard slices. Brilliant idea because eating a whole one is an exercise in damage limitation at the best of times.'

Warlow looked at the pastries resting in the DC's hands before glancing up. Rhys's expression, so full of childlike enthusiasm just moments ago, melted into wariness. 'Don't tell me it's not your thing, sir. I thought—'

'You thought?'

'I mean, everyone likes a custard slice, don't they?'

'Do they?'

'Well, yes, I mean… I—'

'You?'

This time, Rhys's mouth opened, but no sound emerged.

Warlow turned the screw. 'Hang on there, Rhys. You thought that getting me a pastry you clearly like would be the thing to do?'

'You asked for a surprise, sir.'

'I did. And this is what I get. Well, for your information and future reference, Detective Constable… The custard slice ranks in the top three of my favourite pastries, tying with a coconut slice and trailing only slightly after heavily butter-creamed lemon sponge. My number one, of course, is lemon cheesecake.' Warlow reached across and took the pastry and crammed it into his mouth. The noises that emerged next contained no words, but ecstasy came close as an adjective.

Rhys looked on, grinning.

When he'd finished, Warlow said, 'Right, put those away. They'll be for our return journey. What else did you buy?'

'Crisps, sir,' Rhys said it quickly. Despite his obvious

relief at coming up trumps with the custard slice, he could not hide the trepidation in his voice.

Warlow narrowed his eyes. He'd previously banned Rhys from eating crisps in the car because the noise was too overpowering. But the custard slice bite had changed all that. 'Knock yourself out. So long as they're not cheese and onion.'

Rhys shook his head. 'Prawn cocktail, sir. Like I said, I'm not a barbarian.'

'That's debatable. Now, tell me what Gil has found out about Alistair Lyndon.'

CHAPTER NINE

CATRIN ARRIVED JUST as Jess crossed the road to the Markses' property. Jess greeted her and filled her in on the absence of anything terribly useful, other than the enigmatic "thank you" card from "A".

'No sign of violence?'

'Squeaky clean. The neighbours saw us rooting around and came to knock. I'm about to talk to them. Glenda and Hubert Marks.'

Catrin took out her notebook and followed her senior officer through the Markses' open front door.

In contrast to the clean minimalist lines of Lyndon's house, the interior of the Markses' home was a cornucopia of clutter. Next to a push-bike in the hallway, a large and heavy wrought-iron umbrella stand stood next to a bureau stacked high with letters and coupons. Beneath their feet, a garishly patterned carpet led the way towards the kitchen at the back. As she passed open doors to the living room and what might have been a study, Jess noted display cabinets bursting with porcelain figurines and vintage toy cars.

The Markses, it seemed, were collectors. Through the

rear window, Jess caught sight of a colony of gnomes clambering up ladders, sitting on the edge of a little stone well, and clustered around tree stump ornaments. All against a backdrop of flowering borders and a lawn which no self-respecting weed had the temerity to go near.

Their kitchen was all oak and dark work surfaces, the table that the Markses insisted she and Catrin sit at, wooden with wheel-back chairs. Hubert opened the fridge door, adorned with notes and childish drawings. There must have been grandchildren somewhere in the Markses' mix.

But the tea that Hubert put in front of them was hot and strong and hit the spot.

'How long have you known Alistair Lyndon?' Jess asked.

'Since he moved here about four years ago,' Glenda answered. She opened a tin with the word "Biscuits" stamped on the side. No need for subterfuge when it came to baked goods in this house. DS Gil Jones would be horrified, since he hid the squad's *biscuits* –Catrin always thought of the word in French now, courtesy of one of Gil's affectations – in a box labelled "Human Tissue for Transplant", so that inquisitive hands and eyes stayed back.

Jess waved away Glenda's offered digestives and so did Catrin.

'Does he have a car?' Catrin asked.

'Yes. A silver-grey BMW.'

'Model?'

Hubert answered, 'One of the little ones. A1 Series hatchback.'

'Any chance you can remember the licence plate?'

Hubert nodded and reeled it off.

Catrin fought a smile as she scribbled. Nosy neighbours were a wonderful thing.

'And did Alistair live alone?'

A shadow fell over Glenda's rosy-cheeked face. 'Yes, he does now. Since Mirain left.'

'Mirain?' Jess put the teacup back down on its saucer.

'Yes. They were a lovely couple. Mirain was always so bubbly,' Hubert said.

Glenda nodded. 'I feel so sorry for the little girl, Heledd. Of course, she wasn't Alistair's. Mirain had her before they met.'

'What happened to Mirain?' Catrin asked.

'Flown the nest,' Hubert said. 'Ali seemed very upset. He came over to tell us she'd upped sticks… What…?' He looked at Glenda for confirmation. 'Three, or is it four weeks ago now?'

Jess zeroed in on this tidbit. 'Had they fallen out?'

'Oh no,' Glenda sang out the denial. 'They seemed to get on well. And Ali doted on Heledd. She's such a lovely little girl. Back with her real dad now, so I heard.'

'So, no altercations?' Catrin pressed them. 'No fights. No screaming or shouting?'

Hubert looked aghast. 'That's not Ali's style. He's a pretty measured sort of bloke. No, but Mirain… She could be a little moody.'

That earned him a sharp look from Glenda. 'That's unfair, Hubert.'

'Is it? Remember the time she lost it with me offering to clean the gutters? I had the big ladder out and everything.'

'Yes, well, you were fussing and caught her on a bad day, that's all.'

'Is there anyone in Alistair's life with a name beginning with A?'

The Markses exchanged glances, their mouths pouting, heads shaking. A sure sign that Mirain's behaviour had been a topic of conversation over an evening's sardines on toast.

'And you've seen nothing strange going on over there of late?'

Another glance between Glenda and Hubert. This one a little more coy. 'We think he had a visitor last Saturday. Brought a girl home. She left on Sunday morning.'

'And this wasn't Mirain?'

'No, definitely not. This was a younger woman. Blonde hair, heels, you know?'

Jess didn't, but she let it slide.

'What about Alistair's work?' Catrin asked.

Hubert nodded. 'He's a lecturer at the college.'

'The university, you mean?'

'No,' Glenda stepped in. 'At the college. The Further Ed college.'

'So, he's off work now?'

'I don't think he gets the whole summer off, but he's never that busy. They have terms in the college, I think.'

Hubert, who'd been watching the detectives work, took a deep breath. 'I must ask... all these questions... They're the sort of questions detectives ask when something serious has happened. At least they do on TV.'

Jess nodded. 'You're right. And we are very grateful for your cooperation.'

'And for the tea,' Catrin added.

'Something serious has happened,' Jess explained. 'But we are not sure if it involves Alistair yet. That's why we're asking all the questions. To find out where Alistair is. Until we do, we can't be sure of anything, so I can't tell you more until we tick those boxes.'

As explanations went, it lacked much substance, but Jess needed certainty before taking the next step. The last thing the Markses needed to hear was that Alistair Lyndon had been thrown down a mineshaft, only for his BMW to tootle up the road at any moment. Jess doubted that would happen, but corroboration remained a precious commodity in this job.

'Do you have Alistair's phone number?' Catrin asked.

Glenda nodded and fetched her phone.

She also had Mirain's.

When all that had been obtained, Jess stood up, thanked the Markses and took Catrin back to Alistair Lyndon's pristine house, after promising to let the older couple know once they had something definite.

Deep down, she knew that would not be a straightforward conversation.

———

LUNCHTIME CAME and went at the Dressy Fox. They kept the shop open during lunch hour. It could be the busiest part of the day. Tessa took half an hour from one to one-thirty, Ava took one-thirty to two. During her break, Ava left the shop and did some shopping. Her turn to fill up on bread and milk for the flat she shared. Every five minutes, she checked her phone.

Still, none of the messages she'd sent Alistair had been received or read. He must have his phone off. The shop was empty when she got back, and Tessa's smile of greeting was brief and hopeful.

'Nothing?' she asked.

Ava shook her head.

'Me neither. I mean, that's good news in a way. But the hospital has no record of anyone being brought in with that name. Nor anyone who fits his description.'

'What do you mean?'

Tessa bared her teeth in anxious apology. 'In case someone was brought in, I don't know, unconscious or something.'

Ava paled. 'What?'

'Sorry, it's just… You read about these things, right? Anyway, there's nothing. I even phoned Glangwili in Carmarthen in case he went down south. You know what those roads are like. Young racers who think they're rally drivers and—'

'OMG, Tessa.'

'Sorry, Ava. I'm not trying to upset you. I hate to see you like this, that's all.'

Ava nodded. Tessa was right, and she should be grateful to her boss. Phoning around was something she should have done herself but didn't have the guts to do. Truth was, she hadn't wanted to because if Alistair wasn't in a coma in ITU – like a plot in one of the soaps, especially the American ones with River, or Valley, or Bay in the title – it meant he wasn't answering his messages deliberately.

Which meant that he'd sampled the goods on Saturday night and hadn't liked what he'd tasted.

'Maybe you could give his work a ring. Just for peace of mind, right?'

Ava squeezed her eyes shut and shook her head. The last thing she needed was to appear even more desperate than she felt. But she had so wanted this one to work out. So wanted something else besides the cattle market at The Cambrian, or Yoko's on a Friday and Saturday night, and hangovers all day Sunday.

'You really like him, don't you?' Tessa asked, cinching up her lower lip.

Ava nodded. The shop bell rang, and Tessa switched to her professional smile and greeted the customer. Ava slipped into the back and put her milk in the little fridge, trying her best not to feel too sad about Alistair.

An enormous sigh erupted. Why was everything so shit?

The bell rang again.

More customers.

Ava looked in the mirror in the back room. She would not cry. Not again.

No man was worth that.

CHAPTER TEN

THE PLAN WAS that the team all get together for vespers late afternoon. The last two to arrive were Warlow and Rhys, caught up in the inevitable late afternoon commute from Cardiff to all points west. When the doors of the Incident Room opened, Warlow was pleased to see Jess and Catrin already there: the DI busy at a workstation, the DS pinning things up on the Gallery.

'Where's Gil?' he asked.

'Coming through.' The voice, from behind Warlow, sounded business-like as Gil entered with a tray of mugs.

Rhys held the door open but couldn't quite hide his disappointment. 'No *biscuits*, sarge?' He, like everyone else in the department, defaulted to the French pronunciation of biscuit in the presence of the DS.

'Yes, well, as a senior member of the team, I feel it is my responsibility to monitor the consumption of empty calories in the workplace. I think we can all agree, and I accept I am partially to blame, that to expect baked goods whenever we have liquid refreshments is not good for our health.'

Rhys's eyes dropped to look at Gil's ample girth and

then around at the positively svelte Jess and Catrin and the wiry Warlow.

'What the hell is up with you, Gil?' the DCI asked.

'I've made the teas,' Gil said.

'What about the Human Tissue for Transplant box?' Rhys asked, the desperation in his voice obvious for all to hear.

'Put away for the day. Elevenses only for the foreseeable.' Gil handed out the mugs to a very puzzled-looking team.

He looked into each of their faces. '*Bois bach*, I'm not suggesting a starvation diet. You'll all thank me in the long run.'

Warlow appraised the big sergeant. 'It's not your blood pressure again, is it?'

'My blood pressure is that of a racing snake, thank you very much. If you like, I might consider getting some healthy snacks. Crudités or some nuts?'

'Don't worry, we've already got the nuts,' Warlow muttered.

Catrin nodded. 'We could try some fruit.'

'Fruit?' spluttered Rhys, his despair at the absence of something to chew on palpable. 'You can't have a banana with a cup of tea. And there is no way I'll be dunking a mango.'

'Mind your language, Rhys,' Warlow said.

But there was no deflecting the DC. 'You must have a biscuit with tea. It's a tradition. We've always had them. We pay towards them.' The last word emerged as almost a wail. 'Kitty.'

'And they'll still be available,' Gil argued. 'But not with every cuppa. Elevenses only.'

'If you're hungry, Rhys, I have an apple,' Jess offered.

From the look on his face, she might as well have offered him a rotten turnip.

'No, thank you, ma'am.' He slouched away to his desk and shrugged off his jacket.

'Oh dear, Rhys has a cob on,' Catrin said.

Warlow shook his head. 'He has no right to. He ate enough snacks in the car to fuel a medium-sized power station.'

'It's the principle of the thing,' muttered Rhys without looking at either of them.

He had a point and Warlow wondered what Gil's game was here. He was still wondering when the sergeant followed him towards the back of the room and into the SIO's office where the DCI shed his jacket. The August day had morphed into a heavy, muggy afternoon.

'How did the PM go?' Gil asked.

'Rhys is doing the needful. I'm giving him ten minutes to get things together.'

'Good, good.' Gil hovered on the threshold, which, for a man of his size, was no mean feat.

'How about this end?' Warlow asked, glancing at the notes that had appeared on the desk in his absence.

'Yeah, progress of sorts. Lyndon has a mother we're trying to trace.'

'Right,' Warlow said.

Still, Gil hesitated.

'It'll all come out at vespers, I expect,' Warlow said.

'No doubt,' Gil answered, but did not leave.

Warlow glanced around at the sergeant still in the doorway. 'Is there something else, Gil?'

'What?'

'Something bothering you?'

Gil glanced back into the Incident Room before stepping inside the small office and closing the door. 'I wanted to run something past you,' he whispered.

'Not the biscuit moratorium, because I can tell you I stand with Rhys—'

'No, no, not that. It's about your son, Tom.'

Warlow straightened, his antennae twitching. 'Tom?'

'Don't worry, nothing's happened, I just wondered… Think he'd mind if I had a word with him? Being he's a surgeon and all that.'

'ENT. Anything above the shoulders and he's your man.'

'Right, but he knows stuff, doesn't he? About the body and medicine and things?'

'Yes. he knows about… Things. Surgeons all have to do those "things" before they specialise.'

Gil nodded. 'So, you think he'd mind if I called him?'

'Of course not. I'll let him know.'

'I don't want to impose.' Gil sounded earnest.

'It'll be fine. Tom's not precious about his work.' Warlow studied the big man standing in front of him with a fixed smile. 'Is it about you, or one of the family?'

'Me?' Gil's laugh was a good one, though a tad too high for Warlow's liking. 'No, no, no. One of the grand-kids. Something to do with tonsils. Ear, nose, and throat stuff, definitely.'

'Tom's your man, then. I'll text you his number.'

'Would you? I'd be grateful, Evan.'

Warlow fiddled with his phone. 'Done. Right, let me get myself together and we'll have a run through of what we know and what we don't.'

Gil's brows clouded with suspicion. 'Know? What do you think you know?'

'About Lyndon, not very much… If that's who we're talking about here.'

'Lyndon? Of course, it is.' Gil let out a jovial laugh. A highly inappropriate noise under the circumstances given they were discussing a murder victim, but one, Warlow suspected, borne out of misguided relief that the subject was no longer ENT or surgically related. 'Lyndon in the mineshaft. Right, I'll get the troops. See you in a minute.'

Warlow watched Gil walk out and shook his head. ENT my arse, he thought, unaware of just how close to the mark he was with the second part of that idiom.

He gave them all five minutes to settle down and had a lightbulb moment while he waited. He rummaged in the desk drawer for a two-fingered Kit Kat, which he removed before going back out into the Incident Room. The atmosphere remained subdued. Jess had one hand around her mug and typed languorously with one finger of the other. Gil stood back watching Catrin work on the Gallery, arms folded. Rhys sat hunched over his desk, half a quartered apple at his elbow, still uneaten.

Warlow made a great show of unwrapping the Kit Kat and breaking the fingers apart and then in half. He distributed a couple of inches of chocolate-coated wafer to everyone bar Gil, who looked on venomously.

'Cheers, sir,' Rhys said and wolfed down the biscuit.

'Right, now that we've got our sugar levels up,' he sent Gil a pointed look, 'what exactly have we got?'

Since she was the one standing, Catrin led off.

'We have a potential ID found at the scene. We're awaiting definitive analysis. Unfortunately, injuries sustained do not allow identification from photographs. But the driving licence and credit cards found in a wallet at the scene all point to it being Alistair Lyndon who is a thirty-one-year-old lecturer in Art and Design. Neighbours report seeing him last Saturday, but not since. The report of a foul smell emanating from the walkers near the shaft began on Tuesday.'

'I checked with Povey,' Jess said. 'Given the time of year, putrefaction would start to emit odours between twenty-four and seventy-two hours after death.'

'What else did the neighbours tell you?' Warlow asked.

'The Markses are excellent witnesses,' Jess said. 'Lyndon had a long-term partner, a Mirain Hughes, but she left a few weeks ago. They also said that he entertained someone at his home on Saturday night.'

'Quick worker,' Gil said.

'Male or female?' Warlow asked.

'Female. Might be the person who left the thank you note on the bedside cabinet.'

'A?'

Jess nodded.

Warlow stood with hands on hips. 'Though we're yet to have formal confirmation, we've been to Lyndon's house. It's empty. There is no car. For now, it's him until proven otherwise. What else do we have?'

'I've let traffic know about the car. They're on the look-out. Lyndon has no priors. Clean as a whistle.' Gil shrugged.

'There was no phone with the wallet?'

Catrin shook her head.

Warlow nodded slowly. 'Right, Rhys, you're up.'

The DC, buoyed by a quarter finger of Kit Kat, stood with some sheets of paper clutched in his hands. He towered over Catrin and immediately began pinning printed images on the Gallery.

'Oh please, no more PM photos.' Catrin grimaced.

'They're all relevant, I promise,' Rhys muttered.

'You said that last time,' Gil reminded him. 'Those shots of maggot activity under that corpse's scalp were way out of order.'

'It gave us a good indication of how long the body had been there, sarge,' Rhys argued.

'It also gave one of our indexers nightmares for a fort-night. She had to go off sick with stress. I'm surprised she didn't end up on the funny farm.'

Catrin clicked her tongue. 'Can't say that these days, Gil.'

'No? Okay, I'm surprised she didn't end up on the very unfunny farm. Or does that trigger you as well?'

Catrin half-turned away and coughed. The word "Dinosaur" could clearly be heard as she did so.

Rhys finished pinning up two closeup images of the corpse's hand and the unnaturally bent fingers. Blood and dirt had stained the flesh but had also highlighted the deep ridges etched into the skin of the proximal phalanges below the break.

'As holiday snaps go, Rhys, these leave a lot to be desired,' Warlow said.

Rhys pointed out what Tiernon had taken a great delight in confirming to him.

'So, he thinks these marks are from a vice, too?' Catrin asked, arms folded beneath a look of great distaste.

'Yes. Our mineshaft man was tortured.' Rhys pointed to more photographs. This time of linear red lines around the wrists. 'Ligature marks. He was restrained, probably plastic garden ties.' Rhys had one more sheet in his hand. This he had not put up yet. 'This is a closeup of the fatal wound.' He pointed to his head, towards the front on the left-hand side. The photograph he posted was, mercifully, a closeup of a peeled-back scalp to show a smallish crack, but with fragments of bone displaced inwards over the underlying brain matter. It could just about have been anything because no other facial feature was on show. 'It's a ragged trauma. Nothing smooth. There was a lot of dirt and dust from the fall, so Tiernon couldn't say if all that came from before or after. But it doesn't appear smooth enough to be a hammer.'

'So, a blunt instrument?' Catrin asked.

'Something hard with quite sharp edges, Tiernon thought.'

'Like a rock?' Gil asked.

'Possibly.' Rhys nodded.

'Well, what are we thinking? That he was taken somewhere, tortured, killed away from the scene, and then brought back and dumped there?' Warlow waited for responses.

'If you put it that way, it's definitely a vengeful act,' Catrin muttered.

Jess stood up and walked towards the Gallery for a closer view. 'Or someone trying to send a message. Could be a drug thing. Maybe he owed money. Maybe he ripped someone off and they smashed his head in with a rock.'

Warlow nodded. It sounded as good a working theory as any. 'Okay, then we need to dig deeper into Lyndon's life. I want to go to the college, see what we can find out, when he was last at work, talk to colleagues.' He walked over to the brochure that Catrin had pinned up with the map of the trail from the museum past *Yr Het Fawr*. 'I also want to go back to the trail at some point. Walk a bit. I mean, why that shaft of all places?'

'Happy to come with you there, sir. Get my steps in,' Rhys volunteered, his exuberance back with a vengeance. 'I'll bring sandwiches.'

'It's not a bloody away day, Rhys,' Warlow growled.

'I'll still bring a few sandwiches, though, sir. I will.'

And he would, too, thought Warlow. He traced his finger along the line of the track on the shiny paper. 'One thing is certain, the answers are up north, not here in Carmarthen.'

'Are we re-locating, then, sir?' Rhys asked.

'I'll run it past Buchannan, but I see no alternative.'

'Bloody hell,' muttered Gil. 'On the road again. At this rate, we might as well get the Force to buy us a tour bus.'

'That would be so cool.' Rhys grinned. 'We could have

a fridge and a mini kitchen and a gaming area, possibly a home cinema—'

'Can someone take his batteries out, please?' Catrin rolled her eyes.

'What?' Rhys asked, his eyes wide with wonder.

Warlow turned to the team. 'Right, I'm off to see a girl about a dog. I'll text you all Buchannan's thoughts. Stay by your phones.'

CHAPTER ELEVEN

WARLOW DID NOT GET to speak to Sion Buchannan until after six that evening. The call came as he prepared food for his black Lab Cadi, who'd been patiently watching him "prepare" said food, sitting, salivating silently in the corner as Warlow spooned raw meat into a bowl and mixed it with some vegetables. Yet, as soon as he picked up the container, Cadi transformed from patient anticipation into a bouncy fur ball, up on her hind legs, trying to sniff the contents.

'*Y twpsen,*' Warlow chided her affectionately. Labs, more so than other dogs, were food obsessed. He'd read that some breeds, usually smaller and labelled faddy eaters, could pick at a bowl of kibble throughout the day. Put down a bowl full of kibble for a Labrador and it would disappear inside the dog within three minutes.

Not that Cadi ate kibble. Since when did dogs eat grain? No, she was on the raw stuff. Frozen, fresh, and defrosted for her delight. And from the way she demolished the contents of her silver food bowl, delight would be about the right term to use.

'Sion,' Warlow said into the mobile.

'Sorry, Evan. Got waylaid in another blasted meeting. Reorganisation looms.'

'Not another one?'

'Internal this time and only involving the higher ups.'

'You, then.'

Buchannan snorted. 'Much higher than me, thankfully.'

Cadi's bowl clanked against the wall as her snout ploughed in.

'Are you eating?'

'Not me, but the beast is.'

'How is Cadi? None the worse for her experiences last month?'

It seemed the entire Force knew that Warlow's dog got lost down on the Dale Peninsula in Pembrokeshire for a couple of days. 'No. Fact is, I think she milked it. She's certainly reaped the benefits afterwards. Likes a bit of fuss, does Cadi.'

On hearing her name, the dog looked up and registered Warlow's smile of reassurance. That gave her the okay to get on with the business of devouring the pulverised flesh of a duck with added seasonal vegetables, curly kale, cabbage, Brussel sprouts, raspberries, and blueberries. Warlow was in no doubt that sometimes the dog ate better than he did.

'How did it go with you? I hear you may have an ID?' Buchannan asked.

'Yes, work in progress, obviously. But it all points to something local. I think we'll set up a new IR in Aberystwyth nick, if that's okay with you?'

'You hardly need to ask. And why not?' Buchannan said, ever sanguine. 'Give the buggers something to do. And it's always good press when you say a major incident room has been set up outside HQ. Makes us look invested in the task at hand.'

'You been on the cynic pills again, Sion?'

Warlow could almost hear Buchannan smile. 'You'll take all the usual suspects?'

'If possible. Gil can run the office, which leaves me, Jess, Catrin, and Rhys out and about.'

'Good. Jess is off on her course soon. So, another case under her belt at this stage is ideal.' To become a fully-fledged senior investigating officer, hoops needed to be jumped through. One of which was a residential course which Jess had already signed up for.

'Keep me in the loop,' Buchannan added, and ended the call.

Cadi finished her food, urinated on the lawn, and then fetched a toy bear, which she brought to Warlow, nuzzling into his leg by way of a thank you gift for the food. He ruffled the hair on her head. 'Right, looks like more holidays for you.'

The tone of Warlow's voice induced more bum wiggling ecstasy in the dog. 'Glad to see one of us is excited about that.' He sighed, and speed-dialled Jess's number.

———

HELEDD RAMPLEY SAT at the big kitchen table, grinning from ear to ear. They played Harry Potter Dobble; a kind of overblown snap involving matching images on the card you turned over in your hand with something on the card already face up on the table. She was smiling because she was winning. Best of all, her grandfather was losing so badly he could hardly speak. Not that he was useless at card games. But in this game, you needed to know the names of the items on the cards in order to match them. Heledd was a stickler when it came to the rules. Whereas she would say "elder wand", her grandfather might say "knobbly stick" or "magic twig". And no matter how quickly he said "vase" or "cup", instead of the "goblet of fire", Heledd remained unforgiving. And sometimes the words he used were so weird – who didn't know that the broomstick was really a NIMBUS 2000 – he made her collapse in hysterics.

But when 7.30 came, Carwyn Hughes gathered up the cards, much to Heledd's disgust.

'Right, bath for you, young lady, then cereal.'

'Can I have Fruit Loops?'

'Yes. But no extra sugar.'

Heledd wrinkled her nose in disgust, but good-naturedly. 'Mam doesn't let me have Fruit Loops for supper ever. And only twice a week for breakfast.'

Her grandfather had his back to her, reaching into the cupboard. 'Quite right, too.'

'When is she coming back, *Tadcu*?'

Carwyn stopped what he was doing. It only lasted a matter of seconds, but Heledd saw it. Her father was the same. The grownups in her life reacted in exactly the same way whenever she asked about her mother. As if the questions paralysed them somehow. Carwyn turned from the cupboard, a box of cereal in his hand. 'That's a question we'd all like an answer to, Hel.'

'But it's my birthday, and—'

'I know *blodyn*. I know.'

'Can I check Facebook to see if she's left us another message?'

'Alright, but only after the bath and supper. Go on now.'

Heledd climbed off the chair and skipped upstairs but stopped halfway. She'd forgotten Mostyn, her stuffed pig who'd been a constant companion since she was three. Mostyn went everywhere with her. Bath included.

She ran back down fearlessly, as eight-year-olds did.

When she entered the kitchen, she stopped. Her grandfather stood stock still staring out the window, making funny sniffly noises like she sometimes did when she had a cold.

'*Tadcu?*'

He turned, one hand over his eye, blinking furiously.

'Are you okay?'

Carwyn nodded and reached for the paper towel. 'Damn greenfly went into my eye.' He squinted at her through red rims and swatted at the plants on the windowsill. 'I thought you were in the bath?'

'Dad has fly spray. I can ask him to lend you it if you like?'

'Good idea.' Carwyn smiled. 'Now, come on, bath.'

Heledd picked Mostyn up from the table.

'What do you need that pig for, anyway? He'll only get wet.'

'He tests the water to make sure it isn't too hot; I've told you before.' She made it sound as if he'd just asked her why you'd need a seat belt in a car.

'Ah, yes. Silly me.' Carwyn smiled an indulgent smile.

Reassured, Heledd pirouetted, ran back out and up to the bathroom singing the chorus from *I'm Still Standing* – the Elton John classic given new life by a gorilla in Pixar's Sing, which she'd watched earlier.

By Carwyn's estimation, at least a dozen times.

CHAPTER TWELVE

THE COLLEGE ALISTAIR LYNDON taught at had several campuses, but a quick couple of phone calls from Gil established that he was based in Llanbadarn. The office in Coleg Ceredigion's site that Warlow and Catrin now sat in at 9am the following morning, looked to be at the business end of things, dominated, as it was, by a giant wall calendar streaked with coloured tape and Post-It notes covered in scrawled handwriting.

A functional, if untidy, room. Elaine Hunt, the woman who greeted them and showed them to this office, wore a lanyard announcing her as a "Deputy Director of Learning Experience". She also wore a pair of glasses on a chain around her neck and kept her blonde hair in a bob.

'I got a message from Detective Sergeant Jones. You wanted to ask me about Alistair?'

'Yes,' Warlow said. 'We're trying to find him. We thought we'd start with his place of work.'

Hunt nodded. 'He's missing, then?'

'Let's just say we'd like to speak to him or those close to him. All part of an ongoing enquiry,' Catrin stated to put her at ease.

'Of course. But you realise it's not term time. We broke up on the 24th of June.'

'So, could Alistair be on holiday?' Catrin sat forward.

Hunt's tired smile looked painted on. 'I'll forgive you the cliché. Just because the term ends doesn't mean we all swan off to Portugal for three months. Unfortunately, none of us have the entire summer off.'

'So, he should be here? Lyndon, I mean?' Warlow asked.

'Theoretically. We are a big college, though. Seven campuses in all. We're integrated with College Sir Gar in Carmarthenshire with links to both Aberystwyth University and Trinity in Carmarthen. We have open days to organise, fresh courses to set up. Both full-time A level courses and part-time vocational. And, we had our A Level results last week. Most of us will be busy now until September.'

'When does the new term start?'

'8th of September for students,' Hunt answered.

'What does Mr Lyndon teach?' Catrin asked.

'He's in the Creative Arts department. Art and Design mostly.'

'Where would he be if we wanted to find him?'

'Usually in the labs if he's here.'

Warlow stood up. 'Does he work with anyone? An assistant?'

'Some of our tutors are part-time, but I know he's friendly with one of our IT lecturers. Let me try the Computing labs. See if he's there.'

Hunt picked up a phone and punched in some numbers. Someone answered after a few seconds.

'Byron, any idea where Alistair is?'

The two detectives waited while Hunt did their job for them. When she'd finished, she hung up and brought the tired smile back to her face.

'That was Byron. He's friendly with Alistair, but he hasn't seen him for a couple of days.'

'But he knows him well?' Warlow pressed her.

'Yes.'

Warlow stood. 'Okay, if you'd point us in his direction? We'll have a chat with this Byron. Thanks for your help.'

Hunt gave them directions along corridors and upstairs until they found themselves outside a room full of laptops and monitors visible through the windows.

'Hello?' Catrin called out, pushing open the door.

A bearded man with intense dark eyes emerged from a back room. He wore skinny jeans and battered plimsoles and a Hawaiian shirt.

'Ah,' said Catrin, 'You must be—' Her voice froze as recognition dawned on her face. She smiled, then frowned and blushed furiously. 'Byron?'

'Catrin?' Byron grinned. Or at least some teeth appeared within the beard.

Warlow looked on, bemused. 'You two know each other?'

'Yes... I... *We* do. Byron and I were at university together here for a year.'

'Not on the same course, I take it?'

'No.' Catrin's narrow eyes seem to appraise the man in front of her. 'You've lost weight?'

'Yeah. I do a bit of running; you know.'

'My God, how many years has it been?' Catrin asked.

'We were nineteen. Even you could do that maths.' Byron's taunt seemed a little out of place, but Warlow let it slide.

'Too many years,' Catrin said.

'Fancy seeing you here.' Byron's dark eyes had not left Catrin's face.

'Okay,' Warlow said. 'I can see you two have some catching up to do, but we're on the clock, Byron—'

'It's Evans, sir,' Catrin filled in the blanks.

'You okay to answer some questions about Mr Lyndon?' Warlow continued.

Byron held his arms up in surrender. 'Of course.' He flashed Catrin a smile and offered them both a seat.

Warlow took the lead.

'When was the last time you saw Alistair?'

'The last time?' The lecturer looked away and made a sucking noise with his mouth. 'Last Friday, we went out for a beer after finishing here. Just the one after work. Ali left the pub at six-ish. Busy week with the A level results and that.' Byron's accent was English, neutral, but South of Luton definitely.

'Did he have plans for the weekend?'

'He didn't say. I offered to take him out for a curry on Saturday night, but he wasn't up for it. So, the last time I saw him was Friday at the pub before he buggered off early.'

'You saw him leave in his car?' Warlow asked.

'I did.'

'Is that something you did often? Go out for a curry?'

Byron shook his head. 'Nah, hardly. I mean, until a month ago, he was full-on with Mirain and the kid. You know, all loved-up and happy families and all that.'

The lecturer kept glancing at Catrin. Occasionally, his eyes would soften, and he'd shake his head like a man hardly able to believe what he was seeing. What fate had served up.

Catrin stopped writing. 'Why until a month ago?'

'That was when she buggered off. Mirain, I mean. Hit him hard, it did. But if you take something like that on, it's only to be expected.'

Warlow caught Catrin's eye; a signal for her to keep digging. 'Something like what on? A married woman and her child?'

'Nah, there's a lot of those about. I mean someone with a history, like Mirain has. You know, mental health.' Byron put his fingers up to make quote marks around the last two words of the sentence.

Seeing the blank looks on the detectives' faces, he sat back. 'You didn't know.' He sighed. 'I don't suppose I should be the one telling you all this.'

'Oh, no, carry on,' Warlow said. 'It all helps.'

Byron shrugged at the green light he'd been given. 'She was a bit… Mercurial, let's say. Lovely girl. A stunner. And the kid was great. Ali loved them both, but you know what these depressives are like. Up and down like bloody yo-yos. He was mad to take it on if you ask me. All that extra baggage and the kid as well.'

Warlow gave Byron a bit more space, but the lecturer decided he'd said enough on that subject. Still, Warlow pressed him for more. 'And what about this week? Have you seen him?'

'No. You don't, not this time of year. See people, I mean. Not for days sometimes. You'd think the pressure'd be off with students away, but after the exams there's clearing and uni stuff. Some students want to come back and repeat a course. Ali was busy setting up other courses, too.'

'Such as?'

'You'd have to ask him. Depends. From ceramics to animation. Kids are drawn to games these days. There's a Creative Arts department down in Carmarthen. He's been back and forth, chatting with heads of departments.'

Catrin wrote everything down.

'Did he ever mention other family? Parents?'

'I think his mother is still alive. But he didn't have much to do with her from what I understood.'

Byron watched, his chirpy demeanour waning a little as

time went by. 'Mind if I ask what this is about? Has he done something, old Ali?'

'Much as we appreciate the cooperation, we are not at liberty to tell you anything, Mr Evans,' Warlow said.

Catrin jumped in with a change of tack. 'What is Ali like?'

'Like?' Byron snorted.

'Yes, personality wise. Is he happy-go-lucky? Subdued? Is he a home-bird?'

'Not subdued, not when it comes to chatting up women, anyway. And he's good at his job. But he leaves it all here. Not like me. I've got exam papers in my sink at home. But his place. It's like a bloody clinic. You been there yet?'

'We have been to his house. I agree, it's very… Tidy,' Warlow said. 'Is that typical?'

Byron nodded deeply. 'Oh, yeah. His OCD is a pain.'

'What about that house? It's not cheap. How was he able to afford it?' Warlow asked.

Byron grinned. 'That's all part of his dark and dismal past. Ali's been married before. She was a lawyer, and her parents were loaded. When it all fell apart, Ali came into a bit of dosh. Changed jobs and started playing the field again.'

'Do you have a name for his ex?' Catrin asked.

'Yes. Valerie Halpin. Easy name to look up. She's still in business, I think.'

There were more questions, and Byron proved to be an excellent source. But no, he hadn't seen Alistair's car parked in the college. And no, he'd had no communication from him. In fact, he tried texting him there and then, only to shake his head. 'Not receiving. Wherever he is, his phone's off or there's no signal.'

When they'd finished, Warlow thanked him and gave

the standard spiel about not hesitating to get in touch if he thought of anything else.

'We don't have an Incident Room number, but DS Richards will give you hers.'

'DS... That sounds very impressive,' Byron muttered.

For a moment, said DS was surprised, judging by the expression of frozen horror that appeared on her face, but then she tilted her head and fished out a card.

Byron took it, studying it carefully before he looked up. 'Great, I'll text you later. See if we can catch up.'

'Yeah, do that,' Catrin said with a smile that showed no teeth. 'I might not get back to you right away because of... Well, because of Alistair for a start.'

Byron grinned. 'What has he been up to, eh?'

'We'll be in touch, Mr Evans,' Warlow said without answering, and took his leave.

As they walked back to the car, Warlow asked the obvious question. 'You didn't want to give him your card, did you?'

'Doesn't matter about that. Part of the job, sir,' she said, her mouth tight.

'Were you and he...?'

'Once. Yes.'

'Obviously, it didn't work out.'

'No, sir, it didn't.'

They walked on a bit, the day still bright, until Warlow's inquisitiveness got the better of him again. 'And you had no idea he was still around here?'

'No.'

'You didn't keep in touch?'

'That is the first time I've seen or spoken to Byron since I left Aberystwyth halfway through the summer term of my first year.' She said all of this in an overly bright, airy voice.

Warlow nodded, but wisely said nothing else on the matter. If Catrin wanted to tell him more, she would.

By the time they got to the car, she hadn't.

And Warlow was none the wiser by the time they got to Aberystwyth Police Station either. He could have probed further, but then, if you had any sense, you didn't poke a stick into a nest of vipers unless you wanted to get bitten.

CHAPTER THIRTEEN

Rhys Harries followed DI Allanby along the street to where a uniformed officer in a Hi Viz jacket stood, vaguely guarding Lyndon's property. From whom or what, Rhys had no idea. Still, better safe than sorry. While his boss spoke to the Uniform, Rhys assessed his surroundings. The estate was too small and too far away from centres of population for there to be any trouble of the kind that came when you got a lot of people in too small a space. This was the sort of spot that attracted retirees and young families. It was quiet, out of town, a nice place for a starter home or a good place for a buy-to-let. Hardly somewhere you'd expect to find a single man, unless the investment side of things played the bigger part in the decision to buy.

He said as much when Jess Allanby came back to join him.

'Good point. But we don't have the intel on Lyndon's background yet. Maybe he inherited the house?'

'Looks too new, ma'am. Uniforms find anything out?'

'No. Lyndon kept himself to himself. Or he did of late.'

'Quiet family area,' Rhys voiced his thoughts. 'Nice for the partner and his little girl.'

'Not his,' Jess corrected him. 'The girl wasn't his daughter.'

Rhys consulted his notebook. 'No, sorry, you're right. Previous relationship, wasn't it?'

Jess looked at her watch. 'We have half an hour at the most here, because Warlow wants a briefing at eleven. Have you seen the house?'

'No, ma'am.'

'Then let me give you the tour.'

Rhys followed the DI around the back. She opened the door with the key from under the false rock as if she'd done it a hundred times before.

Rhys had one foot on the threshold when Jess pulled him back. 'Gloves and overshoes. You never know.'

He obliged and walked in, taking in the exact same air of sterile functionality that Warlow had seen the day before. 'Tidy sort of bloke.'

'That's one word for it.'

He followed the DI around the ground floor, but then went his own way upstairs. 'Hello,' Rhys said, poking his head around the door to the third bedroom, which, judging by the desk and chair, doubled as a study. 'Seen this?'

'What?'

'A plugged in and charging MacBook.'

'And?'

'Well, at the very least, it means he was expecting to come back for it.' Rhys lifted the laptop lid and the home screen it up, with a "welcome back Alistair" above a text box requesting a password.

'Shall I?' Rhys sent Jess a "dare-me" grin.

Jess let her chin drop. 'Password?'

'I can have a go.'

Rhys sat on a bucket chair and looked around. The desk contained one tray of papers, obviously full of college stuff, with red-ink markings and commentary in the margin next to the handwritten entries. But even this had been stacked neatly and weighed down by a paperweight. Behind, at the rear of the laptop, sat a desk tidy, containing pens and a small notebook. Rhys picked up the notebook. There were about ten pages of entries, numbers and scribbles and nothing much of any sense to anyone but the author. Inside the cover, in the same hand, were the word Ali and an asterisk.

Rhys put his hands on the keys and typed in some letters. At the fourth attempt, the screen changed.

Peering over his shoulder, Jess let out an exhalation of disbelief. 'How the hell?'

The DC reopened the pocketbook and pointed to the word "Ali" and an asterisk. 'Ali and a star. Ali-star, ma'am. That was the password.'

'Not too much of an ego, then?' Jess muttered.

'Mind if we see what he's been up to?' Rhys asked.

'He's unlikely to object, isn't he?'

'That's true.' He clicked open the search engine from the task bar at the bottom of the screen and quickly opened up the search history.

'Looks like Alistair has been a busy boy.'

Jess watched from over the DC's shoulder as Rhys scrolled through and stopped at an entry that was by far the commonest URL there.

'Mostly Fans? That's a subscription website, isn't it?' she asked.

'It's a content-sharing platform, ma'am, to give it its proper name. Big during the pandemic. Quite a lot of people use it for training videos, photography, dance, and—'

'Porn, am I right?'

'You are, ma'am. Anyone who thinks they have anything worth showing can get on there and charge for what they post up. It's a narcissist's dream.'

'What's our misper Alistair been doing?'

Rhys clicked more buttons. 'He has his password saved in Google, I don't even have to log in—' Rhys's sentence ended abruptly as a page filled the screen.

MoulinsplurgeX. Let's play dress up, dress off, and anything else you'd care to suggest.

THE IMAGE of the body that came with it was definitely female, very well proportioned, with very little in the way of clothing covering up the fleshy assets on display. Above all that was a heavily made-up face with a fetching beauty spot – false, Rhys suspected – enormous eyelashes and plumped-up lips around what the Americans called a popsicle.

'She's young,' Jess said.

'Has to be at least eighteen, ma'am.'

'That's still young,' Jess said, trying not to sound too mother-hen about it. But it was difficult when her own daughter was seventeen.

A couple of seconds went by before Rhys asked, 'Do you think those are real?'

'I doubt it. But be careful, lean in any closer and one of them will have your eye out.'

He sat back.

Jess laughed softly.

Rhys went back to the search engine history. 'Looks like Alistair has visited this page at least fifty times in the last two months.'

Jess sighed. 'Okay. So, we know he's not a saint. Who is, these days? Have a look around, see if you can find anything else.'

'I could take the laptop to the station?'

'No. Technically, that would be theft. We still need official confirmation of the dead man's ID before this place becomes fair game. Make a note of everything and we'll take it all back to the others.'

'Will do, ma'am. I'll have a word with Gil. He'll know who to talk to if we need to contact MoulinsplurgeX. In fact, why don't I give him a ring now?'

Jess left him to it.

Gil Jones picked up after five rings. Though he couldn't hear the ringtone, the chorus of Baby Shark had played enough times in the Incident Room for Rhys to imagine it emerging from the sergeant's pocket, and his panicked desperation to put an end to the noise as he fumbled for the phone. He had tried to change it, but a wail of protest from his granddaughters had forced him to leave it as was.

'Rhys, I hope you're on the way in. We could do with some brawn in setting up this Incident Room. Desks need rearranging, chairs moving, and my back isn't what it used to be. Come to think of it, my front has probably seen better days, too.'

'We're still at Lyndon's address, sarge. DI Allanby is talking to the Uniforms.'

'What?' Gil's voice slid up an octave. 'And what are you doing? Sitting in the car stuffing your face, I expect.'

'Wrong. I have Lyndon's laptop open. I've been going through his search history.'

The line went quiet. 'Please don't tell me he's got images of kids?'

'No, at least I haven't found any. But he does have a sweet spot for a certain artiste on MostlyFans.'

'He, she, or neither of the above?'

'She.'

'Okay. Any leanings? Bondage, domination, nappies?'

'Uh, not that I can see. I don't think she needs much in the way of props... I mean, not counting the obvious ones.'

'You mean the type that need batteries?'

'That kind, yeah. No, she likes to wear big ears and a bit of a tail. You know, a round fluffy thing at the back. A bit like Jessica—'

'Thanks for mansplaining a rabbit, Rhys. And she's underage?'

'No. No, I wouldn't say so. But it looks like Lyndon was very much into her. Lots of visits. There's interaction with the messaging portal on that site between him and her. He's paid her to do things online.'

The older sergeant grunted. 'None of that is illegal. Offensive to a well brought-up boy like you, no doubt, but not against the law.'

'I'm not offended, sarge. In fact, she's—'

'*Arglwydd*, get a grip, Rhys.' There was a pause before Gil added, 'Second thoughts, keep your hands where I can see them.'

'Ha, ha, good one, sarge.'

'Yes, well. I will inspect your pockets for crusty tissues when you get back.'

'Sa-arge,' Rhys objected.

'Is there a point to this conversation other than the obvious disappointment in Lyndon's habits?'

Rhys hesitated for only a second. 'I know you've been involved with this side of things.' He didn't need to elaborate. The sergeant's expertise stretched to many aspects of police work, some less salubrious than others. Everyone on the team was aware that Gil had spent years on Operation Alice. For that alone, he'd earned everyone's respect. In DCI Warlow's opinion, anyone who could stomach online investigations into child pornography deserved a bloody knighthood. So, for all the wrong reasons, Gil was a bit of an expert on the sleazy side of the internet.

'I'm all ears,' the DS said, and quickly added, 'not quite like your rabbit lover, but you get my drift.'

'Right, MoulinsplurgeX,' Rhys paused and quickly added, 'that's the online handle she uses to interact with Lyndon and other fans. Lots of other fans. I'm thinking that once DCI Warlow finds out, he'll want us to follow up.'

'He'll want *you* to follow up, you mean? He who smelt it dealt it, and all that. But this girl might be anywhere in the world.'

'Says she's British.'

'And I can say I'm from Timbuktu, but that doesn't mean I am. Everyone knows I'm from Timbukthree.'

'You know what I mean, sarge.'

'I do and your best bet is to have a word with the POLIT team.'

Rhys shut one eye in concentration. 'Police Online Investigation Team?'

'Well done, Rhys. Top marks for reading the memos. Surprised you have the time in between trawling pornography sites.'

'This is work—'

Gil cut across Rhys's protests, 'There's a DS, Pete Donaldson. I'll text you his number. If anyone knows, he will.'

'Thanks, sarge.'

'Tidy. Right, when are you coming back?'

'We'll be back in twenty minutes. Time to get the kettle on, maybe?'

'Less of the cheek. Never mind the kettle, I was going to ring the Optometrist.'

'Why?'

'Get your vision tested when you arrive. You know that stuff you're watching can make you lose your eyesight.'

'You could be right there, sarge. If MoulinsplurgeX turned around a bit too quickly, as DI Allanby pointed out, you could very easily lose an eye.'

'You haven't been showing her this stuff, have you?' Gil demanded, mock horror in his voice.

'I didn't mean to. It just popped up when she was standing behind me.'

'My God, man, show some control.'

'I didn't mean—'

But Gil had already ended the call just as Rhys heard the tail end of a guffaw.

CHAPTER FOURTEEN

ABERYSTWYTH POLICE STATION had a drum tower at one corner of the building. In medieval times, they built these to better protect the inhabitants of castles from siege technology and missiles. The people of Aberystwyth could be a tad boisterous, but not to the extent where anti-siege architecture was called for. Not in a building built in the 1990s. Warlow liked to think that it might be a nod to something Norman, since the street that it stood on had the very non-British name of Boulevard De Saint Brieuc. Of course, there was a Celtic link in that Saint-Brieuc was an old town in Brittany, and since Breton and Welsh stemmed from the same language roots, he might be prepared to let that one go. Plus, the grey stone build made it almost look like a castle if you squinted a bit.

Being on the edge of town meant that there was plenty of parking, with an Army Reserve Training Centre behind, ready to repel all boarders, though there was something fundamentally wrong with that thought, too, since they were not at sea. And the location had the bonus of being opposite the Vale of Rheidol railway. If they were really pushed, they could all tootle off to Devil's Bridge on a train and hike to the spot where Alistair Lyndon, RIP yet to be confirmed, had been interred.

But inside the station, in the co-opted Incident Room – smaller than the one they'd decanted out of in Carmarthen – all thoughts of day trips had long since passed. Teas were needed, but without the bonus of the usual *biscuit*. Gil had the healthy eating bit – or at least the rationed *biscuit* bit – firmly between his teeth.

Warlow looked up from his desk to see the big sergeant fussing at a notice board. They'd spent the best part of half an hour sorting out which desks they'd be working at. They despatched Rhys on a recce to identify where the tea could be made and he'd come back fully armed, but without the Human Tissue for Transplant box, which had remained in Carmarthen, much to everyone's chagrin.

Warlow dropped his eyes back to the screen in front of him and wiggled an unfamiliar mouse. Tiernon's preliminary report had appeared in the team's mailbox, confirming everything that Rhys had said the day before. In addition, the HOP emphasised the fact that the stomach contents were virtually empty, showing that the dead man had not eaten for some time prior to his death. Also, a great deal of vegetation, dirt, and fibre samples had contaminated the body and these would all need to be looked at.

No change there, then.

He also checked over Gil's assessment of Alistair Lyndon. Clean but not squeaky. He'd blotted his pristine copybook twice with speeding offences, both in the Salisbury area, and both when he'd been much younger. He currently had *nul* points (another of Gil's French affectations) on his licence.

Elaine Hunt had taken the time to talk to the College HR and to her bosses. No complaints were outstanding about Lyndon's work. All they had to go on there was what Byron Evans had told them. That he wasn't shy when it came to chatting up the ladies. That he was frighteningly efficient, had a touch of OCD, and knew what he was doing on the work front.

Which gave him an advantage over the state of the investigation. For a start, it would be useful to know if Alistair Lyndon was indeed the body in the mineshaft.

As if on cue, a fresh email appeared in the inbox. This one, too, from the Forensic Path department. Warlow opened it up. Tiernon again, this time informing them all that dental analysis confirmed that the body was that of Alistair Lyndon.

'Right.' Warlow stood up. 'This is a first. Looks like I've opened the email before everyone else.' He strode to the single notice board, divided into two so that one-half functioned as a Gallery, the other as a Job Centre.

Warlow pointed to Alistair Lyndon's name. 'Tiernon has just confirmed that our dead man is indeed Lyndon. No surprises there, but it's good to know. We need to find any living relatives. The house on the Crugiau Estate is now a crime scene. Let's get Povey over there as soon as. Not that I'm expecting her to find anything, but I also want to look inside that locked cupboard.' He turned and regarded the team. 'Right, let's go around the mulberry bush one more time. Jess?'

The DI pivoted at her desk. 'Rhys has had a quick peek at Lyndon's laptop. Be good to get a proper look at it before the tech bods tear it apart.'

'But Rhys found something to work with, yes?' Warlow demanded.

'I did, sir. Lyndon's search history. I'm waiting for a phone call from the POLIT team. It may be nothing at all, but...'

'Chase it up, and while you're waiting, check with Tiernon regarding this other evidence. The dirt and the fibres. Ask him which bit he thinks is the most significant.'

Rhys nodded.

Catrin picked up on his momentary hesitation. 'Don't worry, he won't bite. Anyway, he likes you. I'm surprised he hasn't asked you up to one of his lectures.'

Rhys flushed a bright red.

'He has, hasn't he?' Catrin said, pleased with herself.

'I'm going in a couple of weeks. It's on post-mortem decomposition.'

The look that broke over Catrin's face was priceless. 'We do not want to see any snaps you take,' she warned.

'There'll probably be a handout, you're welcome to have a copy,' Rhys said.

'Or I could simply put my foot in a wasps' nest. I know which would be the more pleasurable of the two.' Catrin sent him a rictus grin.

Warlow turned to Gil, who was massaging his stomach. 'You okay?'

Gil nodded. 'Hunger monster is awake. You may hear him growl.'

'Shame we didn't have any *biscuits* with our tea,' muttered Rhys.

'I heard that.' Gil glowered at the DC.

Warlow pointed to the image of a grey BMW. 'I want to find Lyndon's car. Byron Evans confirmed that he saw Lyndon last on Friday driving his car. So, let's get on to the NVTD, see if they can help.'

This wasn't rocket science. Since 2006, the National Vehicle Tracking Database recorded every vehicle by automatic number plate recognition cameras. Over thirty-five million images were captured every day on the ANPCs that stared down at motorists on poles on every major road. If Lyndon had been driving on one of those roads, they'd find out where he'd been.

'Catrin, where are we with finding the person who left the thank you note for Lyndon?'

'Ideally, if we had his phone, it would help. But we have Lyndon's number and I'm sorting out records from his service provider. Hopefully, that will throw something up for our mysterious "A".'

'Good. Right, that leaves the equally mysterious Mirain Hughes.'

'His missing partner?' Jess asked.

'She's an interesting one,' Catrin said. 'Has a record for outraging public decency. Took her clothes off in a car park, apparently. About four years ago.'

'If she'd done it online, she could have made some money, sir,' Rhys said. It earned him a strange look from the rest of the team. 'Just saying,' he mumbled.

'Okay, well, she's next on my list. And we all have things to do, yes?' Warlow glanced at Gil and indicated the corridor outside. 'A word, sergeant, if you will.'

He led the way and Gil followed, his expression one of guarded interest.

'You okay, Gil?' Warlow asked.

'Not bad,' Gil replied.

'Did you speak with Tom?'

'Tom? Oh, no, not yet. Been too busy with this malarkey. Whose idea was it to move to the North Pole? The Super's?'

'Mine,' Warlow replied. 'And it's hardly the Arctic Circle. We're only forty-five miles from Carmarthen.'

'Then why does it feel so far… North? *Mam fach*, I'm sure I saw a bloody penguin on my way up here.'

Warlow nodded, ignoring Gil's deflection tactics. 'I'm only asking after your wellbeing because I'm doing the maths and coming up with an unhappy Gil. No *biscuits*? The lecture on healthy eating and you wanting to speak to Tom? Are you okay in yourself?'

'Me, I'm fine. Look at me. Know what the current Mrs Jones said as I left for all points north this morning?'

Warlow waited.

'You look like Iron Man.' Gil puffed his chest out.

'Really?'

The DS paused, sticking the tip of his tongue out of the corner of his mouth and making a great show of reconsidering his statement. 'Mind you, it was after I'd complained that my shirt felt a bit stiff around the collar. Maybe what she really said was, "you should try doing some ironing, man".'

Warlow let the laugh come, but it felt a little forced. 'Gil, if it's something serious, then talk with Tom. He'd be delighted.'

'Of course.' Gil was suddenly all smiles. 'As I said, I promised a mate I'd ask an expert. I'll get round to it when I have a spare moment.'

'Good. Make sure you do. We're not very good at discussing our health problems, are we? Us men.'

They exchanged knowing glances. Warlow was a fine one to talk. He'd kept his HIV status under wraps from everyone on the team bar Jess and Buchannan for months. So, he wasn't exactly coming at this discussion from a position of strength. Gil, however, let him off lightly.

'Useless,' the DS agreed. 'Mind you, when you're perfect, there's not a lot to discuss.'

'There is that.'

They grinned at one another and nodded, the chance of either of them expressing real feelings about as likely as seeing a penguin in Aberystwyth. Though it remained an unsaid certainty that if their backs ever were truly up against the wall, both men knew where to turn.

'Right, let's get to it.' Warlow shoved his hands in his trouser pockets.

'Lead on, Gunga Din,' Gil said.

'Ah, Rudyard Kipling reference. Have you used that one with the youngsters, yet?'

Warlow's collective nouns for DS Richards and DC Harries brought a sceptical scowl to Gil's face.

'I would not waste my breath. Rhys would probably think he's a Rapper and Catrin would no doubt play the woke colonialist card. Just to rile me.'

Warlow nodded and pushed open the door to the Incident Room with a smile. Gil was right. Best they keep their powder dry on that one.

CHAPTER FIFTEEN

ONCE WARLOW LEFT on his quest to search out the relatives of the mysterious Mirain Hughes, for those left behind it was a question of manning the phones, trawling through records, and waiting for people to get back to them.

Glamour personified.

The first to get something positive out of the day was Rhys. He took the call from DS Pete Donaldson and quickly explained what they were doing. When he mentioned the name MoulinsplurgeX, the line went silent.

'You're kidding me,' Donaldson said in an accent from somewhere north of Portadown. Marriage to a local girl had brought with it a transfer from Northern Ireland to the supposedly calmer environs of West Wales but had done nothing to diminish the accent.

'Does the name ring a bell?' Rhys demanded.

'It sets off a bloody klaxon.'

'How?'

'MoulinsplurgeX is a real psychology student at the uni in Aber. True name Claudine Barton.'

Rhys wrote it down. 'How come she's known to you, sarge?'

'Ah well, welcome to the brave new world of student debt. Sex workers are entitled to protection, just like everyone else. Though the uni up there may not be as progressive as some, they've recognised the need to support the 6% of students across the country who work their way through uni via the sex industry.'

'But you surely can't go to Aber and do a course in it?'

'Jesus, wash your mouth out with soap and water there, Rhys. You'd be in deep doo-doo if you suggested that. Twitter has already been there and scorched the earth. No, no, this is all about keeping workers safe.'

Rhys paused, trying to get his head around it all.

Donaldson explained, 'We offer support to the uni if they want it. We've even been up to talk to staff about it. You ever heard of National Ugly Mugs?'

'I can't say I have. Though I can come up with a few candidates without much effort.'

'It's a charity set up to collate warnings and incidents about dangerous punters in the sex industry. And there are some choice bastards out there, believe you me. Claudine is an active member. You'd like her. She's a real character. Her partner's a bit of a 'roid monster, but he looks after her. And you say your man, Lyndon, was interacting with her?'

'Online, yes. A lot, judging by his search history. I wondered if there'd been any real contact.'

'Unlikely. Claudine is switched on. Though she isn't shy. She'll chat with you, I'm sure. I can set it up if you like?'

'We've got bugger all else at the moment,' Rhys said.

Donaldson signed off with a promise of a follow-up text.

Rhys put the phone down and turned to Gil. 'That was Donaldson, sarge. I think it might be worth chasing up MoulinsplurgeX. She's local.'

'Okay. That should keep you out of mischief for a while.'

'I'd better speak with Tiernon about the full Path report first, though.'

'You'd better.'

'Could do with a cup of tea and a Hobnob, though.' Rhys's voice dripped with yearning.

Gil flinched. 'Get behind me, Satan. Or, as granddaughter number two was heard to say, after I had used this phrase in context during an open and frank discussion about a takeaway curry with the current Mrs Jones, "get behind me, Stan".'

Rhys chortled and picked up the phone to dial Tiernon's number. 'That Stan can be a bit of a card.'

'He can indeed, Rhys. He can indeed.'

WHILE RHYS WENT full ghoul with Tiernon, Catrin got copies of Lyndon's phone records and went through them. When she'd finished, she took them over to where Jess was working.

'Anything?' Jess asked.

'There is one number that stands out. He texted on Friday and Saturday several times and a dozen times during the week before.'

'Worth giving it a go?'

Catrin shrugged.

Jess picked up the phone and dialled the number. The voice that answered was female and young.

'Hello?'

'Hi, this is Detective Inspector Jess Allanby, Dyfed Powys Police. Who am I talking to, please?'

'This is Ava. Ava Farley.'

Catrin wrote down the name, underlined the capital "A" and hurried back to her desk to begin typing in the details.

'Hi Ava. Sorry for the out of the blue call,' Jess continued.

'Is anything wrong? Is it my gran? Has she fallen again? Is that it?'

Jess felt a sudden surge of sympathy for this girl. 'No, it's not your gran. Your number has come up as appearing on a caller's list that we're investigating.'

'A caller? Who?'

'Alistair Lyndon.'

A choked back sob came down the line before a whispered and tremulous, 'Oh my God. What—'

'I'd rather not talk about it over the phone like this, Ava.'

Catrin angled her screen so that Jess could see. She held up two fingers, palm facing forwards so as not to seem rude. Two Ava Farleys had come up. 'Can you confirm your address for me, Ava? Or, if you'd rather phone the station back to make sure this is me, that would be fine. Just look up the number online and—'

'No, it's fine. I live out near the hospital, Caradog Road.'

Catrin nodded and changed to a thumbs up.

'Is there any chance you can come into the station on Boulevard De Saint Brieuc?' Jess asked.

'The one that looks like a castle?'

'That's the one.'

A silent pause. And then, 'I knew something was wrong. Has something happened to him?'

'This is a serious investigation we're involved in and talking over the phone is never a good idea,' Jess insisted. 'We find these things are much better discussed face to face.'

Ava let out a ratcheting sigh. 'I'm at work. I doubt Tessa can let me go this morning.'

Jess understood. 'It's almost midday. Do you have a lunch break?'

'At one, yes.'

'Tell me where you work. I'll have a car pick you up and drop you back.'

Another pause. 'That makes it sound really serious.'

'The sooner, the better with these things, I've found.'

'You sound nice,' Ava said.

'And you sound sensible. It would be for the best if you could come in.'

'I work at the Dressy Fox on Heol Pren.'

'Would you like the car outside or somewhere else?'

'You worried about my reputation?' Ava asked and let out a hollow laugh.

'Not unless you are.'

'They can park at the back. There's a service road.'

Jess returned the thumbs up to Catrin. 'We'll see you a little after one, Ava. I appreciate it.'

When the call ended, Jess joined Catrin at her desk. 'Ava Farley, aged twenty-six.' Images of a pretty, petite woman in various locations appeared on her Facebook page on-screen. Often with female friends, and with different coloured hair in each shot.

'She looks like fun,' Jess observed.

'Left school at seventeen. Local college, worked at the Dressy Fox for four years. Not in a relationship at the moment, if this is all to be believed.'

'Any record?'

'Nothing on the PNC.'

'Okay, well, we'll find out how well she knew Alistair Lyndon in an hour. We'll do the interview together?'

'Love to, ma'am.'

————

WARLOW MET with Joel Rampley at his place of work: Humphries and Sons, a garage to the northeast of town, sat squeezed into a space between shops. As so often in this area of Welsh speakers, the services offered were written on the wall, first in Welsh and then in English. Who knew that *Adnabod Diffygion* meant Fault Diagnosis? Well, if he'd had to think about it, Warlow probably did. But the garage had it up there, clear as day.

Warlow rang a bell at reception and spoke to a middle-aged man who disappeared wordlessly into the bowels of the workshop and came back with another man in his early thirties. This one was taller, thinner, with a shaved head which, the DCI judged, was finishing a job that nature had already started, opting for the lesser of two evils. Rampley had tattoos on his bare arms and smudges of grease on his jaw. Though it wasn't easy to assess under the overalls, he looked to be a stringy guy; the kind blessed with a fast metabolism. The overalls looked clean on that day, fresh, as did this well-kept establishment. A family business, probably. They likely owned the site rather than rented it; there were better places with easier access to run a garage. Still, people liked consistency, which might be the only genuine explanation for this place's unlikely location smack bang in the middle of town.

Warlow introduced himself and offered his hand before asking, 'Is there anywhere we could chat in private?'

They walked through to a back "waiting room" where

paying customers could sit out of the cold while their cars got the finishing touches of MOTs and services. Warlow turned down the offer of tea and sat on an upholstered bench with Rampley perched opposite him across a table. Not quite the interview room, but it would do.

'Thanks for talking to me,' Warlow began.

'You don't say no when a copper turns up, do you?'

'Some people might. Some people do.'

'Why?'

'Because they think it's their duty to make life as difficult as possible for the police.'

Joel smiled. 'I know the type.'

'I won't waste your time, Mr Rampley. I'm here about your ex-wife, Mirain Hughes.'

Rampley's face took on a pained expression, and he sighed. 'What now?'

Warlow ran with it. 'Now? What do you mean by that?'

'I've been here before, haven't I? You've found her and she's off the bloody rails, right?'

'Not quite.'

Rampley's turn to frown. 'Then what?'

Warlow took out his notebook, a sure sign that things were serious here. It never failed. 'I have to insist that what I'm about to tell you remains completely confidential for the moment.'

'Oh Christ. Something's happened to her, hasn't it? Has she done something stupid? Crashed a car or something?' Though he sounded miffed, Warlow picked up on the undercurrent of concern, too, and Rampley went up a couple of notches in the DCI's estimation.

'No, not as far as we know. This has to do with her current partner, Alistair Lyndon.'

'Him? What's he done, then?'

'Mr Lyndon was found dead two days ago.'

Rampley's mouth fell open and his hands came up

onto the table as he sat back, eyes blinking as if the light were suddenly a little too bright for them. 'Dead?'

'That's the part that has to remain confidential. We haven't informed his next of kin yet. Nor have we informed Mirain.'

Rampley looked down at his hands and suddenly pulled them back across his chest, a fist nestling in each armpit. 'Christ, dead? How?'

'I can't discuss that. The reason I'm here is that we're investigating the circumstances. It's Mirain I want to talk to you about. We don't know where she is.'

Rampley nodded. 'Welcome to the club.'

'What does that mean?'

'The where-the-hell-is-Mirain club, is what I mean.'

Warlow sat forward. A signal for Rampley to expand his explanation. 'I assume you know Mirain left Alistair three, maybe four weeks ago. She's done all of that before. She left us, me and Heledd—'

'Your daughter?'

'Our daughter, Mirain's and mine. She left us half a dozen times over six years.'

Warlow made a note and spoke while he wrote. 'That's… Unusual.'

'Yeah, it is. But not when you understand a bit about her condition. After Hels was born, something happened to Mirain. They say she might have been borderline bipolar before, but after Hels, it kicked in big time. Something about a post-natal exacerbation. Big bloody words, I know. She's okay on meds, but then something convinces her she doesn't need them, and nice mummy Mirain turns into wild frickin' animal Mirain.'

'Are these manic episodes?' Warlow had a grasp of the terminology. He'd come across cases before.

'Yup. Exactly that. Mirain the bloody maniac. Spends loads of money. Gets pissed in strange pubs where she buys everyone a drink. Takes all her clothes off. You name it.'

'You think that's happened this time?'

'Wouldn't you?'

'You've had no communication from her since she left.'

'I didn't say that. She's been texting Heledd. She's on Facebook now and again. What's tragic is that it's Hel's birthday this week and… It's hard explaining all this shit to an eight-year-old.'

'What was the arrangement you had? Were you involved in looking after Heledd, too?'

Rampley nodded. 'Mirain moved in with Alistair, into his nice, new shiny house. Heledd was there all week, and I had her every other weekend, Friday to Monday, plus the odd night when Mirain and Ali had a bloody date night…' He caught himself. 'Sorry.'

Warlow's rancour alarm sounded. 'Did that work okay?'

'It did. Better than now. In the week after Mirain buggered off, Alistair thought it best if Heledd stayed with me. She's with me all the time now, but my shifts start early here. There's a summer school breakfast club.'

'What about afterwards?'

'Mirain's dad helps. Carwyn's been great. Always, right from the start. Salt of the earth, is Carwyn. Heledd thinks the world of him. We sort of shared the Mirain load between us. Sometimes I think what's happened to her hit him hardest of all.'

'Do you mind sharing the recent texts and messages from Mirain with us? I'd really like to get in touch with her.'

Rampley shrugged. 'Sure, I hope you have better luck than we do. Mirain's pretty good at staying hidden when she's off on one.'

Warlow handed him a card. 'I'll get one of my officers

to be in touch for the technical stuff. We may need to borrow your phone for a few hours, that okay?'

'Fine by me.'

They shook hands and Warlow took his leave, wondering just how you explained bipolar disorder to an almost eight-year-old.

CHAPTER SIXTEEN

CLAUDINE BARTON'S flat was on North Parade. A converted Edwardian development which, in the past, would have been a grand terraced house. The sort of establishment with lots of rooms where families stayed for their two-week summer hols, hosted by a landlady with kippers for breakfast and hot water available only between six and nine in the evenings.

But that had long gone the way of separate flats. Number five was two floors up. There may have been a lift, but Rhys took the stairs. The door was royal blue. The girl that opened it was a vision in pink and no taller than about five-three in heels, which were mules under a very short kimono. Though the wrap had been cinched tight, there was enough on show for Rhys to confirm that this was indeed MoulinsplurgeX he was looking at.

'Hiya,' she said in a Valley's accent.

'Claudine, right? I'm DC Rhys Harries.' He held out his warrant card.

Claudine batted ridiculously long eyelashes at the wallet and smiled. 'Yeah, of course. I've been expecting you. Come in.'

The flat was surprisingly roomy, with a spacious sitting room fronted by a bay window looking out onto the street below. 'Wanna coffee?' Claudine asked over her shoulder as she tottered along in front.

Rhys accepted the offer and stood while Claudine went into the adjoining kitchenette. In the bay window, a table nestled holding a laptop and some open textbooks.

'You working?'

Claudine gave him an old-fashioned sort of look. 'I don't usually dress like this for visitors.'

Rhys, a little flustered by her reply, pointed towards the table. 'I meant the books.'

'Oh yeah. That was this morning, though. I'm doing an open university course as well as my degree here. Psychology.'

'Really? A good one to do. I mean, you're probably meeting all sorts of people doing...' he nodded vaguely at her while his eyes tried to find something not too inappropriate to look at, '... What you do.'

'All sorts in all shapes and sizes, yeah,' Claudine agreed. 'I'm staying here this summer. Might as well. There's no seaside in Caerphilly.'

She came back through with two mugs and sat cross-legged on the one sofa. Rhys fetched a chair from the table and sat a good six feet away, trying to decide the best plan of action for the coffee and his notebook. In the end, he placed the coffee on the floor beside him, notebook open on his knees. But then a thought occurred. He was alone with this woman in her flat.

'It would be easier if I recorded our chat.' He wrinkled his nose in apology. 'That okay?'

'Fine,' Claudine said, both hands around her mug, one mule dangling off a bouncing foot. 'Pete Donaldson said you wanted to speak to me about the business?'

'You as MoulinsplurgeX, yes.' Rhys took a sip of coffee

and fixed his eyes on the beauty spot on Claudine's left cheek. 'Mind if I ask how old you are, Claudine?'

'I'll be twenty in six weeks,' she said and smiled. 'I know I look younger. My voice doesn't help. But it doesn't do any harm either, for the business, I mean.'

Rhys nodded. He understood where she was coming from, but it only added to his discomfort. 'I saw your website…'

'Did you?' she sounded genuinely interested. 'What did you think?'

'… As part of the investigation we are running into an unnatural death,' Rhys added the qualification quickly and saw Claudine's big eyes double in size.

'Oh, my God. Really? Like on Netflix?'

'No. Not at all like on Netflix. I mean, it's nothing like that, really. Lots of hanging about, interviewing people. Gathering information. Hardly any car chases.'

'But like, you're a homicide detective, then?'

'We don't use that term… So no, not… Well, yes. In this case, I suppose I am.'

Claudine sat up. 'That's amazing.' Shifting in the seat made the kimono stretch tightly across her chest and the gap showing her cleavage widened perceptibly. Rhys reached for his coffee and made a very conscious effort to keep his eyes on her face when he lifted it to his lips.

'Is this where you do the camera work?' The words came out from behind his mug, almost an octave higher than he'd intended.

Claudine shook her head. 'Mostly in my bedroom. I can set it all up in minutes. The Webcam stuff is easy money. I dress up and chat. People, mainly men, ask me to do things. Sometimes it's just putting lipstick on. Other times it's more… Involved.'

Yep, I know exactly what "involved" means, thought Rhys,

casting his mind back to the MoulinsplurgeX showreel she had on the site. But all he did was nod in encouragement.

'I mean, people pay me to do the strangest things. And I don't mean the obvious.'

He nodded again. Claudine had a girl-next-door vibe about her. A butter-wouldn't-melt-in-her-mouth quality, which, given the things that she'd been asked to put in her mouth online, probably left very little room for any churned dairy products, salted or unsalted.

'Good money, is it?'

'Amazing. I've done other stuff before. Never stripping, but a couple of times I've answered funny adverts. Once I had to go to someone's house all dressed up just to eat a salad in a thong and heels.' She paused, turning over what she'd said in her mind. 'It was me in the thong and heels, not the salad. I nearly bloody froze. But the customer was really nice. Didn't speak much, did what men do, on his own, while he watched me eat. When he'd finished, I left with one hundred quid. He did all the clearing up. Of himself and the salad.'

Rhys couldn't help but grimace. 'Isn't that risky?'

Claudine nodded. 'Afterwards, I thought probably not the best idea. That was before I met Luca, my boyfriend. But what people do, and what turns them on, is their business, as long as no one gets hurt, right? I don't hold it against them. Plus, I only get half my tuition fees paid. All the rest is a loan. But I want to be debt free when I finish here.'

'So, for you, this is a job?'

Claudine smiled. 'Exactly. And it pays a shit load better than serving lunch at Café Clec.' She sipped at her coffee before adding, 'I've done that too, by the way.'

Rhys sipped some more coffee. He took in the smile and the siliconed attributes that were perkily straining against the fabric of her gown, fighting the urge to let his eyes stray down over her smooth legs.

Get a grip, Rhys. You're there to do a job. The voice in his head was Gil's.

'Does the name Alistair Lyndon mean anything to you, Claudine?'

She shook her head.

'Can I show you some screenshots we found on Lyndon's computer?'

He picked up his phone, found the images, and watched as Claudine scrolled through the shots he'd taken from Lyndon's laptop of his recorded interactions with MoulinsplurgeX.

After a while, she looked up. 'He's not Alistair Lyndon on here, though, is he?'

'No, he's signed in as Clean Unit.'

Another nod. 'I wondered where he'd got to. He's a regular. Private client. That's a good £3 a minute. Group chats are half that price. From what I remember, he liked me to spread cream over...' She waved a hand with sparkly pink nail extensions over her chest.

'Ah,' was all Rhys could drag up from his lexicon.

Claudine smiled apologetically. 'Whipped cream. Which I then wiped off with a finger and had to eat.' She handed back the phone.

'So, you've never seen Lyndon in the flesh?'

'No, I wouldn't know him from Adam.'

Rhys showed her a photo of Lyndon. She looked at it before flicking her eyes back at Rhys with a shrug.

'How long had he been a regular?'

'Ooh, no idea. I can probably check. I can search and see when he first appeared. I don't keep tabs, though. Once it's done, it's done, you know? It's all an act. A performance. All the baby talk and heavy breathing.'

'Donaldson told me you're an active NUM member, too?'

Claudine gave him a big Jane-next-door smile. 'When I tell people that, they think I'm a miner. The underground type, not the underage type. But I'm on the Mugs' committee. It's a great thing to share.'

'You're conscious of safety?'

'Of course. Except for the salad and thong thingy. Which I definitely don't do now.'

Rhys gave her a thin smile. 'Do you live here alone?'

'That's a Pete Donaldson question.' She grinned. 'No, I live with my boyfriend.'

'Good,' Rhys replied.

'You sound surprised.'

'Do I? It's just... What you do could strain a relationship.'

Claudine smoothed down the hem of her kimono. All two millimetres of it. 'He can get twitchy sometimes. But it's make-believe. That's what I keep telling him.'

'And it doesn't bother him?'

That gave Claudine pause. 'He knows we need the money. This place is almost £700 a month, so I have to keep working. His wage hardly pays for our Friday night pizza. He gets moody sometimes when I'm at it for too long.'

Rhys thought about asking what "at it" might be but thought better of it. He'd got enough for now. 'Okay, thanks for your time. If you could let me have the timeline, how long Lyndon was a client, that would be great. If we have any more questions, we'll be in touch. My number's on here.' He handed over a card.

'Any time,' she said and stood up.

The sound of a key in the door drew their attention. It opened and a man wearing dark gym clothing walked in with two Lidl carrier bags. The T-shirt he wore might as well have been sprayed on over a barrel chest and biceps the size of rugby balls. He was shorter than Rhys but made up for that in the width of his built-up torso.

'You're back early,' Claudine said.

'Who is this?' asked the man, staring at Rhys with unbridled suspicion.

'This is Rhys Harries.' She turned, smiling towards Rhys and back again. 'Rhys, meet Luca, my partner.'

Rhys stepped forward, hand outstretched. But Luca did not let go of the bags, preferring instead to double down on the challenging glare.

'Fair enough,' Rhys said. He turned back to Claudine. 'As I said, you have my number. Anything at all occurs to you, give me a ring. Luca.' Rhys nodded at the boyfriend and walked towards the open door.

He'd gone down one flight when the argument began. Raised voices. Well, mainly a man's raised voice.

'Again, Claudine. Again?'

'It isn't like that. He's—'

'I don't want to hear it. He's a student, isn't he? One of your nerdy boyfriends from the uni?'

'No, he's not. For God's sake, Luca—'

'Don't for God's sake me. I'm not stupid. No more people coming to the flat, we said, didn't we?'

'I can't stop people knocking on the door. And those others, they were part of my tutor group.'

'Tutor group my arse. Just the internet stuff, we said, right? Just the cameras and shit.'

Rhys slowed down, wondering if he should go back up and intervene here, because if Luca had an inside voice, he'd left it at the checkout in Lidl.

'You think I don't know, Claud? What if I hadn't come home now? What would have happened, eh?'

'Nothing.'

'Bollocks!'

'Luca, shut up,' Claudine said.

'Shut up? No, I won't shut up. I told you what would happen. I told you what I'd do when your punters come to call.'

'He's not a punter—'

Rhys half turned in time to see Luca barrelling down the stairs towards him, his face red and twisted in anger.

'Hang on, Luca, you have definitely got the wrong end of the—'

He never finished the sentence. Luca put one hand on the banister and one on the wall, lifted himself up and aimed a foot square at the DC's chest. All Rhys heard after that was Claudine's high-pitched scream. And there were words of warning in that scream.

'Luca, he's a copper!'

But then came a second sound. The noise of his head hitting the half-landing wall as he flew backwards towards it. After that, the fading noise of clattering footsteps on the stairs and another scream from Claudine reached him before the world around him faded and finally went very dark.

CHAPTER SEVENTEEN

AVA FARLEY WAS on her second tissue.

Jess chose the least austere space she could find at Aberystwyth station to talk to the girl and ended up in a room with four rows of chairs, six across, in front of a lectern. She'd pushed the inevitable flip chart to one side and rearranged the chairs into something less formal. Catrin sat off to one side, Ava sat opposite Jess. The chairs were plastic, the walls bright white under harsh fluorescent strip lighting that buzzed angry-wasp style above them.

It still looked like an interview room, no matter what.

'In your own time, Ava,' Jess said.

'Sorry... I... sorry. I guessed something had happened. I thought he'd changed his mind about me, you know?' She sniffed and dabbed at her nose.

Jess took in the short blonde hair, curling at the bottom, the full makeup, the stylish clothes. Not her taste, and certainly not Molly's, but smart, nevertheless. She looked fit. A runner perhaps. Some girls went through their late teens and early twenties believing they could do whatever they wanted before the booze and the crap food took their toll. The awakening sometimes came at thirty or just after, but Ava seemed to have realised earlier than some. Jess hoped she'd instilled some of that wellbeing into Molly already.

So, Ava looked after herself. Up to now, Jess saw nothing to dislike. Alistair Lyndon must have thought he'd won the lottery, judging by what she'd seen of the man in photographs. Not bad, but nothing to write home about. Whereas Ava would merit half a dozen pages of descriptive prose. Clearly, she'd seen something else in Lyndon. But then, attraction was a strange old beast and Jess didn't have to stray far from her own little patch to rattle its cage. Tricky Ricky was a case in point. Physically, he'd be everyone's idea of beefcake, but underneath it, he'd been an emotionally needy egomaniac who craved approval by flirting with anyone who'd listen, when he wasn't trying to be the best at golf or five-a-side or whatever other pursuit sucked at his time. She'd put up with it for years. She'd never understand why it had taken that long for her to realise he couldn't help himself.

But that was total BS, because you could always help yourself. All you needed was willpower and a sense of loyalty and maturity.

Bloody Ricky.

Contemplating him again irritated Jess immensely. He had no place in this room. Nor in her life. Not anymore. She sucked in a deep breath and banished him from her thoughts.

'How long had you known Alistair, Ava?'

'Six weeks, that's all. The first time I met him, he'd come into the shop to buy something for his girlfriend. Said they were going through a rocky patch. So, I helped him buy a cropped cashmere jumper. He came back in a week later. I thought he'd come back to return it because she hadn't liked it. That happens. But that wasn't why. He'd come in to thank me. Sort of.'

Jess picked up on that. 'Why sort of?'

'He looked a bit down and when I asked him why, he said that the jumper, his peace offering, had come too late and that his partner had left him.'

Out of the corner of Jess's eye, she saw Catrin taking notes.

'He was nice. Chatty,' Ava continued. 'Didn't push anything, but I felt sorry for him. A couple of days later, he came back in again, looking a bit rougher. He said it had been so nice to chat with me. Said it had helped because I was a stranger. All his friends had taken sides in the split-up. He asked if I'd have a coffee with him. So, I did.'

'You felt sorry for him?'

Ava nodded.

'When did you first go out together?'

'A week later. He took me for a meal to a place I'd never been to before. He was nice. Not pushy as I said. We got a little drunk, and he told me all about what had happened. His partner had gone off and left Alistair and her little girl. I couldn't understand why anyone would do that. The little girl had gone back to live with her real dad because... Well, because he was her next of kin. But that was awkward because the real dad worked long hours. So awful.'

'Did you sleep with Alistair then?'

Ava frowned. 'No, not then. I did fancy him. He was older and very different to the blokes I normally met up with.'

'How so?'

'Less grabby, for a start. A bit more grown-up if you know what I mean.'

Jess smiled. She felt for this Love Island generation. All the men grew up thinking they were porn stars, and expecting the girls to react accordingly. 'So, how did it progress from there?'

'He was pretty cut up about his partner leaving, but gradually, he became…' She contemplated her next words carefully. 'I'd say more angry than sad. He said he was so glad that he'd met me and that I was helping him loads by just listening. Said he wanted to make it up to me and cook me a proper meal. Show me his house, that sort of thing.'

'Had he ever been back to your flat?'

'Once, after a night out. He came in for a coffee. My flatmate was there. Not very romantic. He kissed me the first time then. It was nice. But he didn't stay. Like I say, not pushy.'

'So, the first time you slept with him was…'

'Last Saturday. I stayed the night at his house.'

'What was your impression of it?'

'Lovely. Big and clean, and he was right. His partner, Mirain, she'd gone and taken everything. He showed me her picture and one of Heledd, the little girl. He said he missed her, too.' Ava's bottom lip quivered, and she broke down again. 'Sorry, I can't believe he's gone. I thought he'd changed his mind about…' She looked up suddenly, staring straight into Jess's face. 'Please tell me it wasn't suicide. Please tell me he didn't do this to himself.'

'It wasn't suicide, Ava. We don't know exactly what happened yet, but we are treating his death as suspicious.'

'What?' she breathed out the word in horror.

Jess nodded. 'So, you understand why I have to ask you some of these questions. What time did you leave on Sunday?'

Ava looked down at her hands. 'Time? I was going to my mum's for lunch. I said I'd cancel, but Alistair insisted I went. We were in bed and… He got up to make me coffee and even ran me back to the flat. So sweet of him. The last time I saw him was at half nine on Sunday morning when he dropped me off.'

'Was your flatmate home?'

'Yes. Alistair waited until I was inside and I waved to him from my window. My flatmate said it was cute because she saw me do it.'

'So, if we ask her, she'll attest to Alistair being alive at nine-thirty on Sunday morning?'

Another sob as Ava squeezed her eyes shut, and a big fat tear rolled down her cheek.

'One last thing,' Jess said. 'Did you leave him a note?'

Ava nodded. 'Just to say thank you for a lovely evening.'

Jess glanced across at Catrin and then at her watch. 'It's almost 1.45. We'll get you back to the shop. Sorry to have taken up your lunch break.'

Ava shook her head. 'I'm not hungry. I couldn't eat anything.'

'We'll get you a cup of tea while we rustle up transport. Catrin will take some details of your flatmate's number if that's okay.'

Ava nodded.

Jess sorted out the tea and they packed Ava off. On their way back to the Incident Room, Jess asked Catrin the obvious, 'Well? Is she telling the truth?'

'I'd put money on it, ma'am. No one is that good an actor. But the timing is off. I mean, as far as I remember, Mirain was still around six weeks ago.'

'Yes, that is odd. We'd better—'

'Ma'am!' Gil's voice from down the corridor stopped the women in their tracks. The big sergeant hurried over, the effort making him wheeze. 'Glad I caught you. We just took a call from A&E in Bronglais. Rhys is there.'

Catrin's eyes went ceiling-wards. 'What has he done now?'

'Hit his head. They're stitching him up as we speak.'

'What happened?' Jess demanded.

'Pretty garbled so far, but according to Claudine

Barton, her boyfriend accidentally pushed Rhys down the stairs.'

'Honestly, that boy,' Catrin began.

'Okay.' Jess took control. 'Does Warlow know?'

'I'm about to phone him.'

'Do that. Tell him I'm on the way to Claudine Barton's address and I'll meet him at the hospital. Catrin, you check Ava Farley's story with her flatmate.' She turned and hurried up the corridor without looking back. 'Text me the address, Gil. My God, it never just rains, does it?'

————

WARLOW FOUND RHYS IN AN A&E cubicle when he arrived, sitting in a chair and drinking tea. The DC looked a little sheepish, but none the worse for his adventures.

'How many stitches?' Warlow asked.

'Five, sir.' Rhys bent forward and Warlow inspected a neat wound to the left of the DC's crown.

'I just spoke to the charge nurse. He says you're fine. But I've asked them to do a CT scan.'

'There's no need for that, sir—'

'There is. I want them to check to see if there's a bloody brain inside that skull of yours.'

'Not fair, sir,' Rhys protested. 'He came at me from above. Lucky there was a landing, or I might have fallen all the way down.'

Warlow shook his head and made a show of looking the man up and down. 'At least you're in one piece. I'm counting four limbs and a head. Though you're going to want to call in to the men's at some point. Your shirt looks like something from a slasher movie and you've got blood…' Warlow waved a finger vaguely over his own face and hair.

'I was going to, sir. They said I might need to stay here for a while until I got the all-clear.'

'All right, for some. Enjoying that tea?'

'It's a good one, sir. None of the machine rubbish. The charge nurse made one for me.'

'Good. While you enjoy your break, you'd better tell me what the hell happened.'

'Claudine Barton, sir—'

'Hang on.' Warlow's gaze drifted off to the right. 'Ah, here comes DI Allanby.'

Jess appeared and gave Rhys the exact same kind of look – a pained mixture of exasperation and relief – that Warlow had worn a minute before.

'My God, Rhys,' she said. 'Are you alright?'

'Fine, ma'am. I just didn't see it coming.'

'That'll be a huge consolation to your mother when she reads that written on your gravestone,' Warlow muttered. He turned to Jess. 'Rhys was about to tell me all about the peculiar series of events that brought him here.'

'I'm all ears,' Jess said.

Rhys puffed out his cheeks and threw up his hands. 'I'd taken a statement from Claudine Barton who admits that Lyndon had been in contact with her, but only online and that she wouldn't recognise him as all contact had been virtual. Her partner, Luca, turned up. I went to leave, and he threw a hissy fit. I was going back up to the flat to explain when he came at me down the stairs and drop-kicked me. I fell back and ended up here. Like I say, it could have been worse.' He blinked a few times and grinned.

Warlow grunted. 'Glad you think so.'

'I've just come back from Barton's flat,' Jess said. 'Her story tallies with yours. Her partner is one Luca Domacini. Third-generation Welsh Italian. Apparently, he's a bit possessive.'

Warlow frowned. 'What? And he's living with a sex worker?'

'She said he was fine with it being all online,' Rhys said. 'What he can't cope with is her getting attention in the flesh.'

'I also spoke to another resident from a flat downstairs,' Jess continued. 'He was coming home when the ruckus broke out. He heard Domacini yelling and saw him come at you. He says that when Claudine shouted out that you were a police officer, Luca was about to thump you, but thought the better of it and fled.'

'I don't remember him thumping me,' Rhys said.

'Did you pass out?'

'I don't know, sir. I felt dizzy and disorientated, and I vaguely remember someone running downstairs, but then Claudine helped me up and called an ambulance.'

Warlow sat on the edge of the cubicle bed and picked up a clipboard with Rhys's admission statistics. He opened and shut the clip a few times, pondering the information that Rhys and Jess had given him and weighing it all up. 'Now we have Luca Domacini in the mix as a hothead. And you say Lyndon was a regular of Claudine's?'

Rhys scrubbed at some dried blood on his cheek with a forefinger. 'He often paid for private interaction, so Claudine said.'

Jess narrowed her eyes. 'You think Domacini might have turned into a green-eyed monster?'

Warlow voiced his ideas. 'If Lyndon's obsession went beyond the internet, it can't be ruled out. Any idea where Domacini is now?'

Jess shook her head. 'In the wind, I suspect.'

Warlow contemplated Rhys once more. 'Every cloud, eh, Rhys. Thanks to your skill at getting into scrapes, we now have one Luca Domacini as a person of interest.'

'Are we going after him, sir?'

'We are. But not you. Back to the Incident Room for you and Gil will run you home as soon as he's able.'

'There's no need, sir. I'm fine.'

'I'm sure you are. But you look like Dracula's apprentice. We can't have you scaring the innocent people of Aberystwyth. Before you know it, we'll have a mob with pitchforks and wooden stakes besieging the station. Finish your tea and I'll find the charge nurse, see if I can get us all out of here. Meanwhile, I'm going for a nice long walk up in the hills.'

CHAPTER EIGHTEEN

R<small>HYS'S</small> <small>INJURY</small> put a dent in the afternoon's activities. But the investigation needed time to ferment, for enquiries to be fielded, reports to be obtained, scalp wounds to stop throbbing.

The others all went home at five knowing they would not be kicking off their shoes in their own living rooms much before seven; knowing they'd have to repeat the journey bright and early the next morning for a briefing at 9.15am. Once more unto the Castle Keep, as Gil had already christened the Aberystwyth Incident Room.

While the rest of the team negotiated twisting roads in slow traffic, at around six, Warlow drove the dozen miles back to Ystumtuen and parked in the same lay-by next to the copse that he'd parked in yesterday morning. This time, he'd come prepared and dressed more appropriately in a tactical T-shirt, Rohans, and walking shoes. All with a view to re-exploring the route that the walkers who'd reported Alistair's rotting odour had taken.

He'd walked no more than thirty yards before he stopped and took in his surroundings. Just the one property in view, half a mile up the hill to his left. And trees obscured even that. The road passed the little machinery graveyard whose gate was closed and secured only by a knotted rope. Warlow stood by the entrance and gave the place a little more attention this time, taking a closer look at the slowly rusting hulks in the makeshift yard.

A couple of old cab-less tractors, one big yellow backhoe excavator, some generators, fridges heaped drunkenly one on the other, vans, trailers, ride-on mowers, and three caravans. These were all the old type, oval shaped, room inside to barely swing a hamster, let alone a cat. Oddly enough, you often found these mobile homes in out of the way rural places. They found their way to these isolated spots as temporary accommodation for itinerant workers and farmhands. But the ones he studied now had seen much better days. Two didn't even have doors, never mind windows.

Warlow frowned. How or why, you'd find a breakers yard in this remote spot remained a mystery. Probably a little side hustle for diversifying farmers, no doubt.

He brought the route up in an OS map on his phone. He passed a couple of spots opposite walking trails on the map, but with no obvious entry points off the road that he walked on. An indication that these paths were not frequented so that the vegetation, and a farmer's fence, had eradicated the old ways. Nothing for it but to continue another hundred yards to the stile and retrace the steps he'd taken with Rhys yesterday morning. Definitely a bridleway on the map, but he saw no sign of horse traffic underfoot, nor any tell-tale mounds of grassy manure. He moved uphill towards where the Apache Village had been on the higher ground, an area marked on his map as *Ochr-Fawr*, or big side. The white tents still up but personnel free. Not even a uniform to ward off nosy beggars.

Not that the area teemed with nosy beggars today. This

part of Mid Wales was as sparsely populated an area as Warlow could remember seeing. If you excluded the sheep.

No guards meant that Povey's team had done what they had to do and packed up. But blue and white police tape still marked off the area.

This time, Warlow took his time ascending through the sheep-dotted fields, noting his progress on the map and more than once taking in the odd cairn and abandoned shaft or two. These, close up, were almost hidden, or only roughly indicated by ragged arrangements of stones and sparse vegetation.

No fences or signs, other than the tape strung on temporary stakes. Just as there weren't any around *Yr Het Fawr*, the curious flat-topped stones that showed the old mineshaft. He retraced his steps from the tents, back to the bridleway and followed it up towards a pool, *Llyn Yr Oerfa*. They didn't mess about when it came to place names up here. Cold Lake looked exactly as described. An open expanse of water on high ground, unprotected from the wind. He spotted a couple of properties with lake views. One whitewashed in the vernacular style, the other grey and yellow brick. But they'd been built in the lee of the hill behind, out of the worst of the westerlies.

No view of *Yr Het Fawr* from there.

From the lake, the bridleway crossed a narrow road and then ascended once more towards the higher ground of *Bryn Rhosau* with its clutch of wind turbines feeding the grid off to the northeast. He paused at the top to look ahead and then back. Up here was completely empty, rolling moorland. No trees, no houses. Below him, the bridleway angled north towards the out of sight A44 and the associated Mining Museum and, further up, the Red Kite feeding Centre at Bwlch Nant Yr Arian, where walkers had reported the bad smell coming out of the ground which led to the discovery of Lyndon's body.

The walkers would have come this way if they followed the OS map. South from the Visitor Centre at Bwlch Nant Yr Arian. Following the same route on the map that Warlow took, but in reverse. As an experienced walker, with Cadi at his side, Warlow had hiked long stretches of the coastal path and the wilder moors and mountains. And he'd seen much better signage than on this route. Looking around at this unpopulated spot, its openness struck him. Unless you knew there were old mines and shafts here, there was nothing to show that there'd been such activity in the area.

Not here.

Not unless you'd visited the Mining Museum or Bwlch Nant Yr Arian Centre and reconnoitred the land. And you certainly would not know your way around the myriad little side paths leading up the hills. That required local knowledge.

Food for thought, that.

But it was the thought of food that finally made Warlow turn around and retrace his steps to the Jeep. He'd booked a room in a hotel a couple of miles away. The only hotel with rooms in the area, in fact.

Despite the horror that had brought him to this sparsely populated locale, as Warlow headed east along the A44, the sun had not yet set, and the evening remained warm, he couldn't help but wonder at the natural beauty around him.

Empty roads, the light almost surreal. The kind of evening film directors pray for.

Living in Pembrokeshire, Warlow had become used to stunning views and lush beaches, but here was something different again. These were the Cambrian Mountains. Gentler than their towering cousins in Snowdonia, and less harsh and rugged, too, than the Beacons further south. They rolled away on either side of the road as he drove, lush and green, here and there broken by stony outcrops and patches of darker fern. There was something almost alpine about it, this plateau of the Mid Wales massif. He'd been further north and east only once, to visit Pumlumon, the very heart of this "Desert of Wales", where the Severn emerged from the earth and began its journey south, bringing commerce and lifeblood to the English cities of Hereford, Gloucester, and Bristol.

But it had been a winter trip, and he vividly remembered the bitter wind that froze his fingers. Even Cadi had wanted to turn back.

But here and now… This was chocolate box stuff.

Warlow ate a good meal in the hotel bar, glad of the time to be alone. He rang Rhys and found the DC in good spirits and none the worse for his injury. He said goodnight and retired to his room, sat on the bed and started humming a tune that came unbidden into his head.

What the hell was that? Warlow ran it through, layering words onto the melody, dragging them up from a seventies memory bank he didn't even know existed. An old song: *Alone Again, Naturally*. Gilbert O'Sullivan's melancholy examination of suicidal thought. In his head, Warlow heard Gil's scoffing voice. Not my choice as a karaoke track at the rugby club, let's put it that way.

But it was more the title than the song's content that had bubbled to the surface in Warlow's brain. Alone Again. The SIO's curse. By necessity, too, because, yes, it could be tough at the top.

As a concept, "the top" was a square peg that didn't fit easily into Warlow's round egalitarian core. But some things, murder enquiries included, were not run well by committee. Someone needed to take the helm and steer the ship through the uncharted waters at the beginning of an investigation. And yes, it could be isolating; a better word in Warlow's mind than lonely, since he did not consider himself a lonely person. More a self-sufficient and self-contained sort of person. Both natural extensions of self-made… Christ, that made him sound like a Lego kit. He paused his musings there, fighting another smile and another imagined Gil put-down.

Of course, there were things he missed. A furry head to fondle for a start. And, now and again, some adult conversation with another member of the human race. Someone with XY chromosomes and an infectious laugh, preferably. Yet, it did no good to dwell on these things because he had enough to occupy him for now. Besides, internalising your thoughts made you a malcontent. And disenchantment with one's lot was a dangerous mindset that could manifest in misguided ideas and actions. He sensed some elements of that in this case already. If someone asked him to put his finger on what he meant, he'd struggle. But that was the general direction his thoughts leaned towards. All he needed now was to add substance to the framework of his nebulous ideas and all would be well.

Sighing, Warlow lay back and closed his eyes.

———

DS CATRIN RICHARDS, as was her wont, went for a quick run immediately after she got home to the house she shared with PC Craig Peters. A traffic officer, Craig was on a night shift and left her a portion of the chicken and broccoli bake he'd made, plated up and covered in cling film in the fridge, ready for the microwave.

The fact that he could cook, quite apart from his humour, made him a real catch. The fact that he was a nice man who looked after himself, shared her view on life and the law, and cared a lot about her made it doubly so.

Run finished, Catrin showered and sat in their kitchen,

forking broccoli into her mouth while she read through some of the reports she'd brought home, namely Alistair Lyndon's bank statements. She glanced through them and found nothing of any note. Alistair was in the black. His mortgage repayments were small. Compared to hers and Craig's, definitely. And there were no odd amounts, no large sums either in or out over a six-month period that might raise suspicions. Cash might be king, but in this day and age of instant BACS transfer and PayPal, hiding transactions had become difficult.

And they'd found nothing stuffed into his mattress at his home, either.

Whatever happened to him did not seem to have anything to do with money.

She drained her glass of iced water and was on the way to the fridge to replenish it when her phone bleeped. A text message from a number she didn't recognise:

> Hi Cat. Great to see you. Be even better to meet up for a proper chat. It's been too long. Let me know when you're back up, or I can come down to stay maybe? Dug into my photo archive for this one. Good Times. You are looking more than great BTW. Almost as good as you did back then. Check this out. Byronski.

ALL THE HAIR on the nape of her neck stood to attention until she finally let out the breath she'd been holding. Then she read the message again and squeezed her eyes shut.

'Shit,' she hissed out. Byronski. A name she had genuinely hoped never to hear again, and yet here it was, echoing in her head. He'd shaved his head once for a bet.

After a heavy night on the booze and… Other things. He'd been nineteen then and a loose cannon. When his father saw what he'd done, his response was derision and an insult, comparing him to Jimmy Somerville after a bad night on the town.

'Jimmy Somerville?' she'd asked. 'Who the hell is he?'

'The falsetto singer from Bronski Beat. My dad's least favourite group when he'd been into pop music.'

A reference that had meant little to the still teenage Catrin Richards, but which she'd since come to understand was probably homophobic in intention. But Byron Evans had run with the insult and christened himself Byronski there and then. A little intimate in-joke between the two of them.

The two of them.

Catrin cringed. The memory that she'd once been in a relationship with Byron seemed more like a bad dream. Something from a different existence in a past life. Her life as a wild child in her first year at university. A year during which she and Byron had become bosom buddies and, to her shame, friends with benefits.

She could hardly believe what she'd allowed herself to do then. What she'd given herself up to. What had she been thinking?

They'd met early in the term. He was a funny drunk. And persistent. And she, nice girl Catrin, had revelled in the freedom of being away from home, as some kids did. She'd done everything, gone to every party, every dance, tried every drink and other artificial stimulant that people offered. Easy to excuse in a silly, naïve eighteen-year-old. Except she now knew that it was a slippery slope upon which some people lost all their footing, ending up at the very bottom of a steep hill, an inch from the gutter.

She and Byronski had been a feckless couple, both

academically unchallenged by their first-year course, both majoring in hedonism instead.

Her rude awakening had come one late morning when she'd risen with a blinding headache to find him in a pool of vomit next to a pile of white powder on her nightstand.

Not that she had it tested, but she doubted it had been talcum powder.

That morning had been her epiphany. Not so for Byron.

She'd left. He'd stayed, drowning his sorrows by clinging to the student lifestyle until the bitter end.

Another bleep from the phone. Another Byronski message:

> SOZ, forgot the snap.

THE PHOTOGRAPH FOLLOWED. A nineteen-year-old Catrin Richards on the way to a tarts and vicars party. She'd gone all out as a hybrid bunny girl, a la Bridget Jones, complete with bodice, black stockings, and gloves to the elbow. She was heavier then thanks to all those booze calories. But even so, she'd carried it off well.

God, what had she been thinking?

Another message followed:

> Brilliant, right? The after-party shots are even better. Text me.

She remembered the party. The start of it, anyway. In some grungy flat with half the rugby team singing their heads off, slopping beer in a boat race, which she'd been a willing participant in. But she couldn't remember much after the half bottle of vodka she'd downed. Rites of passage? Or a narrow escape?

No doubting which of those two questions she had an answer to now.

But the photo was harmless enough, if a little too revealing. Way too embarrassing to show to Craig.

'Bloody Byronski,' she muttered and texted back:

> Busy. I will text you. No more photographs, please. They are not for an internet audience.

He texted back:

> Yes, sergeant. I'll be waiting. Be good to scroll through them again, though. Just the two of us.

No, it damn well wouldn't, she thought. Not on your Nelly, Byronski.

CHAPTER NINETEEN

WARLOW GOT UP EARLY and ate a hearty breakfast. Even though he rarely indulged, based on principles drummed into him as a child, he decided to get his money's worth. After a full English with a Danish chaser and cup of so-so, over-stewed drip coffee (why was it that hotels always got this so wrong?) he wandered into the Castle Keep and logged on to his computer one minute before 8am.

Tiernon had updated his report overnight. The latest addition dealt with a white substance found around Lyndon's mouth. Preliminary analysis suggested an adhesive gum-like material.

So, someone had taped Lyndon's mouth shut somewhere along his journey towards and across the River Styx.

Warlow turned that thought over in his head as a smile curved up the corner of his mouth. He'd cut back on using that particular Greek mythological reference in Rhys's company since he'd once found a Post-It note-to-self stuck on the DC's monitor screen with a scribbled.

'Styx? Tributary of the Towy?'
Does he mean Sirhowy, or Seiont or Sawdde?

.   .   .

THANKFULLY, he'd put Rhys right before Gil had latched on to the slip.

But taping added grist to the theoretical mill that Lyndon had been held captive somewhere away from the mineshaft to start with. Some fibres found on Lyndon's body also suggested coarse matting. Two things to work with, then, but utterly useless unless you knew where to look.

The first team member to arrive, a little after 8.25, was Gil. Warlow was on his way back to the Incident Room with a fresh mug of tea to wash away memories of that too-bitter coffee, when the sergeant came barrelling around the corner, clearly in a hurry.

'Early bird,' Warlow said.

'Catches the nematode. Not much traffic this time of day.' Gil had a plaid sandwich bag in his hand, the kind you kept in the freezer overnight because it had some kind of refrigerant built into the material.

'Lunch?'

Gil screwed his mouth up. 'Not under the trade descriptions act. Anwen calls it a salad. Lettuce, tomatoes, half a tin of tuna, and cucumber. I mean, cucumber? *Er mwyn yr Arglwydd*. I can think of several things you can do with a cucumber, but eating it is not one of them.'

'So long as everyone is a consenting adult, eh?'

Gil feigned primness. 'Must you lower the tone, Detective Chief Inspector.' Gil opened the Incident Room door and inhaled through his nose loudly. 'Ah, the smell of great expectations. Can't beat it.'

He held the door open for Warlow, who stopped as a new thought struck him. 'Get a chance to chat with Tom?'

Gil shook his head. 'Unfortunately, no. We've all been busy.'

Warlow glanced at a clock at the far end of the room, remembering to avoid the classic mistake of looking at his watch while holding a mug of tea. Many a damp sock and shoe had resulted from that. Not to mention, on a couple of occasions, a hot, but thankfully never scalding, moist groin. 'Now is a good time. Unless he's operating, Tom will be free before clinics start.'

'There is that,' Gil replied, with a distinct lack of commitment.

Both men stood regarding one another, having reached a conversational impasse with no clear path out of it.

The awkward paralysis ended when a Uniform appeared out of the lift, and received the inquisitive, and oddly grateful, attention of both detectives.

Slightly taken aback by this unwarranted interest, the Uniform stammered, 'Uh… Downstairs… Someone to see you, sir. Says they're from the uni. To do with what happened to your DC Harries, I think. They weren't too clear on that point.'

'Okay, I'll come straight down,' Warlow said.

'Names?' Gil asked.

'Name, sarge.'

'You said they,' Gil said.

'As in, that's what they wanted to be called. There's just the one. Not he or she. Wants to be known as Myst.'

'As in water particles floating in the air?' Gil asked.

'No, with a "y". I've put them in the family room.'

'Good idea.' Warlow looked down at his mug. The tea was too hot to down in one.

'Why don't I come with you, sir?' Gil kept it formal for the Uniform's sake, though there was no mistaking the glint in his eye. 'You can finish your tea while I sit there and listen to them, wearing my serious listening face.'

'Intriguing,' Warlow said. 'That implies you have a non-serious listening face.'

Gil nodded. 'According to the Lady Anwen, it's mainly a non-listening face, serious or otherwise.' He took a big step and launched his sandwich bag at a desk, where it slid off and landed on the floor.

'That's buggered your salad,' Warlow said.

'Probably all it's good for. And a suitable role for the cucumber. Right, lead on. Myst is waiting for us downstairs. I hope to God they're not Scottish or we'll never find them.'

The Uniform snorted a laugh but snuffed it out in the light of Warlow's glare.

'Please don't encourage him. Think of him as a zoo animal. One you're not supposed to feed.'

'Right, sir.' The Uniform's face twitched as he fought the laugh.

'Just pretend he's a rare Orang Utang.'

In front, out of sight and halfway down the stairs, Gil's voice filtered up. 'I heard that.'

———

CATRIN OFFERED to pick Rhys up for the journey back north to Aberystwyth the following morning. He was waiting outside his parents' house when she arrived, all smiles and armed with a steel water bottle and something wrapped in a kitchen tissue balanced in one hand.

'What's that?' Catrin asked as he adjusted the passenger seat and slid it back to its limit to allow his long limbs a little space.

'My mother made some cherry and coconut slices. She insisted I brought a piece for you.' He opened it up and a mini cascade of dried coconut dandruff'd onto the seat.

Catrin frowned.

'I know,' Rhys said. 'I said you wouldn't want it. You're like Gina.'

'How so?' Gina Mellings was Rhys's partner. A fellow uniformed officer who always looked as if she'd just stepped out of a fitness magazine whenever Catrin met her.

'Gina wouldn't eat it. She'd look at it and salivate and make me keep her a corner of mine, something about the size of my thumbnail. Then she'd eat that and regret not having a bigger bit. I don't know how you do it.' Rhys shook his head with a bemused half smile.

'By you, are you referring to me and Gina, or women in general?'

Rhys paused for thought. 'I suppose you and Gina. I mean, I can't speak for women in general. I only really know you and Gina and DI Allanby and my mother. But you're not the best sample if we were going to look at it statistically.'

'No?'

'No. You lot are all… Principled. I suppose I ought to include the groups of women I sometimes see outside the Cock a Doodle Fry on a Saturday night. I suspect that these two slices would not have touched the sides had one of them been in the car.'

Catrin's eyes crinkled, but she kept a straight face. 'You are so judgemental, Rhys.'

'No,' he protested. 'That's pure observation, not obesism. Though I did read that there's a pandemic of that about, too.' He looked down at the little wrapped items. 'What shall I do with them, then?'

'If you can manage a little self-control, we could take them in to Gil. Tempt him with them.'

'That's cruel.'

This time, Catrin did smile. 'Yes, I know.'

The radio was tuned to BBC 6 and Cream was giving *White Room* an outing. Rhys patted his hand on his knee in time. 'The Wolf would be in his element with this stuff.'

He leaned forward and placed the little parcel between his enormous feet in the footwell before changing tack. 'How did you get on with the bank statements?'

'Nothing. He's clean as a whistle. You?'

'Nothing new. DI Allanby asked me to look through his divorce stuff. It all went smoothly, according to the papers I read.'

'You going to speak to his ex?'

'Probably.'

They drove on. At the eastern edge of Carmarthen, the car headed north towards Peniel. Catrin glanced over. 'Talking of exes, how would you feel if someone from your past suddenly appeared with some embarrassing photos?'

'How embarrassing?'

'On a scale of ten, do you mean?'

'Well, yes, but I meant in what way embarrassing. I mean, my mother showed Gina some photos of me aged twelve being a zombie in *Thriller* at an Urdd competition. That was embarrassing.'

Catrin nodded. Most Welsh-speaking kids had been roped into some kind of activity involving Wales's national youth organisation, foreshortened in the language to Yr Urdd. Usually concert parties, choirs, and sketches, supported by schools in an annual national competition. But for every opera or pop star it spawned, there were hundreds of others left scarred by their involvement. Okay, maybe that was a little harsh; it wasn't the Hitler Youth for God's sake. But she knew where Rhys was coming from. Unfortunately, it wasn't the direction of travel she wanted to take.

'No, I meant embarrassing in a social context, perhaps even salacious context.'

Rhys's eyes widened and, as per, he leapt in with both feet. 'What, like if Gina had done some page three stuff, you mean?'

'Yeah, maybe, that sort of thing.'

He didn't answer her right away. If Clapton's sublime guitar solo hadn't been filling the car, Catrin was certain she'd have heard Rhys's cogs whirring. 'Depends. I mean, if Gina had done that and someone else showed me, I'd be miffed. If she showed them to me, full disclosure, and all that...' he gave her a sideways glance, 'I wouldn't complain. I mean, I might want to inspect the goods to make sure they still worked.'

'Oh, for God's sake.'

Rhys threw his hands up. 'Well, I don't know what you mean exactly.'

'I mean, what if they were properly embarrassing photos?' she dropped her voice low, which brooked no logic at all since they were the only people in the car. 'Meant for personal consumption.'

'Oh, right. Then I might not want to see them. But if I did, I might want an explanation. Not of why they were taken, but why I needed to see them.'

Catrin nodded. The one thing you got with Rhys was an honest answer. It might not be the one she wanted to hear, but he was right. She couldn't remember what kind of photographs Byronski wanted to show her. There were a good six months of her first year in university that she struggled to remember. She wasn't proud of that. She also had a sneaking suspicion she would not be proud of whatever Byronski wanted to share. Definitely not for sharing with Craig.

And anyway, she had no intention of getting back in touch with Byronski. If they needed to see him again in relation to the investigation, Rhys could handle it.

She glanced down at the little parcel at Rhys's feet.

'Cherry and coconut?'

Rhys nodded.

'Right, come on, then,' Catrin said. 'Share and share alike.'

Surprised and grinning from ear to ear, Rhys unfurled the cakes. Catrin took one and bit in. Sugar and fat dissolved in her mouth, and she made a noise halfway between a whimper and a moan. Not exactly Harry met Sally, but close.

Cake really was the best way to forget your woes.

CHAPTER TWENTY

MYST TURNED out to be exactly what Warlow and Gil had been expecting.

Both detectives were conscious of the fact that preconceptions were a dangerous thing in investigations, as indeed, in life. These days, you walked a tightrope when it came to identity politics. Not just as a police officer, but as a member of the public. It was a rabbit hole where the law, science, shouty politics, and free speech often locked horns, while common sense stood by holding its ribs with laughter. And in these days, where even discussion could bring the wrath of the God of cancellation down upon you, it was better to stick by the letter of the law and otherwise keep your powder dry and your mind open.

He'd discussed these and other issues with Gil on several occasions and was aware of how the sergeant stood. As police officers, they had to keep their minds open, to consider what made people tick, and sometimes tock. But, by and large, the men shared the same worldview. They were even proud of their country and that kind of seditious thinking could earn you a burning at the Twitter stake these days.

Just as well neither man went anywhere near it.

So, when the Gen Z calling themselves Myst turned out to be an early twenties bearded person with a skull T-shirt, a lip ring, and both little fingernails painted black, Warlow wasn't surprised.

Myst stood up when they entered the room and studied their lanyards with interest.

Their first words were, 'There are no pronouns on your badges?'

'No,' Gil said. 'We're non-binary, here. I'm Sergeant Jones, this is DCI Warlow.'

'They're labels, but that works,' Myst said, untouched by, and probably unaware of, Gil's sarcasm. Their accent placed them somewhere in the valleys east of Merthyr, if Warlow was any judge.

'How can we help you, Myst—' Warlow asked, just managing to chop off the added "er" at the end of Myst, which would have been a categorisation disaster.

'I'm a neighbour of Claudine Barton's. I heard about what happened yesterday.'

'Right,' Gil said.

'I live with my cis partner in a ground-floor flat in the same building.'

Warlow could see Gil calculating, his brows a ploughed field of concentration. 'So, you're cis?'

'I am.'

Gil nodded. 'Ah, cis, right. Cis. Right.'

Both Myst and Warlow glared at the sergeant.

'Sorry. For a minute there, when you said your cis partner, I heard sis partner. Which of course suggested a whole different can of worms in a very *Game of Thrones*, Cersei and Jamie Lannister kind of way.'

That earned him a quizzical look from Warlow. Gil responded with an unvoiced mouthing of the word "siblings".

Myst, who had lost what negligible amount of humour he might have been born with along the angst-ridden way of his teen years, stared back. 'I refused to watch that. Its themes were a perpetuation of binary stereotypes with little or no concept of gender choice. I've made *my* choice of name by adopting a non-limiting mid-identification which allies me to nature. I go by Myst and use they. My partner prefers "nya" as a cat gender identifier.'

That little piece of information exploded a silence grenade in the room. It took a good few seconds to clear.

'They're identifying as a cat?' Gil asked eventually.

'They like cats.'

'Not many cats in *Game of Thrones*,' Gil said. A response which, under the circumstances, was as good as any. 'Dragons, yes. And a lot of barbecued meat as a result. But cats,' Gil shook his head, 'not so many.'

Myst didn't answer.

'Do you have any information for us, Myst?' Warlow asked, quickly realising that wherever this was going was not a destination he had any real appetite for.

Myst cleared their throat. 'I do. On my way home last night, Luca, who prefers a binary handle, came running out of the house and jumped on a motorbike. I'd not seen that before. He used to have a cycle, but not a motorbike.'

Gil nodded. 'Number plate?'

Myst shook his head.

'Make or model?'

Another shake.

Gil made a show of writing something down. 'We'll get this out to the rest of the Force pronto. On… A… Motorbike.' He looked up. 'At least he's not on roller skates. Continuing the Cats theme. The musical with them all dressed up like… Cats.'

'Thank you, Myst,' Warlow said with a fixed smile. 'That is useful.'

Myst stood up. Warlow offered a hand, which Myst declined. 'There's too much inference of a power relationship in a handshake. I prefer to keep to my own space.'

'Lovely,' Gil said. 'Thank you again. If you could give me a phone number, in case we need to contact you?'

'Do I have to? It's just that the account is in my deadname.'

'Deadname?'

'The name I had to use before identifying.'

'Ah,' Gil said with a smile so fixed it looked as if it had been sculpted on. 'We'll try not to use that, then. Just the number will do.'

When Myst had gone, both detectives walked back upstairs in silence until, finally, and as inevitably as sunshine after the rain, Gil broke it. 'Did I hear that correctly? She wanted to be identified as a cat?'

'You did.'

'Does that mean she sits in front of the telly licking her own—'

'That imagination of yours should come with a bloody government health warning,' Warlow interjected.

'I was going to say paws. Only people with their heads in the gutter would have assumed otherwise.' Gil shook his head and sighed. 'I don't know. Do you sometimes feel that the world has moved on a bit too far and that somehow, we've been left stranded by the tide?'

'Maybe. Or perhaps I'm bloody glad I'm not at university again. Those are choppy waters to navigate.'

'Only if you seek to be in the same boat. Me, I think I'd be on a windsurfer, on my tod, earphones on, hair in the wind, and shiver me timbers.'

'The idea of you on a windsurfer shivering your timbers needs a great deal of imagination. I might require a biscuit before I can stretch to that.'

'Ah well, that image will remain an enigma, then. We are biscuit free again today, I'm afraid.'

Warlow sighed. 'You can go off people, you know?'

———

THE SATURDAY MORNING'S catch-up meeting took place in a business-like tea, but *sans biscuit*, atmosphere. Rhys's scalp wound was inspected by the team and the general agreement was that the nurse who'd sutured him up had done a fine job.

'Must have been hard stopping all that cotton wool from coming out while she was tying the knots.' Gil peered at the wound.

'It's a nice, neat job,' Jess said, flashing Gil an admonishing glance.

'And it's given us someone we need to question.' Warlow explained what they'd learnt from Jess's visit to Claudine and their brief interview with Myst. Then he updated them on Tiernon's report.

'You think Alistair Lyndon was abducted, then?' Jess asked.

'Perhaps. Or drugged. We need a toxicology report to know that. Either way, it looks like gagged and bound, if you remember the ligature marks on the wrist.'

'What about the other fibres Tiernon was antsy about, sir?' Catrin asked.

'Nothing yet. Rhys, keep an eye out for more intel on that.'

'But in the meantime, we need to find out as much as we can about Luca Domacini.'

'The bloke with the ninja skills that poleaxed Rhys,' Catrin said with glee.

'I wasn't even looking,' Rhys objected.

'What, as he was coming downstairs to meet you?' Gil asked. 'Did you have your eyes shut?'

'No, I don't mean that. I mean, I wasn't expecting him to kick out like that. He took me unawares.'

Gil frowned. 'He took me unawares on the stairs? That's a line straight out of *Lady Chatterley's Lover*, isn't it?'

'Was she in Downton Abbey?' Rhys asked.

'I doubt it very much,' Warlow said, realising they were getting side-tracked quickly.

'I've got some background,' Gil said. 'Domacini is a hothead. A couple of arrests for affray. But since he works as a bouncer in somewhere called the Cat's Whisper—'

'A misprint, surely?' Jess grimaced.

'Afraid not. Let's hope it's deliberate and not ignorance.' Gil posted an A4 sheet up on the Job Centre. 'Although I have my doubts. Domacini also works as a personal trainer, sometimes home visits, sometimes at a gym. He's also got some form with drugs, possession, nothing huge. He's also registered at a second address.'

'Right, we need to find him as a priority,' Warlow said. 'Let's see if there's any CCTV in and around where Claudine Barton lives. Send some Uniforms round to the second address and let's find this motorbike of his.' The DCI got up and walked to the Gallery half of the board, and looked again at the crime scene photos. 'I walked the path last night. Not quite all the way to the Visitor Centre, but two-thirds of the way. To get a feel for it.'

'And?' Jess joined him at the board.

'It's wild country. Wide open, but uninhabited. The question is, was he brought down from the higher ground, or taken up from lower down? There are no signposts. You need an OS map to keep track.'

'So, you're thinking that whoever put him there must have known about these shafts?'

'I do. But what the link with Ystumtuen is, I have no idea.'

'Yet, sir,' Catrin said.

'Quite right, Catrin. Not yet.'

Then it was Rhys's turn to fill them in on what they'd learnt about the dead man. His previous marriage and his divorce settlement.

'No children, then?' Jess asked.

Rhys shook his head.

Jess turned to Catrin. 'Do you have a photograph of Ava, the mysterious "A" of the thank you card?'

'I do, ma'am. Sorry, slipped my mind.' Catrin pinned up a snapshot of Ava Farley. 'She seemed genuinely confused by Lyndon's absence. At the moment, she and her flatmate are the last to have seen him alive last Sunday morning when he dropped her back at her flat.'

'And he'd said nothing to her about where he might be going?' Warlow asked.

Jess shook her head, arms folded, staring at the photograph. 'No. And no communication from him since then.'

'Do his phone records confirm that?' Gil turned to Catrin.

'They do. No phone activity after two pm on Sunday afternoon.'

'The one odd thing about this is the overlap in timing.' Jess pointed at Gil's posted up timeline. 'Ava Farley told us that Lyndon had made contact and asked her out because his partner had left him. That was over five weeks ago. But, according to the neighbours, Mirain was still living with Lyndon at that time.'

'Could she have been mistaken about the timing?' Warlow asked.

'It's possible, of course. I'll double check.' Jess made a note.

'Which brings us back to the mysterious Mirain.

Despite going off, she's been communicating with her daughter through social media. I think we ought to talk to her, agreed?'

Everyone nodded.

Warlow continued, 'We'll need access to her Facebook account. I said we might need to borrow her ex-husband's phone.'

'She doesn't sound very reliable, sir,' Rhys observed.

'If mental illness is one thing, it's unpredictable. That doesn't mean we shouldn't follow it up.'

Warlow went to the SIO office and sent Joel Rampley a message. He came back quickly:

> At work, can't help. Try Mirain's dad, Carwyn

A NUMBER FOLLOWED. Warlow dialled it and got an answer immediately.

'Mr Hughes, my name's Evan Warlow, I'm a Detective Chief Inspector looking into a serious crime. I—'

'I know who you are,' Carwyn Hughes interjected. 'Joel told me you'd spoken to him.'

'We'd like to speak to your daughter, Mr Hughes.'

'Wouldn't we all.'

It might have been an odd response from a father, but then this wasn't Carwyn Hughes's first ride on the ghost train when it came to Mirain.

'Joel suggested I speak to you. He said she'd been communicating via Facebook and messaging services.'

'She has been. She's done that before, but not for a while.'

'Would it be convenient to come and have a word with you?'

'I've got Heledd... That's Mirain's daughter, with me.'

'I promise it wouldn't be for long.'

A prolonged beat of silence followed.

'Aye, alright.'

Warlow wrote down the address and went back out to the Incident Room.

'Jess, fancy a trip out to meet Mirain's father and her daughter?'

CHAPTER TWENTY-ONE

LUCA PRETENDED to adjust something on the rear wheel of his cousin's Honda 125. He'd parked behind a Sky van with his front wheel against the kerb, so he could stare through the spokes of the wheel up the street to his flat. He'd been there for about fifteen minutes after hiding out at his mate, Tapper's place, overnight. After leaving Claudine's, he'd panicked and gone hell for leather up the coast to Aberdovey and Tapper's house in the hills.

Luca was not the kind of man who had doubts about his decisions. Throughout his life, he'd acted first and thought about it afterwards. But this time, all he could think about was Claudine screaming at him. *'He's a copper!'*

Why hadn't she said something before he'd gone down the stairs? The bloke hadn't looked like a copper. Too young. Too fit looking. Okay, he had a jacket and trousers on, not jeans like the other scruffy students that had called at her flat, but he would pass for a student. That fresh face could not have been a copper's face.

He'd panicked. The adrenaline had kicked in and he'd legged it without even stopping to see if the bloke was okay. That wasn't going to go down well. Neither would be them finding the stash of pumpers and skittles in his flat.

Fuck!

He needed to get in and out of his uncle's place like a rat up a drainpipe. He'd hide the stash of steroids and methylphenidate and then, yeah, then he'd maybe see his cousin and give the bike back. He didn't want to be caught on it. The no licence and insurance crap would piss off his cousin, never mind the fuzz. They'd be after him, the fuzz. He would not hide out. Not his style. Now it was all about damage limitation. He'd already lost a customer that morning. Had to cancel with big Russell, whose journey towards weight loss had begun only a week before. At twenty-five quid an hour, it was good money for bugger all work, other than telling the lardass that he was doing "great" when he lifted a five-kilo kettle bell. Russell had a long way to go on his journey. A cash cow if there ever was one. Maybe a year or two, judging by the way he'd lasted only three minutes on the running machine. Or, in his case, the walking machine.

If and when Luca went to the cop shop, he'd say he didn't know the bloke at Claudine's was a copper, but some kind of rival or a punter from the Cat's Whisper come looking for trouble. There was always one idiot threatening to knife him when he stopped them from going into the club, or "helped" them out through the door. It wasn't as if he made that stuff up. Yeah, when he saw the bloke on the stairs, he'd been in fear for his life.

Never mind that he'd left his girlfriend alone to fend for herself.

No, he'd say he ran away to draw the punter off. Though Claudine's texts had told him the bloke had hit his head and they'd called a fucking ambulance.

Shit.

Luca got up. He'd taken off his helmet and put on a beanie instead. The bloody thing itched like a bastard.

'In and out like a rat up a drainpipe. Come on,' Luca whispered to himself. He looked up and down the street. No sign of anyone. No one sitting in their cars watching for him. So, as good a time as any. He stayed on the side of the road opposite the flat, head down, feet moving quickly over the pavement until he got to where he could cross.

He looked up and down, and then up again. He'd taken two steps when the response vehicle came around the corner fifty yards away. Luca did an about-turn halfway over the road and tried to make it look as natural as possible. He stopped, tapped the back of his pocket as if he was looking for something before pirouetting and heading back to the pavement, walking quickly away from the flat and the bike, barely resisting the urge to sprint. He'd gone twenty yards when he ducked behind a Range Rover and watched as the cop car stopped outside his place.

Luca whimpered.

An officer got out and knocked on the door. Tudor Street was a row of terraced houses. Luca'd kept the place going, even though he spent half the week at Claudine's. Working at the Cat's Whisper meant he wouldn't get home until three and this was much more convenient, as well as not disturbing Claudine. The house had belonged to his uncle, now having his nappy changed twice a day in a nursing home and being fed through a straw, so he didn't need the place anymore. There'd be no one home and the fuzz couldn't get in without a warrant. All he needed to do was stay out of sight until they left.

The dog was not big. Its owner stopped to let the terrier cock its leg up against a tree. She had no idea Luca was squatting down out of sight between the Alder and the front of a parked Range Rover. Neither did Pickles the dog until he caught sight of a creeping hand and immediately let forth a salvo of barks.

The noise startled his owner badly. But not half as much as it startled Luca whose one weakness – though Claudine would later attest to him having many – was a fear of dogs of all sizes.

Luca shot up and ran with a wail onto the road. Pickles, on a long lead, followed him with yelps of joy at having flushed out this hidden prey.

The police officer thirty yards away turned to look.

Luca, with a scream, sprinted past three cars back towards his flat, sidestepped onto the pavement and grabbed his bike.

He didn't see the police officer lean in to talk with his partner. Didn't stop when the officer shouted at him to do so. All he could think of now was firing up the Honda and sodding off as quickly as possible.

Headless panic ruled. Probably the root cause of why he chose to only look behind him when he reversed the bike out and not glance ahead at what might come the other way as he kicked the bike into gear.

With luck, it was an Asda delivery van that Luca collided with, trundling along looking at house numbers. Still, Luca had been accelerating and the collision sent him over the handlebars and splat against the windscreen of the van which screeched to a halt while he, like an egg on a greasy plate, slid off and down onto the road in time to see, through one already swelling eye, two police officers running towards him.

———

'DADDY'S TAKING me to the pictures and to MacDonalds today because it's my birthday. And tomorrow, *Tadcu* is taking me to Kartwheels.'

'Is he now?' Jess grinned at the little girl. She was turning out to be a real chatterbox. They were sitting in Carwyn Hughes's kitchen in Bow Street, a village three miles to the north of Aberystwyth. *Anwylfa*, the dear place; a white-painted bungalow a stone's throw from the railway line with a large garden to the rear.

'You like going to the pictures, then?'

Heledd nodded eagerly. 'Dad buys humongous popcorn and a Pepsi and sometimes chocolate.' Her face became serious. 'But only Dad. Mam makes me take an apple. She doesn't go to the pictures a lot.'

'An apple isn't quite the same, is it?' Jess wrinkled her nose.

Heledd thought about this and backtracked on her disloyalty. 'I still like going with Mam. She can do funny voices like the cartoons.'

Warlow listened and then caught Jess's eye, pointed to himself and Carwyn, Heledd's grandfather, and nodded towards the window.

'Tell you what, Heledd,' Jess said, getting up. 'Can you show me your *Tadcu*'s garden? I hear it's full of vegetables.'

Heledd's eyes doubled in size. '*Tadcu*'s got massive onions and beetroots and tomatoes in the greenhouse.' She was on her feet in an instant.

'That okay, Mr Hughes?' Jess asked.

Carwyn Hughes smiled indulgently and raised a finger. 'Remember, keep those pigeons off my beans.'

Heledd made a sound in her throat like a pigeon coo-ing and led Jess out through the back door.

'She's a one off, that one,' Carwyn said.

Warlow watched him move to the window and follow Jess's progress down a narrow path that split the neat rows of planting in two. He wasn't a big man, but still had a mop of trimmed silver hair and a face brown from hours outdoors. The jeans and work shirt he wore looked clean but well used. But it was the man's hands that struck Warlow. The fingers were thick and calloused from hard manual work.

'Is she like her mother?' Warlow asked.

'*Yr un spit*,' Carwyn's reply emerged automatically in his first language. *Yr un spit*, literally translated meant the same spit. The less tawdry translation might have been "cut from the same cloth", though that didn't carry the same punch. He turned back from the window with an apologetic look at Warlow. 'Sorry, do you…'

'I do.' People of Carwyn's generation living in this part of West Wales often felt much more comfortable communicating in Welsh. Warlow switched effortlessly into it now.

'Can we speak about Mirain?'

'Of course. Did you want to go through to the living room?'

Warlow had turned down the offer of tea. Though it was a hard to break habit, he didn't want to impose any more than he had to on the little girl's birthday. Carwyn led him through to a neat room with a sofa and one armchair, a sideboard, and a TV. A few family photos adorned the walls, but no art.

Carwyn answered the DCI's unspoken question, 'We moved here after I retired and then Eluned became unwell.'

Warlow took in the photographs. Faded wedding snaps of a younger Carwyn and his bride Eluned. The same woman, smiling and holding a baby that must have been Mirain, along with a bigger snap of an older Carwyn and Eluned and a pretty woman holding another baby next to Joel in front of a caravan under a blue sky.

'That Mirain?' Warlow pointed.

Carwyn nodded. 'That's her with Heledd down in Aberaeron. Last time we were all on holiday together. We'd been here just a year when my wife passed. It was quick. Ovarian, they said. Heledd was only two.'

'Sorry to hear that.'

Carwyn shrugged and pointed to the armchair. Warlow sat while his host took the sofa.

'Heledd's dad, Joel, mentioned a group chat you all had,' Warlow said.

'Yes. I'm no expert on these things. Heledd's like a little wizard on the computers and things, but I just about manage the phone.'

'Would it be okay to see your messages from Mirain?'

Carwyn retrieved a phone from the sideboard and put on a pair of glasses. He pressed buttons and made some exaggerated swipes until whatever he was looking for appeared and then turned the phone around to show Warlow. 'It's called Heledd's Gang. Her choice.'

'And her most recent messages are here. Since she went missing?'

A pinched expression was the only response Carwyn gave to that question.

Warlow eased back. 'Must be hard, knowing your daughter is unwell.'

'Harder than anyone could know.'

'I understand it got worse once Heledd was born.'

Carwyn nodded. 'But it's not her fault. No fault, either of them.'

Warlow's turn to nod. He was a father, too. 'But these episodes, they always end, don't they?'

'They have, up to now,' Carwyn said, tight-lipped.

Warlow stopped scrolling through the message app and glanced at the sideboard, taking in the cups and certificates. 'Yours?' he asked,

'Gardening club. Bit of a hobby of mine.'

'You know your onions, then?'

A little smile curled up Carwyn's mouth. 'Something to

do after I retired. I'm busy enough. Mate of mine keeps horses and I help with that sometimes. I grow veg and, of course, there's Heledd.'

'What did you do, Carwyn?'

'Electricity board. SWEB then SWALEC. I worked down south a bit when it was Southern Power.'

Warlow's eyes dropped back to the phone. 'Would it be okay if you took some screenshots of the last few weeks' messages and emailed them to me?'

'I could try.'

'We could do it now if you like.' Warlow was no IT wizard like Heledd, but he had his skills. Within five minutes, he'd sent over a month's worth of messages. 'Does Mirain know about Alistair?'

'I haven't said anything about him.'

'I'm sorry I must ask you these questions, but it's my job. At any time during her illness, has Mirain ever been violent towards anyone?'

The man's eyes fell away, and he exhaled thinly.

'We'd like to find her, too, Carwyn,' Warlow said by way of reassurance.

A barely perceptible nod followed. 'That won't be easy. I've been looking for a long time now. We all have.'

Odd words, but Warlow assumed there was a deeper meaning here. Perhaps Carwyn Hughes had lost his daughter, in the figurative sense, years ago.

'I'm sure she'd want to know about Alistair.'

'She would.' Carwyn jerked his chin up in agreement. And though this expression didn't change, a solitary tear ran down from the corner of one eye.

Warlow moved to the edge of his seat and reached a hand across to touch the older man's arm. 'Sorry. I realise this is hard for you.'

'It is. It's bloody hard.' The words were now barely a whisper.

Warlow handed back the phone. 'We'll find her. I promise you that.'

An unnamed emotion passed over the older man's face, like a cloud over the moon. 'I know you will. I want you to. For Heledd's sake, if not for mine.'

Jess appeared in the doorway, Heledd holding her hand.

'I've just had a call from Gil,' she explained, her grey eyes animated.

'Progress?' Warlow asked.

'Of sorts. An RTA. Our motorbike man has been in a little accident.'

CHAPTER TWENTY-TWO

CATRIN WAS WADING through Mirain's phone records when her phone chimed an incoming text message notification The name came up on her screen and she lifted her chin towards the ceiling with a sigh.

> Byronski: It's Saturday. You up for a coffee? Magda's is still here.

> Remember those post hangover fry-ups? These days it's lattes and macchiatos

> and almond croissants. Here's another snap from the archive.

THE PHOTO, this time, showed the younger Catrin on a bed, face down, her hair, a lot longer then, half covering her face. Bed sheets covered only part of her backside. The rest was all on show. Her pale skin in the dim light of a dark bedroom looked oddly darker than usual. She remembered that Byronski had a couple of cameras that he was always playing with. This shot looked grainy, something to do with how you processed the image, no doubt.

But it wasn't so much the image that bothered her now. The term "archive" sent a flutter through her gut. How many more of these did the sod have?

She began texting back a firm refusal of the offer but stopped halfway through. There was only one way to find out how many "snaps" Byronski had in his archive, and that meant confronting him. This needed nipping in the bud.

She sat back, eyes on the screen in front of her, but her mind somewhere else altogether. Trying and failing to piece together the details of that flighty ten months of her first year of university. She hadn't thought about all that for a long time. She'd moved on. A different degree, a career, a couple of boyfriends in between, and then Craig.

She glanced around the room. A few Uniforms had been co-opted as indexers and researchers, but Gil looked busy at his desk, so did Rhys. She turned around and found Jess Allanby on the phone.

She'd tried talking to Rhys about this, to no avail. Gil might be a little more sympathetic, but ideally, she wanted to run all this past another woman. She'd spent a lot of time with Jess Allanby and, although the DI kept an air of composed professionalism at work, she had her own cross to bear regarding a breakup. To an extent that that made her personal life off limits, other than discussions over Molly's teenage antics.

Because of that, Catrin never truly opened up to Jess, but Byronski seemed like a special case. More than anything, she needed advice about how best to deal with him.

The Incident Room, with Warlow gone, felt relatively calm. Now would be as good a time as any.

Catrin got up from her desk, smoothed down her

trousers, and started across the room just as Jess finished her call. She took two steps when the DI fixed her with a look that she recognised. Animated, and a little flushed. The kind of look she got when something significant had happened in a case. And when she spoke, she used a voice meant to be heard by everyone in the room.

'Listen up. That was Sergeant Nixon on a street near Bronglais hospital. They're responding to a call from a paramedic. It's Luca Domacini.'

'What's happened?' Gil asked, on his feet in an instant. 'Don't tell me the bugger's had a heart attack?'

'No,' Jess said with a simmering anger underlying her words. 'Worse than that. He's done another runner.'

'What?' Rhys swivelled around in his seat.

'Catrin, can you get on to traffic and see if there's any CCTV footage in that area?'

'Ma'am.' Catrin turned back to her desk, all thoughts of Byronski thrust to the back of her mind.

For now.

———

WARLOW STOOD at the side of the road with a diminutive paramedic called Rita Yelland. She was still a little shaken, but thankfully unharmed.

'We were five minutes from the hospital. He was semi-conscious when we got to him at the site of the RTA. His BP and heart rate were stable, but he responded to questions, so I thought—'

'We both did.' Her partner, Bob Armitage, stood next to her. A good foot taller than Rita, with iron-grey hair, he looked more upset than his partner. 'I was driving. If I'd have been in the back, things might have been different.'

Warlow ignored him. He'd deal with his guilt his own way, no doubt.

'As I say, only five minutes out when he sat up and pushed me down,' Rita said. 'He took me by surprise. One minute, he looked like he was sparked out, the next thing, he was on top of me, hand in my hair, then on my throat. He didn't hit me but he drew his fist back so I shouted to Bob to stop.'

'I didn't have much choice,' Bob muttered.

'Once we stopped, Domacini opened the doors and ran off. It took ten seconds.'

'Had he said anything at all on the journey?' Warlow asked.

Rita shook her head.

'Did he have a weapon of any kind?'

'Not that I could see.' She stood with hands on hips. Angry and trembling from the adrenaline. But Rita looked like a tough cookie. Paramedics had to be to deal, on a daily basis, with things most people would run a mile from. But this was different. Yes, they got threats from drunks and people who didn't know any better, but this was a perpetrator who'd added actual bodily harm (of a female health worker) to a list that had previously contained assaulting a police officer. Not to mention the damaged pride and disappointment he'd caused Rita. Her job was to help people. When those same people ended up not wanting help, or worse, being obnoxious and violent, it hurt.

'He didn't hit you?'

Rita shook her head. 'But he looked capable of it.'

Warlow put a hand on her arm. 'You did the right thing, stopping and letting him go. He's desperate.'

'What has he done?' Bob asked.

'We don't know, but he took out one of my officers, too. As time goes on, it's looking worse and worse for him.'

He left them to it. Conventional wisdom said that Rita ought to go home for a strong cup of tea and a lie down, but even as Warlow walked away, he heard a call come over the radio that there was a possible burns incident at a house on Greenfield Street. If there was any suggestion that these two should call it a day, it ended within thirty seconds. Warlow saw Bob and Rita climb into the front seats of the ambulance and the next minute, they were off, blue lights flashing.

CHAPTER TWENTY-THREE

'Who the hell escapes from an ambulance after an RTA?' Rhys asked Catrin while they searched for known camera positions on their screens.

'Exactly. What the hell is he up to?' Catrin looked perplexed.

'He'll have no idea,' Gil said. 'Scrotes like him can't stand the thought of getting caught. It's a macho thing.'

'But why?'

'Well, he wants to get back to his house,' Rhys offered. 'There's a chance that—'

Rhys's mobile rang. Not a number he recognised. He picked up.

'Hello. DC Harries. It's Claudine. We met at my flat.'

Rhys moved the phone away on an outstretched hand and put the other to the side of his mouth so that he could whisper to the team, 'Domacini's partner.'

He brought the phone back. 'Yes, Claudine, how can I help you?'

'I was ringing... I wanted to find out if... Are you okay?'

'Great, thanks.'

'There was a lot of blood on the stairs.'

'Yeah, sorry about that. I'm a good little bleeder, so my sergeant tells me. Though sometimes he leaves out the good bit.'

'I'm so glad. Luca can be wild. He has an awful temper.'

'He hasn't ever—'

'I knew you were going to ask me that. No, never. Not with me. It's always with other people.'

'That's good, then. Although, I'm other people, so not so good for me.'

Catrin, a couple of desks over and listening to Rhys's side of the conversation, held up her hands with a scrunched-up face in a gesture of amused confusion. A state of mind Rhys's ability to torture the language often evinced in her.

Rhys, not wanting to be distracted, turned away only to see Gil on the other side of him gesturing a circular motion with one hand and an opening and closing motion with the other.

Rhys twigged that they wanted him to keep talking.

'Has Luca been in touch with you, Claudine?'

'No.' Claudine did not sound convincing.

'Are you sure about that?'

'He said he was going to his uncle's old place, but that was ages ago. I haven't heard from him in hours.'

Rhys wondered if the RTA had damaged Luca's phone more than it had damaged him. 'If he does contact you, it's important you contact us right away.'

'Is he in trouble?'

'I won't lie to you. Yes, he is.'

'For kicking you in the chest?'

'Let's just say it doesn't show him in a very good light.'

'He isn't a thug, honestly.'

That was debatable. 'Okay, but if he contacts you, please tell me.'

'I will.'

In the silence that followed, Rhys tried desperately to think of something else to say, but it was Claudine who ended the stalemate.

'Actually, there was something I wanted to ask you. I couldn't before because I'd only just met you and then when Luca turned up—'

'All hell broke loose.'

Claudine giggled. She used her little girl voice for that one. 'Can we meet? I know it's a Saturday, but a quick coffee in town. Just you and me. Do you know the Quayside?'

'No, but I can find it.'

'Half an hour?'

'I'll be there.'

When he'd finished, Gil clapped him on the back. 'Well done, Rhys.'

'She said she wanted to say something, but not on the phone.'

'Think Domacini's with her?' Catrin asked.

'Don't know. I didn't get that feeling. I'm meeting her in town.'

Jess nodded. 'Off you go, then. Find out as much as possible about Domacini. He may have some places he frequents. If anyone'll know, it'll be his partner.'

And so, paradoxically, it wasn't Catrin that went out to coffee with an old flame, but Rhys, with a new acquaintance. One with expertise in the sensual arts, who was closest to their person of interest in a murder enquiry.

She was sitting on a stool near a window bench in the coffee shop when Rhys entered. The last time he'd seen her, she was dressed to thrill. Now she'd adopted a student uniform of tight skinny jeans and shapeless hoodie.

Though her eyelashes were still long, she'd scrubbed most of the makeup, including the mole, off her face and had opted for glasses to correct her obvious short sightedness instead of the tinted contacts she wore for her "clients".

'Can I get you anything?' Rhys asked with a nod at her empty cup.

'Tap water will be fine,' Claudine answered.

The place was full. Shoppers, a group of teens being conspiratorial in the corner, and random couples leaning in, their worlds constricted to the air around and between them.

Rhys ordered a coffee at the counter. An Americano. He'd suffered the wrath of Evan Warlow for ordering a white chocolate Frappuccino with whipped cream once and would not do it again. Though there was no one here to wag a finger, he felt he'd moved on from that sugary delight to something a little more mature.

He sat on a stool next to Claudine and smiled the kind of smile that harbingered bad news.

'Before we start, I ought to tell you that Luca was in a minor accident.'

Claudine blinked furiously behind her glasses, which were perched a little too far forward on her nose than was sensible, to avoid eyelash damage.

Rhys held up his hands in placation. 'Don't worry, he's fine. But on the way to the hospital, he attacked a paramedic and ran off. The uniformed officers who were accompanying him had gone on ahead in their own vehicle.'

Claudine clutched an open hand to her mouth. 'Oh my God, what an idiot. Don't tell me he hurt someone?'

'No, he didn't. But we need to get to him before he does anything else silly. You can see that, can't you?'

Claudine nodded.

'So, once more. Has he contacted you?'

She shook her head, earnestness personified. 'Not for hours. The trouble is, he doesn't think things through.'

'Was that what you wanted to say to me?'

The big eyelashes batted up and down. 'No.'

'Okay,' Rhys said, wary now.

'Luca and… We're kind of a couple, but kind of not. He's a bit too possessive, even though he knows what I do. I mean, lots of men have seen my body. And I mean lots.'

'How many would you say?' Probably not a relevant question, but Rhys couldn't help himself.

Claudine puffed out an exhalation. 'Thousands, definitely. Maybe hundreds of thousands. It's the internet, so who knows.'

'Aren't you worried about that?'

Claudine shrugged. 'No one recognises me like this.' She swiped a hand down over her clothes, top to bottom. 'And I get no complaints when I do my stuff. You've seen it. What do you think?'

Rhys's turn to nod. Because no words would come. Instead, he picked up his coffee cup and sipped.

Claudine leaned forwards and dropped her voice low. 'The reason I wanted to see you has nothing to do with Luca.' She smiled and there was something very… Professional about that smile. 'I was wondering if you might help me out. Work wise. You and me in a bit of a double act.'

Rhys had a mouth full of coffee as he stared at Claudine over the rim of his cup, his eyes widening with each word she spoke. Somehow, he managed not to spit it out.

'You look very fit and, though I haven't seen you with no clothes on, I'm sure you're not carrying much fat,' she explained. 'Neither does Luca, but he's turned me down point blank. I mean, I'd do all the work. All you'd have to do is lie there, or stand there, or crouch there. No one would see your face. I'm pretty good at camera angles. And it wouldn't be your face they'd be looking at, anyway. It'd be my face and a certain part of your anatomy. I get requests for the real thing all the time. We could charge a special rate and we'd make an absolute killing.' She let out one of her little giggles. 'We could put a small policeman's hat on it and I'd call you Mr Truncheon.'

Rhys swallowed. Or rather gulped. And the coffee in his mouth found its way into a tube that was never meant for hot fluids. He managed, to his credit, to get a paper towel over his face before the worst of the regurgitated stuff came back up from his larynx and out of his mouth in an explosive cough. More of it took route B via his nostrils. He lurched back, his stool scraping over the floor, and tried to clear his airways, tears streaming down his face, the tickle in his larynx unstoppable.

For a good two minutes.

Someone even came over to pat him on the back, but he waved the bloke away.

'I'm fine… Fine,' he gasped.

When he finally looked at Claudine, she was still sitting there, contemplating him impassively. 'Obviously, that has come as a bit of a shock. Have a think about it. I mean, I'm not going anywhere. You're a busy man and you know where I am.' She got off the stool and picked up her bag. 'Oh, and if Luca tries to contact me, I'll text you. 'Kay?'

And with that she walked out, leaving the detective alone to mop himself up and wonder if there were any hidden cameras or microphones in the place. He jerked his head up and around in panic. He could almost accept it if it *had* been a wind up. But something told him it had not been, and no one was taking any notice of him now. They'd all gone back to their flat whites and cappuccinos. He picked up Claudine's untouched tap water and sipped.

It helped.

Mr bloody Truncheon?

Rhys shook his head and pondered just how weird this world he was living in could be.

Was he ever going to tell Gina about this?

She'd be the only one. He'd never tell anyone else. And even Gina was not scoring high on his possibles list. The sound of her throaty, hysterical laughter bounced around in his head in anticipation.

Of course, he'd never do it—Mr Truncheon. Not in a million years. And as of this moment, Claudine didn't need to come anywhere near the investigation because she had nothing else to contribute. Of that, he was sure.

He needed to keep her away from Gil and Catrin at all costs; that was certain.

He couldn't bear the thought of them ever mentioning the word "truncheon" ever again.

CHAPTER TWENTY-FOUR

When Warlow got back to the "Castle Keep", Jess stood outside, mobile to her ear, pacing back and forth. She waved a greeting and mouthed 'Molly' to him as he pushed through the main entrance doors.

The shared Gallery and Job Centre boards looked pleasingly full as Warlow stripped off his jacket. He nodded at Catrin and raised a hand to Gil but noted Rhys's absence.

'Where is he?' Warlow asked. 'Getting the tea on?'

'Alas, no. He had a mysterious phone call from Luca's partner, uh, Claudine Barton. Said she had something for him. Jess suggested he follow it up, "our man in Aberystwyth" style. I've had a text. He's on the way back.'

'Has she told him where Domacini is?'

'If she has, he didn't put it in his text, which read, and I quote: "Claudine a damp squid. Back soon."'

Gil held up the phone by way of confirmation.

'We're both hoping that's a predictive text error on the squid, right?' Warlow raised one eyebrow.

'We can but hope. However, this comes from a man

who has been known to use "nip it in the butt" when he's wanted to quickly end something unpleasant.'

'I put it down to the education system,' Warlow said. 'And to think his mother is an English teacher, too.'

'Ah, but she insisted on sending him to a school where she did not teach,' Gil said.

'She'd have been better off keeping an eye on the bugger and teaching him the difference between squid and squib. Christ, she must be rotating in her grave.'

Gil's turn to cock one eye. 'You realise Mrs Harries is very much alive and well.'

'Someone better dig her up, then.'

The sergeant nodded his appreciation of Warlow's very old joke coincidental with Jess breezing back in.

'Just saw Rhys pull up,' she announced.

'Right, I'll get the kettle boiled.' Gil sauntered out of the Incident Room whistling the tune to *Rocky*.

'All okay with Molly?' Warlow asked.

Jess dipped her head low to answer. 'Her dad's just informed her he might be out of circulation for a while. Of course, she thinks that means he's going to jail. So, she is now doing the headless chicken in our kitchen.'

'Still, nice to know she's concerned for her dad.'

'More concerned for her street cred, more like.'

'That's a bit harsh, isn't it?'

She sank into a chair. 'I suppose so. Sometimes I wonder who is the biggest drama queen, Molly or Ricky.'

'If he is going to go undercover, though, he will be off-grid for who knows how long.'

'He'll be out of my sodding hair, that's for certain.' Jess's eyes stayed hard.

'And I wouldn't say Molly is a drama queen. She's a teenager, that's all.'

'Isn't she just.'

The Incident Room door swung open, and Rhys

walked through, took in the inquisitive faces of the rest of the team, stood stock still, went bright red and said, 'What?'

'Nothing,' Catrin said. 'But why are you looking so guilty? What have you and Claudine been up to?'

Rhys shrugged off his jacket. 'Waste of time, that's all. She hasn't been contacted by Domacini, that's for sure.' He turned to Warlow. 'Hello, sir. Did they find a phone on him, do you know?'

'Didn't ask.'

'I'm wondering if it got damaged in the RTA.'

'Good point,' Warlow agreed.

'If she didn't want to speak to you about Domacini, what did she want?' Catrin persisted.

'She realised he might not be around for a while, so she was angling for some police protection. For her work, you know.' Whereas this wasn't strictly true, it wasn't exactly a lie, either. After all, the offer she'd made Rhys would have involved him being a presence and an obvious one if the policeman's helmet thing was ever in play.

Catrin's eyes narrowed. 'Why is it I get the impression you are only telling us half a story here?'

'Ah well, sarge, it must be all that detective training.' Rhys's smile beamed out.

Catrin said no more, but her glare could have stripped paint.

Thankfully, his ordeal ended when Gil pushed through the door, phone in hand.

'I've just taken a call from one of the Rural Crime Team. I think you know him as Tomo?'

Warlow nodded. He knew Tomo. They'd worked together on a case over on the far eastern edge of Powys where two farmers were murdered.

'Tomo? What does he have to say?'

'Someone said they'd seen something in a quarry over

at Ystrad Meurig. Some stuff floating in the water there. Looks like it belonged to Alistair Lyndon.'

———

THE JOURNEY south and east took twenty-five minutes. It might not have been far on the map, but the roads wound up and down towards one of the oldest villages in Ceredigion. Warlow drove with Rhys as passenger.

'What can you tell me about this place?' Warlow asked.

Rhys had his phone out, googling. 'Not much, sir. I mean, we did touch on Ystrad Meurig in school because it had a castle a thousand years ago. Not anymore, of course. All that's left is a mound of earth. But it had strategic importance. Quite a few battles in the area. Us against them.'

'Them?'

'The Normans, sir.'

Warlow turned one sceptical eye towards the DC. 'And you're in the "us" camp, are you?'

'Clue is in the name, sir. Lots of Rhys's around this part of the world. Mainly kings and princes.'

'Don't tell me you're the heir to the throne?'

Rhys laughed out loud. 'Someone already pinched that, sir.' He flicked through pages on his phone. 'Ah, right, looks like there is more than one quarry here. It's a big area. But the place we want is just to the east. Not the main quarry. I have instructions.'

Warlow followed them and parked up next to a Ford Ranger with the usual blue and yellow checkered side panels. They were at the bottom of a gouged-out area of countryside, once again no houses or farms within sight, with a track leading up to the higher ground and another Apache Village of white tents. Away to their left, the sloping land fell away to reveal a deep, scoured-out area with a flat expanse of water within it. But his eyes were drawn to the huge orange mobile crane with its telescopic boom extended out over the tallest edge of the quarry fifty yards away and seventy or so feet up from where they had parked.

The thick cables of the crane's load line led straight down into the water.

Warlow walked across to the edge for a better view. Here, they were about thirty feet up. For once, the gods had been kind, and the day remained still and calm. No wind to rattle the crane cables. There were divers in the dark waters and a small inflatable boat. Someone signalled and the crane's winch took the tension while the divers in the water hung back. The cables ran, and the water stayed calm until the rear of the vehicle approached the surface. It glinted like some exotic fish under the water until it emerged, number plate attached.

'That's it, sir,' Rhys said.

'What? You can read the number plate from up here?'

Warlow had his hand over his eyes to cut out the glare. He had a pair of varifocals on, but the numberplate was a mere black and white jumble. But Rhys reeled off the letters and numbers.

'Christ, are you part kestrel?'

'Young eyes, sir.'

'Watch it,' Warlow warned.

In the quarry, water streamed out of the open windows on both the passenger and driver's sides. Someone had left them that way to ensure the thing sank, no doubt. One and a half tons of metal bled water as the crane did its thing and dragged the vehicle clear. It glinted in the sunshine against the grey and brown rocks of the quarry wall. Once it was clear of the top edge, the crane's boom arm swung ninety degrees and gently lowered the car onto solid ground.

Warlow was already making his way up as officers secured the vehicle with chocks and released the crane's cables.

By the time Warlow arrived, Povey was already out, tyveked to the gills, kneeling to inspect the outside of the BMW.

'I hope to God you're going to tell me that there's no one inside,' Warlow said.

'Can't speak for the boot, but the seats are all empty. No sign of external damage. Hasn't been in an accident.'

'We should look in the boot,' Warlow said. 'Can we do it if the battery's flat?'

Rhys stepped forward. 'It's a hatchback. I reckon if we open the back doors, the rear seats will fold down.'

Warlow turned to look at his junior with admiration.

Povey went to it. Water trickled out of the footwell and dripped down from the inside of the door once she'd opened it. She looked inside and reached up to the catch on the top of the rear seat, released it, and folded the seat down. Warlow could hear his pulse thrumming in his ears as the seat-back flattened.

The boot wasn't empty. Inside was a shoulder bag and scattered remnants of papers that stuck soggily to the inside of the rear window and the boot lining. But that was all.

'Those papers were what someone saw floating on the surface. They're exam papers from the college. Some walkers phoned it in.'

If it had not been for the papers, no one would have known the car was at the bottom of that quarry.

'Any signs at all of a struggle in here?' Warlow bent at the waist to peer into the soaked interior. A futile question, he knew, but he asked it anyway.

'Nothing that I can see, but we need a better look. As you know, any DNA evidence will have suffered from being in the water, but you never know. We've successfully recovered evidence from prolonged water exposure before.' She stepped back, hands on hips, in contemplation. 'But it'll be a job. Sooner we get this back to the compound, the better.'

Warlow left her to it and strode back to the stoned track they'd walked up. It went on towards a sheep pen and petered out. You could drive a vehicle up here, that was clear. But there were no signs, and someone had to have known about its existence.

Only one thing was for certain: that person was not Alistair Lyndon.

CHAPTER TWENTY-FIVE

THIS TIME, when they got back to Aberystwyth, Gil had the tea ready. Warlow reined back his disappointment over the lack of biscuits, but Rhys couldn't hold it in.

'Something to dunk would be nice,' he muttered.

'Your head in a bucket?' Catrin grinned.

Rhys took offence. The team recognised his hangry mode, and another snipe was all it needed to trigger a response. 'You okay, sarge? You seem a bit... Tetchy.'

Catrin shuffled some papers on her desk. 'I'm fine, thank you. As Sergeant Jones says, it'll do us all good to stay away from refined sugar for a few days.'

'Speak for yourself,' Rhys grumbled.

The tea, at least, was hot and sweet. They formed a half circle and Warlow took the lead. 'Povey has Lyndon's car for now, but it looked undamaged. Theories?' He glanced around.

Rhys replied first, 'Someone killed Lyndon, then took his car to the quarry and drove it in from a great height.'

'Good observation, Rhys. Now colour in the missing bits for me.'

Rhys frowned.

'The who and the why?' Warlow demanded.

Rhys, sitting with his long legs straight out in front of him, arms folded, let his chin fall to his chest for a minute, thinking. 'Someone didn't want the car found because there's evidence in it?'

'Possibly.'

'Or wanted to buy some time?' Catrin's turn.

'Or didn't think at all and wanted it out of sight,' Jess said.

'All three sound pretty valid,' Warlow agreed.

'And if that person is Luca Domacini, it might fit,' Rhys said.

That earned him a team glare.

Rhys sat up, realising he needed to expound his thinking. 'Claudine says he's a spontaneous sort of bloke. If he killed Lyndon, he may have panicked, wanted to get rid of as much evidence as possible as quickly as possible.'

'It's a bit out of the way, though, this quarry,' Gil said. 'How would he have got back?'

'It's not that far. Half an hour at most from here,' Rhys answered.

'Presuming he can't fly; he'd have needed transport back.'

Warlow walked over to the map. He put his finger on Ystymtuen and ran it down towards Ystrad Meurig. It made the third leg of a triangle joining the quarry, where they found the body and the town they were sitting in now. 'If you look, where we found the body is directly north of where the car got dumped. What, fifteen miles at most? There is a road that joins the two. The...' he paused and put on his pocket reading glasses, '... B4343. And a spiderweb of smaller roads.'

'You think that's significant?' Gil asked.

'Who knows? Domacini's a fitness freak. Don't tell me

he can't ride a bike. But we need to establish whether there's public transport.'

Catrin made a note.

'But as of now, we still have Luca Domacini in the frame?' Jess asked.

'Until we can eliminate him, he's our strongest candidate. Though I would have liked some firmer link between him and Alistair Lyndon apart from the vague possibility that the victim was hassling Ms MoulinsplurgeX online.' Warlow turned away from the board and removed his glasses. 'What about our other lines of enquiry? Any joy with finding Mirain?'

Catrin nodded. 'I'm still working on her phone records, sir.'

'Gil?'

'I'm waiting for a call back from Lyndon's ex. I've left messages. I'll try again now.'

Jess pushed off the desk she was leaning on. 'Let me have a go. Where does she work?'

Gil nodded. 'Lawyer at a big accountancy firm in Cardiff.'

She glanced at her watch. 'Right, I'll get to it.'

———

JESS DIDN'T BOTHER with Valerie Halpin's direct number. Instead, she looked up the company's directors, found a likely candidate and rang her.

'It could be that Ms Halpin hasn't received our messages or, as is sometimes the case these days, thinks it's a scam,' Jess explained after laying out her credentials and adopting a no-nonsense approach. She was that by default, but more so when she needed to be.

While she waited for the director to contact Ms Halpin,

Jess checked her mobile for more texts from Molly. Since they'd spoken, there'd been only the one:

> Is he going undercvr mum?

JESS SMILED. It had taken her all of fifteen minutes to run through all the possibilities for her father's enigmatic chat and, discounting prison, come up with this. She texted back an acronym:

> TAIL

THE ACRONYM WAS something she'd come up with to let her daughter know that whatever the perceived teenage urgency, Jess could not discuss it now because she was busy. They would "Talk About It Later". The acronym annoyed the hell out of Molly over the years. To be fair, the number of times Jess had needed to use it had diminished considerably. And this time, it had more to do with security than Molly wanting to impinge upon Jess's paid police time. She waited. Molly didn't text back. Message received, then.

She got a call from Cardiff a minute later.

'Hello?' said a female voice.

'Is this Valerie?' Jess asked.

'It is. I've been asked to phone you.' No doubting the frisson or irritation in the tone. It didn't matter. Jess was used to much worse. From resistance to downright violent threats.

'Thanks for getting in touch. Okay to call you Valerie?'

'Yes... I suppose.'

'Good. I'll get straight to the point, Valerie. I'm ringing about your ex-husband, Alistair Lyndon.'

A deep sigh. 'What's he done?'

'I don't like doing this sort of thing by phone, Valerie, but it's bad news. I'm afraid Alistair Lyndon has been found dead.'

No sigh this time, just empty silence. At this stage, regardless of history, a sob normally broke through. But nothing came from Valerie. And her next sentence was matter of fact.

'How did it happen?'

'I'm not at liberty to say other than we are treating Mr Lyndon's death as suspicious. We wanted you to be aware before the press statement which is going to happen soon.'

'Thank you.'

'When was the last time you spoke to Alistair, Valerie?'

'In court. Eighteen months ago.'

'Nothing since?'

'He sometimes sends me a card.'

'Birthday?'

'Could be. I wouldn't know. If I recognise his hand-writing, I burn the envelope before opening.'

Wow. That made her and Ricky's relationship seem positively cordial. 'I take it your divorce was acrimonious?'

'You could say that.'

Jess wrote the word down and underlined it.

'Would you say that Alistair had any enemies?'

'Besides me, you mean?'

'Excuse me?'

'Sorry, I didn't mean it that way. When did it happen?'

'We think about a week ago.'

This time, there was a sigh. Small but perceptible. 'I was in Portugal. I have an alibi.'

Valerie Halpin, as Gil would say, took no prisoners. Jess was quick to correct her. 'No one is accusing you of—'

'I am sorry to hear all this. Sorry for his mum.'

'We're having difficulty tracing her.'

'That's because she's in France. They were estranged. I have a number if you need it.'

'We will. She'll need to be informed. Legally, she is next of kin.'

'Look, Alistair was a shit of spectacular proportions. A flirty liar that had his eyes on every bit of skirt that walked past. How the hell he got to be a teacher I do not know. But if you're expecting floods of tears, you are going to be disappointed. He's a narcissist… Was a narcissist. And you know what they're like. Con artists who do not give a crap about who they hurt. Biggest regret of my life was bumping into him at a nightclub. I can send you a transcript of my court statement for the divorce. It still hurts. Mainly because I had to share all my bloody assets with that bastard.'

'That won't be necessary.'

'I'll email you the number of the man I was in Portugal with, too. He's not perfect. What bloody man is? But compared with Alistair, he's a saint.'

'Okay, that would be good. Thank you.'

After a beat, Valerie asked, 'I suppose his partner will get the house?' An odd question, but a sign of how raw the previous relationship was.

'I have no idea what's in his will.'

'Poor woman. She won't thank me for saying this, but if he's out of her life, then she's a lucky woman to have escaped unscathed. You can tell her that from me.'

'What about his mother.'

'I can speak to her if you like. She's a good woman.'

'No, I need to do that. But thanks for the offer.'

Jess gave Valerie her email, put the phone down, and made some notes. Not quite what she'd been expecting, but useful. She walked over to Warlow's desk and quickly précis'd the conversation.

Warlow listened and tilted his head. 'Not coming out of this at all well, is he, old Alistair?'

Catrin, looking a little agitated, bustled over to join the senior officers.

'Sir, ma'am, I am so sorry about this. I picked up an email that I should have seen earlier. It's from Morton's gym, where Domacini sometimes works.'

'As a personal trainer?'

'Yes. Anyway, the manager there has been through his list of members and, surprise, surprise, Alistair Lyndon is on that list.'

'So, there is a link,' Jess said.

'I don't know how solid this is. I mean, two men in the same gym don't add up to much.'

'But it adds up to something,' Warlow said.

'And Domacini's record confirms that he was under suspicion of supplying illegal anabolic steroids and other banned substances. He'd done it all before,' Jess added.

Warlow sat up. 'That might explain why he's so keen to get back to his old uncle's house.'

'He'll want his stash,' Jess agreed.

'Do we have people watching the place?'

'CID,' Catrin said.

'Okay. Let's pull them all away to make it look like we've lost interest. See what Luca does next.'

Both women nodded their agreement. Jess moved back to her desk, but Catrin stayed. 'I'd like to apologise for not seeing this earlier, sir.'

'Not like you, Catrin. Everything okay?'

'It is, sir. I'm dealing with some stuff, but it's all fine.'

Warlow doubted that. 'Well, if there's anything I can do. Or if not me, then DI Allanby has a very sympathetic ear.' Warlow had the sense to see that sometimes these things were gender-related. Nothing sexist in that. Sometimes women wanted another woman to confide in. And it was unlike Catrin Richards not to be on top of things.

'Thank you, sir. I'm sure it'll all go away.'

'Well, my door is always open,' Warlow said and added, in a low growl, 'Except there is no office up here to put a door on. But you get the gist.'

'I do, sir. Thank you.'

Warlow took in her unconvincing smile but said nothing more. Instead, he called over the room. 'Rhys, cancel the photo shoot with Hello for this evening. We've got somewhere to be.'

CHAPTER TWENTY-SIX

LUCA HAD FOUND A BETTER place to watch his uncle's house from. They were laying fibre-optic lines in the roads and had conveniently left two or three areas dug up and surrounded by red plastic barriers. There were three on his road and another four on the street around the corner. Much of this work had been sub-contracted, and whoever had done the digging was out of sync with the optical ducting guys. Which meant lots of holes.

He'd felt dizzy after getting out of the ambulance. He hadn't passed out when he hit the delivery van, but it had shaken him. Still, he'd done the right thing in getting out of there. Now, if only he could stay ahead of the cops for a while and get his stash out, all would be good. He'd nicked a hoodie from a clothesline and, under the added camouflage of a baseball cap he'd found in a skip, he'd made his way back to his uncle's place.

Seeing the works on the pavement had cemented his plan. Hardly any people anyway in this part of town and, whenever anyone came near, he simply ducked his head and pretended to be doing something important down the hole.

He'd been doing that for three hours now. And during all that time, a police car had sat outside his uncle's house. As if he would just saunter up like a muppet.

Bloody coppers. Clueless, the lot of them. And having no phone was a bastard. He'd lost it somewhere along the way. But then, he'd seen enough TV and films to know they could track you if you had your phone. Better to be a stealth ninja.

He'd called into a shop for some water and now sat on an exposed pipe at the bottom of the trench to take another sip. His neck hurt, but that didn't matter. He would split with Claudine. He liked her, but the punter thing was doing his head in. He didn't mind blokes fancying her. He didn't even mind some of the stuff she did on camera because that was acting, right? And taking money from mugs who paid by the second to look, well, that was easy money.

But when the dirty bastards turned up on your doorstep, or you overheard people say her name in the gym, that was definitely out of fucking order. Big time. He couldn't handle that stuff.

He'd lost his shit on the stairs with the copper because of all that. Luca shook his head.

He still couldn't believe it. He looked nothing like a copper. For a start, he wasn't a fat slob.

Luca ran a hand through his hair. He had more than usual thanks to that Wicks bloke. Him with the hair. Ever since lockdown, Claudine had been on at him to grow his hair like fitness guru "Joe".

But that would change now. No more bloody Claudine and all those pervs.

A car started up on the street. Luca poked his head up to pavement level. The response vehicle parked in front of the house signalled and pulled away.

Probably called to something a bit more important than babysitting a property.

Or a change of shift.

In which case, Luca needed to act and act now. But not through the front door this time. Speed and stealth were his friends. He climbed out of the trench, stood for a minute to let his dizziness pass, and walked towards the next junction of streets. Some developer had converted a big house, *Llys Hafren*, into flats in a property behind and a couple of doors up from his uncle's, accessed from another road. His uncle's garden backed onto the parking space in the courtyard of that flat conversion, fenced off with wooden boards.

Luca kept his head down, walked around and up the next street. The parking area for *Llys Hafren* was unguarded. He walked straight in and clambered over the fence to drop into a pile of crap that had accumulated over the months and years at the bottom of his uncle's garden.

At one time, this place had been full of flowers. Now it doubled as a wildlife jungle. No mow May had turned into no mow never. But this was no time for regrets. If his uncle ever left it to him, he'd do something about it. Find some Poles to knock the place into shape. Convert it into student flats and start raking in the dosh.

But first, he needed his stash.

He walked quickly up the narrow gap between the encroaching wall of thistles and dandelions until he got to the little extension that poked out of the back of the house. The key was inside the door but the window on the left never closed properly, and he yanked at it until it came open enough for him to get a hand in and release the stay. Paint flaked off the rotting woodwork as he got one leg through the window space, and he tried to shift his weight so that his testicles didn't get caught on the aluminium frame.

With an ungainly hop, he managed it and stood in the kitchen he knew so well, listening.

No sound except some traffic noises from the wide-open window. Luca didn't close it. Better to leave it as it was so that he could get away sharp-ish. He stood stock still, listening hard.

Nothing.

Now he hurried through the tiny extension and into a hallway past the kitchen. He swung a hand up to the balustrade and took two stairs at a time to stand on the landing.

Still no sound except a creak of a floorboard under his foot as he shifted weight.

He went straight to his bedroom and shoved the door open.

His bed was as he'd left it. Was that only yesterday morning? He'd stayed here because of his bouncer work and because he'd needed to get up to meet with a client at the gym at eight-thirty. Not that his lack of time would excuse the state of his bed.

That was par for the course.

A big, heavy, dysfunctional brown wardrobe stood in one corner. An heirloom from the days when everything in his uncle's house had been brown: furniture, sideboards, cupboards, the lot. But that would all change once he was gone.

For one brief second, that thought pierced Luca's single-minded obsession, and he paused, remembering when he'd loved coming here to be with his uncle and auntie. Those days when they'd play in the garden, and she'd read to him. Talk to him about the old days and their life as kids in Italy.

But that was then, and this was now.

Luca pulled open the wardrobe door, ripped out his hanging clothes and reached up to push up the false roof he'd put in. Above that, a shallow plastic toolbox no more than four inches deep hung from a hook screwed into the wood. He unhooked it, pulled it down, put it on the rumpled bed, and unsnapped the lock.

Everything was as he'd left it. No one had touched the stash. He made two fists and, standing alone and with his teeth clamped shut, hissed out a, 'Yessss. You beauty.'

It was then that he heard another creak on the landing. In a heartbeat, all his elation evaporated.

He snatched up the plastic bags of drugs and turned in time to see a man in a suit walk through the bedroom door and say, 'Police. Stay calm. Stay exactly where you are.'

Luca didn't know this man, and he wasn't big. Nowhere near as big as Luca. He took a step forward.

'I can see you're not inclined to take my advice there, Luca. No weapons? Good. Now, there are one or two things you need to know.'

Luca stopped.

'That police response vehicle you saw leave earlier has been replaced by a much bigger van. And there's another one in the little car park you jumped the fence of. All full of helpful officers who will be delighted to accompany you to the station. And I use the word accompany advisedly.'

'You can't be in here. You don't have a warrant,' Luca's voice barked out. Adrenaline made his legs tremble.

Warlow flourished a bit of paper. 'The other thing you ought to know is that—'

Luca ran for it. He lunged at the man, who simply stepped aside and let Luca go for the door. He had one foot over the threshold when something big and hard caught him in the chest and drove him backwards into the room where he landed, arse first, on the bed.

Winded, Luca tried to sit up but only managed a wheezing spasm ending in his falling back again.

The man in the suit stepped forward, holding up a lanyard with his warrant card clearly displayed. 'DCI Evan Warlow. As you will have probably sussed out, the chap you met outside the bedroom door is Detective Constable Rhys Harries, the officer you kicked down the stairs at your girlfriend's flat. And believe you me, there is nothing in the world that he would enjoy more than apprehending you were you to flee again. But then you've already found that out the hard way.'

Rhys stood, tensed for more action, his fists balled, while Warlow continued.

'He has several stitches that he wouldn't have if it weren't for you. I am almost certain it would please him enormously to return the favour.'

With a flourish, Rhys flicked open a metal baton.

Luca looked down at the drugs in his hands and dropped them to the floor in a hot potato fashion.

'Those aren't mine,' he said.

'Of course not. Probably your iron pumping uncle's. Now turn around and my colleague Detective Constable Rhys Harries will put handcuffs on you.'

Luca didn't move.

Warlow shook his head sadly. 'Or don't and resist us, in which case we'll be joined by my colleagues, eagerly awaiting my signal. They're all out there, champing at the bit, and one of them has a big red battering ram which will make a mess of your front door. You've seen them on the telly, all shouty and pissed off. My point is, we'll end up apprehending you anyway, but with a lot more swearing and a rainbow of bruises. None of which will be mine. Either way, I'm easy.'

'I didn't know he was a copper,' Luca said.

'Strangely enough, that might have helped a lot if it hadn't been for the illegal substances you came back to get.'

'Red-handed, sir,' Rhys added without taking his eyes off the man hunched forward on the bed.

'Indeed.' Warlow turned to Rhys. 'Detective Constable Harries, please arrest this man on suspicion of causing actual bodily harm and on suspicion of possessing a Class B drug, which is what Ritalin is, if I am not mistaken.'

Luca looked up from the bed, all the fight leeching out of him. 'I'm sorry about…' He pointed at Rhys's head.

'I'm sure you are,' Warlow said. 'Now let's get you along to the station so we can find out what else you're sorry about.'

CHAPTER TWENTY-SEVEN

The person lucky enough to be dragged in to sit at Luca Domacini's side during his initial police interview did not look enthralled to be there. Warlow put Gil and Catrin together for the interrogation, while he and Jess observed on a screen in a separate room. The woman next to Luca was a police station representative. It was late, and the law firm had sent down the poor sod on the roster. After all, the potential charge at this stage was actual bodily harm and possession. Nothing tabloid worthy. Not yet, at any rate.

The firm, and their senior partner, were entities Warlow had come across before. But said senior partner was at home with a glass of chardonnay, feet up, no doubt watching some crime drama and laughing her socks off.

Keri Nichols, however, was a trainee solicitor who had done the Police Station Representatives Accreditation Scheme, which was all you needed to do to be invited to "advise" a grumpy Luca Domacini under the bright lights of the interview room.

Nichols wore thick-rimmed glasses and had declined the offer of tea, preferring a paper cup of water. She reminded Warlow of a skittish bird, painfully thin, all in black with a grey shirt. She twitched her gaze between her client, the officers, and the pad on her knees.

Luca, on the other hand, sat forward, forearms on the desk, while Gil did most of the talking, and Catrin sat back, waiting.

For now.

Gil had been through the events leading up to the attack on Rhys Harries, adding his own calming interpretation to draw Luca out. Luckily, after three attempts at, 'I would suggest a no comment in answer to that question,' as a mantra, the legal rep shut up and turned her attention to writing down everything that Domacini said. It wasn't as if there was any doubt about what had happened as Gil had pointed out. Attacking police officers and paramedics would not go down well in the courts. And the drugs he was selling were found during a lawful police raid.

'So, you turn up at Claudine Barton's, with whom you are in a relationship, see a strange bloke there, and assume that this person had been bothering her, correct?'

'Exactly.'

Gil nodded. 'Understandable, given Miss Barton's line of work. You were wary. Protective.'

'I didn't know who he was.'

'And did Miss Barton seem upset at all?'

Luca thought about this, knowing full well she hadn't. But he accepted the gift for what it was. 'Maybe. It all happened so fast.'

'Yes. We have a statement from the victim.' Gil picked up a sheet of paper. 'He flew at me without warning and kicked me in the chest.'

Luca glowered. 'I was worried he might become violent.'

'He is a violent-looking sort of chap, DC Harries,

wouldn't you agree, Sergeant Richards' He glanced across at Catrin. She returned it with her eyelids at half-mast.

Gil turned back and slid his glasses down from where he'd pushed them up over his forehead so that he could use them for their intended purpose. 'Now, about the drugs. Not yours, you say?'

'No.'

'Even though you removed them from a box hanging from a hook in a hidden space in your wardrobe?'

Luca's forehead seemed to be doing a dance all of its own. Next to him, Ms Nichols leaned over. 'I'd suggest a no comment to that one.'

Gil ignored her. 'Good idea. Especially since the witness we have who saw you do that is a Detective Chief Inspector.'

Luca shrugged. 'When I say not mine, I mean, they are mine, but I would not sell them or anything. They're for me.'

'So, they are yours,' Catrin remarked.

Her voice brought Luca up short. 'I got confused. People breaking into your house... It's stressful.'

'It would be,' Gil agreed. 'I can see that. Right, we'll make a note of that. Personal use for the drugs as opposed to flogging them all down the gym, then.'

Luca watched Gil scribble and looked across at the legal rep. 'That's good, isn't it?' he whispered. 'Me not knowing who it was I attacked and the drugs being for personal use?'

Nichols looked up and gave him a twitch of her lips that didn't last long enough to be a genuine smile.

'I expect you come across a lot of violence in your job, Mr Domacini,' Catrin said.

A derisory smile flickered. 'I'm a bouncer. It's in the job description.'

'Might in part explain the attack on DC Harries.'

Luca sighed. 'I already told you; I didn't know he was a copper.'

'Should that make any difference?'

'Of course, it should. I'm not bloody stupid. I wouldn't have attacked him if I'd known, would I?'

'But fair game if he was an innocent member of the public?' Catrin framed the word as a question and dropped her chin to add a dollop of disdainful scepticism.

'What about your job as a personal trainer? Any violence there?' Gil asked.

'Violence, no… What are you on about?'

Catrin pressed on, not giving Domacini time to think. 'Claudine Barton, or MoulinsplurgeX as she is better known, has built a name for herself. All her fellow students know who she is and what she does.'

'Yeah?' Luca spiked his response with a challenge.

'Did anyone ever mention Claudine at the gym? Did you ever lose your temper there?'

'What… No. Okay, sometimes I heard her name, but I didn't let on. Not then. But I never forget a face, so if one or two of those student twats turned up at the nightclub, then it was game on.'

'Is that what happened to Alistair Lyndon?'

'Who?' A deeper frown from Luca now. Real confusion this time.

'Alistair Lyndon. He's a member of the gym and he's also one of Claudine's fans, judging by his internet history and his bank account.'

'She has more than one fan.'

Gil crossed his arms over his chest. 'But Lyndon was local. On the doorstep. Not some anonymous bugger a thousand miles away.'

'I don't know an Alistair Lyndon,' Luca persisted.

'Sure he isn't someone you "gave" drugs to?' Catrin

made quotation marks in the air to emphasise the word "gave".

'Like I told you, I don't—'

She didn't let him finish. 'Did he say things about Claudine? Did he have a filthy mouth? Is that why you abducted him and smashed him over the head with a rock?'

Luca's posture changed in an instant. 'What? No... What? Who is this Lyndon bloke?' He threw Nichols a wide-eyed glance. 'What the fuck?'

Nichols, all credit to her, took up the challenge, her back straightening. 'I thought we were discussing actual bodily harm and a drugs charge, here?'

'We are. But we think they both might be linked to something else, and so we're asking questions about Alistair Lyndon,' Catrin replied.

'I don't know an Alistair Lyndon,' Luca said again.

Catrin turned back to Luca. 'Maybe you saw him hanging around Claudine's flat? Or, more likely, heard him say something at the gym? Maybe he turned up at the nightclub? We'll find out if he did easily enough. We're at the beginning of our enquiry into his death.'

Death.

The "D" word.

It had the desired effect on both Luca and his representative. A locked and loaded silence followed, during which the officers kept their eyes on Luca's face while his danced all over the room and ended up on Keri Nichols. 'What the hell is this? You didn't say nothing about this?'

'I didn't know,' she spluttered, turning back to the officers. 'We were not told—'

'We're telling you now,' Gil cut across her. 'Alistair Lyndon was abducted and killed a week ago and his dead body hidden down a mineshaft. Lots of violence involved in that sort of thing. Some of it before, some of it after death. We are giving Mr Domacini here the opportunity to tell us what he knows about that situation.'

'Nothing,' Luca blurted out. 'I don't know nothing.'

'I'd like to take a break,' Nichols said, already reaching into her bag for a phone.

'Sure. Here, or would you like us to take Luca back to the custody suite?'

Nichols looked across at the man sitting next to her, whose foot had begun bouncing up and down on the floor and whose face looked like a pot about to come to the boil. 'Best I make a call before consulting with my client,' she said, hastily.

'Fine. Fifteen minutes?' Gil said.

'And then we'll show you some photographs of Mr Lyndon. See if they'll help jog your memory, eh, Luca?' Catrin was all smiles.

'Can we get you a sandwich or anything?' Gil asked.

Catrin sucked air in through her teeth and tilted her head like someone asked to consider a very tricky little conundrum. 'Let's not be hasty, Sergeant Jones. I'd suggest Mr Domacini refrains from eating for now. These photos are best seen on an empty stomach.'

Luca's face blanched. And as for Keri Nichols, she was almost out of the door before Catrin finished the sentence.

———

GIL AND CATRIN joined the senior officers in the observation room while Luca made his way back to the cells, making it known to everyone, and loudly, that 'I haven't killed no one, you bastards.'

'Well?' Gil asked as soon as the door behind him closed.

'He has all the attributes,' Jess observed. 'He's power-ful, quick-tempered, not a fan of Claudine's admirers.'

'He isn't subtle, I'll say that about him,' Warlow said, but he couldn't hide the nagging doubt that tugged at the edges of his mouth.

'You're not convinced, sir?' Catrin asked.

'I saw his face when you mentioned Lyndon. I read genuine surprise. And I doubt old Luca would pass the interview for RADA. He doesn't know what the hell you're talking about.'

Gil and Catrin exchanged glances.

'But we still show him the photos,' Warlow added. 'He stays top of the list until we can establish his movements on the Sunday that Lyndon disappeared. Get a cuppa while you have the chance.'

When they'd gone, Warlow arched his back and an ominous click resulted.

'That doesn't sound good,' Jess said.

'Sleeping in a strange bed does wonders for my lower back. You know what it's like.' He glanced at his watch. Eight pm had come and gone. 'You need to get home to that daughter of yours.'

'And your dog.'

Warlow nodded. 'She's going to forget what I look like. I'll sit in with Gil and let Catrin get off, too...' He paused before adding an observation. 'Is it me, or do you get the feeling she's not quite firing on all cylinders?'

'You've noticed, too? Something's bothering her.'

'I asked, but she's keeping things buttoned up. And that's not like her.'

'Who knows what goes on behind closed doors, eh?'

'You think it's domestic?'

'I'm a sodding fine one to ask,' Jess replied.

'Me, too. No chance either of us opening a marriage guidance counselling business on the side, is there?' Warlow's split from his wife was old history. Her recent death had only rubbed salt into a festering wound. If he'd hoped that Denise's passing would have given him closure, he'd been wrong. And though he'd left with a modicum of concern for her, not hate, there were things left unsaid between them which would now never be spoken or heard.

'Definitely not,' Jess said at the door. 'We're better off helping the dead get some restitution, you and me.'

'There is that.' He smiled at her, but there was not a jot of amusement in it.

CHAPTER TWENTY-EIGHT

BY THE TIME Luca got back from his break, Nichols's message had finally got through. When they showed him the photographs of the scene, he pushed them all back towards Gil with a shake of his head. His response to all questions pertaining to Alistair Lyndon was now a firm. 'No comment'.

Just before 9pm, Warlow called a halt to proceedings. They were getting nowhere.

Gil looked drawn and tired and Warlow suspected that if he dared look in a mirror himself, he'd probably see much the same sort of picture. Gil headed for home.

'Take your time coming back up Monday,' Warlow said.

'Yeah,' Gil replied in a way that told Warlow he'd be back by eight on the dot, just like everyone else.

Warlow checked the group emails for anything else before he headed for the hotel and found nothing new. But fate had one more hand to play. It came in the form of a text from Povey:

> Nothing significant so far. No sign of violence.

> You still at it?

Povey replied:

> Do bears?

Warlow grinned.

> Where are you?

She sent him a pin and, ten minutes later, Warlow drove to a garage to the west of town where the recovery vehicle had taken Lyndon's car. A white Technical Investigation van stood in the yard, side doors open. The silver BMW had been parked inside and the big mobile arc lights had been switched on, illuminating the scene like a film set. There were two white-clad "snowmen" – another of Gil's nicknames for the Tyvek suited investigators – besides Povey.

'Bloody hell,' she said when Warlow walked up. 'I don't have any excuses, but you should be tucked up in bed, or at least in a bar with a pie and a pint.'

'It's not ten, yet,' Warlow said, as if that explained everything.

They'd set up an evidence table to the rear, ten feet from the car which stood, all doors open, boot and bonnet lids up.

'What have you found?'

'The remains of a box file with some papers inside. They're from the college where Lyndon taught. In the glove box, we found insurance documents, the car's instruction manual, and a bottle of hand sanitiser. In the driver's side visor was a credit card.'

'Anything in the box file?'

Povey pointed to a green box whose lid had detached. Next to that was a pile of drying papers. 'The file must have come apart, and some papers floated out and up to the surface. They were what drew the attention of the walkers.'

Warlow looked at the marked-up exam papers and nodded. 'Bit of luck, then. Otherwise, we'd have never found the car.'

'The only other thing stuck in the cargo net behind the driver's seat was a pink purse.' She pointed at something that looked like a box with eyes.

Warlow frowned.

Povey put him out of his misery. 'It's called a glam bag. All the rage with eight-year-olds. That, believe it or not, is supposed to be a unicorn's face.'

'That yellow thing sticking up is its horn?'

'It is.'

'Right. Nothing in it?'

'Lip balm and a pound coin.'

'Okay. I think we can safely assume that's Heledd Rampley's. She and her mother were living with Lyndon until their split. You won't get much from fingerprinting the car, then?'

'I doubt it. But we'll try.'

'Blood?'

'If there was any, it's all washed away. But if I find something, you will be the first on the list. We're about to call it a night. Let things dry out and look again tomorrow.'

Warlow thanked her and headed back to his car. He cast his mind back to Lyndon's house and the way he kept it neat and tidy. It looked like he had the same approach to his BMW. The only thing that was perhaps out of place was the kid's toy stuffed behind the seat. Easy to miss there. Warlow had once found a copy of a five-year-old magazine in his, stuffed there by one of his sons. Depended how long you kept a car, he supposed. And finding a child's toy was hardly significant.

He filed it away. You never knew in cases like this what tiny piece of information set all the dominoes tumbling.

———

HE THOUGHT about those fragments of information again on Sunday morning as he woke up in the hotel and wrote up his reports, and again during the afternoon when he drove home to pick up Cadi from Cold Blow and share a cup of tea with Jess and Molly. He deliberately stayed away from mentioning the case. And, since Molly didn't bring it up, Tricky Ricky remained on the back burner, too.

Though his thoughts never strayed far from that wind-blown spot in the Cambrian Mountains where Alistair Lyndon's corpse had been found, an afternoon watching a black Labrador chase a ball on a beach was a balm for the soul. And, as with so many things that needed to be seen from a different angle before they made any sense, this playtime with the dog played an important role. The trick, he'd come to realise after a long career, was to know when to stop. He could have spent Sunday interrogating Domacini further. Could have gone back to the scene of the crime. Hassled Povey or Tiernon for more. But that could wait until tomorrow. This downtime, in his experience, had a stimulating effect on his subconscious. The cauldron where abstract thoughts marinated. And out of that marinade, ideas, sometimes even unseen answers, came. Not always, but often enough for him to understand that pushing through when there was little or no juice left in the tank paid no dividends.

And Cadi, on her favourite beach reached only by a meandering path with no parking for tourists, sand all over her nose, an indestructible blue and orange rubber ball in her mouth squeaking in protest as she chewed it, was as good a distraction as any. Only when she finally admitted fatigue by lying down on the sand did Warlow give up. He drove back to *Ffau'r Blaidd*, his cottage in Nevern, fed the dog, and took her back to Cold Blow at 8.30pm, and Molly, before driving back to Aberystwyth, hoping that his R and R might at least give him a course to pursue in the investigation.

But he still had found nothing to light the way by the time he pulled into the hotel car park.

————

CARWYN HUGHES DELIVERED his granddaughter Heledd to her father's flat at 8pm on Sunday evening. Joel opened the door, and she ran into his open arms.

'Hey, birthday girl,' Joel said. 'How did it go at Kartwheels?'

Carwyn answered with a grin. 'Ha, we've got a genuine racer here, alright.'

Heledd pushed back from her father's arms and looked up into his face. 'We had races, and I won three times.'

'Three times?' Joel asked.

'She beat them all. Some of them a couple of years older than she is. She's not an under eight anymore, so she raced in the under tens.'

Joel, genuinely delighted, hugged Heledd once more. 'Don't tell me I'm going to have to buy you an old jalopy.'

'What's a jellypee?'

'What your *tadcu* drives,' Joel said.

Heledd spun around. 'Do you drive a jellypee, *Tadcu*? I thought it was a Nissan?'

'It is, *cariad*. Your dad is trying to be funny.'

'And *Tadcu* took me to see Gem.'

'Did you ride her?' Joel asked.

'Ye-eah,' Heledd said. Another perk of Carwyn being mates with a horse owner.

'You hungry?' Joel asked his daughter.

She shook her head. 'We had chips on the way home.'

'Bring me any?'

'No,' said Heledd with a big smile.

'Right then, upstairs and have a bath and get into your PJs. We can watch some TV for half an hour before bed, okay?'

Heledd ran back to Carwyn and hugged him again, speaking once more in her native Welsh. '*Diolch, Tadcu.*'

'*Penblwydd hapus,*' Carwyn said and watched her sprint up the stairs.

'Thanks for that,' Joel said when he heard the water running in the bathroom. 'I got some repairs done on the car, and I fixed the two-doors-down bloke's bike. Made a fifty out of that.'

'Any time, you only have to ask.'

'You want a drink? Cup of tea?'

'No, I'll be off. Give you and Hel a chance to catch up. It's been a big weekend for her.'

'Eight. Can you believe it?'

'Hardly.'

Joel paused and clenched his jaw. 'Did she mention Mirain at all?'

Carwyn's brows twitched at the mention of Heledd's mother. 'A couple of times. She wants to send Mirain a message on Facebook. Tell her all about today. But she also said she wished she could have been there to see her win the races.'

Joel shook his head and looked up at the ceiling. 'Jesus. It's never been this bad. I thought she'd be back for Hel's birthday, you know? And yes, we can't blame her for the blasted illness but... Her daughter's birthday? Come on.'

'It's an unpleasant situation, Joel.'

'You don't think it has anything to do with Alistair, do you? You don't think she's done something bloody stupid—'

'No,' Carwyn interjected. 'Can't be that... She had nothing to do with what happened to Alistair. You can't start thinking like that.'

'Heledd misses her so much.'

Carwyn nodded. 'We all do.'

'Not me. I gave up missing her because it was way too painful.'

'It's been hard for you.'

'I just wish we'd hear from her, for Hel's sake.'

'She won't stay hidden forever. We both know that.'

Joel nodded. 'Thanks again for today. I'm grateful and Heledd is, too.'

'She's a treasure. It's her day.'

CHAPTER TWENTY-NINE

CATRIN SHARED another journey up to Aberystwyth with Rhys on Monday morning. Bank Holiday Monday morning. They discussed the case and everything that went with it. Neither of them knew what on earth was up with Gil, whose new health kick – or anti-biscuit kick –left them baffled.

'Do you really think he's trying to be healthier and lose weight?' Catrin asked as they reached the outskirts of the town.

Rhys shrugged. 'Why would a "racing snake", his own words, want to lose weight?'

'For racing snake, read bloated Anaconda. And the fact that you keep quoting him proves to me you are spending too much time with him.'

'But he's my mentor.'

'Exactly. Half of everything he says is bull.'

Rhys, who'd been tapping away at a song, stopped and turned his incredulous face towards Catrin. 'Sarge! You cracked a mentor-minotaur pun joke.'

She grimaced. 'See, he's even influencing me.' The truth was, not having heard from Byronski by text since she'd replied to him had buoyed her mood.

'Wait until I tell him.' Rhys went back to tapping with vigour.

'You will do no such thing. There is no need to encourage the man.'

'He spends a lot more time in the toilet these days, though. Have you noticed?'

'I can't say I have,' Catrin replied.

'On Friday, I was in there and he mumbled something from inside a cubicle. I'm sure it was *Red Red Wine*, the old UB40 song?' He hummed the tune.

'What?'

'I mean, usually he sings other songs when he knows someone is in there.'

Knowing she was going to regret it, Catrin asked, 'What other songs?'

'Oh, you know,' Rhys said airily, clearly wondering if he should backtrack.

'No, I do not know. But I now need to know.'

'Well, it's either, *Oops I Did it Again* as in Britney Spears, or that old Western song that was in the Blues Brothers' film. What's it called, *Rawhide*? That one about rolling. Except he sings wiping, wiping, wiping.'

'My God, what the hell is wrong with you men and toilet humour?'

'Gil's got some crackers. He said he'd recently bought a toilet brush and, long story short, he was going back to toilet paper pretty damn quick.'

'Right. That's it.'

'I'm just saying.'

'Well, stop just saying.'

Rhys smiled and sat back, muttering to himself, 'Half of everything he says is bull. Genius.'

Of course, the man in question was already there when they got to the Incident Room. He tapped his watch when he saw them.

'I hope you've got a note signed by your parents explaining why you were late for assembly?'

Rhys grinned. Catrin walked past with her eyes half shut, shaking her head, but she was also fighting a smile.

Jess arrived a few minutes later and explained that Warlow was on the phone with the CPS regarding extending Domacini's custody and had gone to a quiet spot downstairs to do that and prepare a press statement. Gil then filled them in on the suspect's lack of cooperation in answering questions.

'So, we need to establish his movements on and around the Sunday that Lyndon dipped off the radar.'

Catrin got back to her desk as her phone signalled a message and her mood evaporated upon seeing who it was from.

> Byronski. Okay, I get it. The silent treatment. Not like you. Fine. But I have another snap from the archive for you. I'm still here.

ANOTHER SNAP. This one cropped to show the young student Catrin, sitting naked on a bed with a beer bottle in hand in a very suggestive pose. Her other hand was handcuffed to a bedpost. Behind her, the upper half of a male body stood with the head pixilated out.

'Shit,' she muttered. It came out unplanned and way too loud.

'Language, please,' Gil said without looking up.

Rhys was too busy on the phone to hear it, but someone else did.

'Everything okay, Catrin?' Jess called over.

Catrin's head flicked up. 'Me, ma'am? Yes… It's…'
Her smile faltered. 'I need a minute.' She got up and
quick-stepped out through the door.

Gil watched her with a wary expression. Rhys
remained oblivious. But Jess knew trouble when it raised its
head. She was up out of her seat before the door swung
shut.

Catrin hurried to the ladies. The only real haven in
this place and somewhere she could process what had
just happened. She felt flushed and angry and… Shit,
shit, shit. What other photographs did this idiot have?
She paced back and forth, trying to remember. Trying
and failing as she had done over the last twenty-four
hours.

When the door opened, she was half hidden behind it
and Jess Allanby had to walk into the room before swivel-
ling to find Catrin.

'You okay, Catrin?' Jess asked.

'Fine, ma'am. Bit of an icky stomach. Left-over pizza
last night.'

Jess nodded. And Catrin understood it was a disbe-
lieving nod. She'd delivered enough of her own over her
career. 'You are not a left-over pizza kind of woman,
Sergeant. Now, you can tell me to piss off because it is
none of my business and you have the right to do that. But
I am concerned. I have never seen you rush out of the
Incident Room like that before. If it is something medical,
then we ought to get you sorted so that you're firing on all
cylinders because we need that. We need you. If it's something else, then fair enough. Like I say, tell me to take a
walk, but if there's anything—'

Catrin held up her phone with the sent image still on
the screen.

Jess took it and frowned. To her credit, she didn't ask

who or what it was, simply looked at it and took in the details, realisation slowly dawning.

'You?' she asked finally.

'Yes, ma'am. DCI Warlow and I went to interview a colleague of Lyndon's at the college. Turns out I… I knew him from old.'

'From your time here?'

'Just for a bit of the first year.' Catrin nodded. Her mouth quivered and her hands shook when she pulled back the phone. 'I left to change courses but also, if I'm honest, to get away from what had become toxic. From Byron. I thought we'd both moved on. Seems like he hasn't.'

'Are there other photos?'

'Yes.'

'Like this?'

'Not as bad. But they've progressed in degree if you understand what I mean?'

'I do,' Jess said.

Catrin's next deep breath stuttered into her lungs. 'I'm not sure what to do, ma'am. This is personal crap, but I wouldn't want Craig to see these. It's not me. Not now.'

'What does good old Byron want?' Jess made Byron sound like something you wiped off a shoe.

'To meet me on his own. To talk about old times.'

'And you?'

Catrin shook her head and skidded out a sigh.

'Right,' Jess said. 'Text Byron and invite him to the station. Say that you have a few more questions and that you can play catch up, too. Then I want you to forget about this and leave it to me. I may need to borrow your phone for an hour at some point.'

'For the photos, ma'am?'

'Yes.'

'I could send them—'

'No. I don't want you to. I want you to put it out of your mind and do what you do best. Work this case.'

'Yes, ma'am.'

Jess pulled her in for a hug.

'Thank you,' Catrin said in a broken voice.

———

GIL GOT up from his desk and massaged the back of his neck, stiff from staring at the screen, then pulled back his shoulders in a stretch. He stopped when the creak of the buttons across his belly became too ominous.

'Just off to spend a penny,' he said to Rhys.

The DC didn't look up but came back with one of Gil's own stock phrases. 'Here's hoping it doesn't turn into £3.50, eh, sarge?'

'Indeed,' Gil said. 'I'll get the kettle on while I'm in the vicinity.'

'But the kitchen isn't in the same direction,' Rhys said.

Gil didn't bother to turn around when he replied, 'And your point is?'

In the men's, he chose a cubicle instead of the urinal and, after relieving himself, only then did he look into the water at the base of the bowl.

Another pink tinge.

'Ay, Caramba,' he whispered.

He zipped up and walked to the sink to wash his hands. No escaping the mirror, though, and he glanced at himself with a shake of his head. It was a fact that he'd never been handsome. He'd been a little too jowly for that. But once, a long time ago, admittedly, someone had commented that he bore a resemblance to Marlon Brando. And yes, it had been on a work night out and the lady in question wore glasses made from the bottoms of bottles, but he'd never forgotten it. In the right light, there was still something there, he liked to think. That no one else thought it except, in weak moments, the Lady Anwen, as he liked to call his wife, didn't matter. And as you got older, these things mattered less and less. But disease and ill health cared nothing for how old you were or what you looked like.

Bloody ironic that all this should happen now when he and Anwen had decided they had to do something about their weight, plural. She'd mentioned scary words like five and two and alcohol-free nights in. She'd even suggested the odd vegetarian meal, or at least a meal without red meat, once or twice a week. They should eat more fish, definitely. He saw the sense in all that and, since Anwen ran the kitchen, he knew he'd go along. They both wanted to enjoy their time with their granddaughters, and the job wasn't getting any easier. They'd settled on a transitional period for the dietary change and, thanks to his brother-in-law's allotment, a surfeit of home-grown vegetables seemed to arrive in a constant stream since they'd moved down to Llandeilo.

He'd even taken to bringing a salad to work, freshly prepared by the Lady Anwen every morning. And, of course, he'd cut down on the *biscuits*. But there could be no denying the evidence of his own eyes and the change of colour in the bowl. No denying, too, that every day brought him closer to an appointment with Coldfinger.

Gil shuddered.

For now, though, there was the job.

He held his hands under the blower until they were dry and headed towards the kettle.

CHAPTER THIRTY

WARLOW HATED this part of the job. The higher the case
profile, the shinier the brass who came to speak with the
press. Every murder case had its own quirks. And Alistair
Lyndon's death was no exception. But, after talking with
Buchannan, it had been pointed out that, as yet, they had
no motive, no weapon, and nothing concrete in terms of
who, or where, or how the crimes had been committed.
But the press were, like the Red Kites that wheeled and
whistled their eerie refrain above the crime scene, carrion
feeders. And, in cases like this, conjecture could very much
be your enemy, and scaremongering in an area dependent
on tourism at the height of the summer was never a good
idea. He understood where Buchannan was coming from.
He might not have been deliberately channelling his inner
Sheriff Brody from *Jaws*, closing the beach to all-comers,
but dangers from sinkholes and mineshafts were one thing:
a killer stalking the trails another altogether. Far better to
share with the press what they had and stay in control.

Sort of.

The Force's liaison had sorted out the statement, but it
needed a senior officer to deliver it. They'd spun the bottle,

and it ended up pointing at Warlow. And so, on a grey, but dry, Monday morning outside the main entrance of Aberystwyth Police Station, with the "Castle Keep" forming a backdrop, Warlow waited for the TV cameras to set up and deliver his blurb. He'd checked his appearance in the loo before coming out. There was little or no wind. Nothing was more distracting than an unruly lock of hair, or famously, in Buchannan's case, a tie that appeared to have a snake-like wandering life of its own.

On a signal from the press officer, Warlow began, 'Following suspicions raised by the public, the South and Mid-Wales cave rescue team examined a mineshaft near a walking trail near Nant Yr Arian six days ago and discovered a body. This has now been recovered and a formal identification procedure undertaken. I can confirm that the body is that of Alistair Lyndon. We have been in touch with Alistair's family and the thoughts of the whole of the Dyfed Powys Force are with them at this distressing time. Our investigation into the cause of Alistair's death continues, and I am pleased to be leading a team who will be looking into his disappearance. Following a post-mortem examination, there are indications that Alistair was forcibly held against his will prior to his death and an attempt made to secrete his body in the shaft. There is no doubt in our minds that crimes have been committed in relation to this death, but the exact nature of these crimes is yet to have been established. This is distressing news for the community and for users of the walking routes in this area. I can assure you all that we are determined to ensure that this wonderful part of Wales remains safe. As of this moment, there is a man in custody helping us with our enquiries. And, as you will all appreciate, I am not at liberty to answer questions at this time. Thank you for your patience.'

Short and sweet, but the whole hullabaloo had taken a

chunk out of the day, which he could have spent a lot more profitably. The press officer walked back into the building with him.

'Well done. That came across well. You're good in front of the camera.'

Warlow shrugged. 'Thanks. Having no Q and A helps.'

'We'll save that for the conference when it comes.' The officer, a large woman with a friendly smile, delivered all this with enthusiasm.

'It won't.' Warlow punctured her balloon with a pithy reply. 'Not if I have anything to do with it.'

He sent Rhys a text and, fifteen minutes later, they were sitting once more in the interview room with Domacini and a still nervous-looking Nichols.

'Right, Luca,' Warlow began once Rhys had started the tape and said all the right words. 'Here we are again. Hope you had a good night's sleep.'

'They're shit beds.'

'Okay, next time we'll see if we can get you an upgrade.'

Nichols's lips thinned in annoyance, but Warlow ignored her.

'Once more, would you care to tell us what your relationship with Alistair Lyndon was?'

'No comment.'

'Alistair was alive and well on Saturday the 20th. We know that because he was out with a friend and that has been confirmed by CCTV. Including this clip from the Cat's Whisper, which is where you work. Am I right?'

'No comment.'

Rhys had a laptop open on the desk, positioned to make it visible for all four seated people. He pressed a button and the video clip rolled. Time and date stamped; it showed a time of 21.22. There was no sound, but the camera, situated up and to the right of the main entrance, showed a queue of people waiting to get in and two black-clad, armband-wearing bouncers. One of those was Luca Domacini. Into the frame walked two people. One, the male, looked older than his female companion but wore a shirt outside his jeans and had a trimmed beard and very white teeth. This was Alistair Lyndon. The girl on his arm was Ava Farley.

On screen, Lyndon spoke. But the words he exchanged were with the other bouncer, not Domacini. However, as he walked in through the doors, Domacini's eyes followed him in.

'So, what we have here is clear evidence you were, in fact near Alistair Lyndon for the time he was in the club. And that you recognised him.'

Nichols sent Luca a strong warning look, but this time, he ignored it. 'Is that who you are talking about? I don't know him. I seen him up at the uni is all. When I went to pick up Claudine sometimes. In the Union Bar there. I seen him a few times. A creep, trying to hit on the younger girls.'

Warlow saw Rhys trying to form a word on his lips that no doubt might have included spring-chicken, but luckily, he refrained. Luca's hypocritical awareness for what he'd just said was obviously lacking.

'But you can see how much of a problem this gives us, eh, Luca?'

'I was working. I wasn't in the club.'

Warlow nodded. 'But you had breaks.' Warlow glanced at Rhys, who ran a second clip. An identical view. The time stamp this time 23.12. Two bouncers, still. But this time no Domacini. The doors opened and out walked Lyndon and Farley.

'So, you weren't there when they left?'

'No. There are three of us. Fifteen-minute breaks between eleven and midnight.'

'Time enough for you to follow Lyndon, then. To a car? Or a taxi? How did he get home?'

Domacini sat forward. 'I told you; I don't know this guy. I didn't follow him. Why would I follow him?'

'To find out where he lived so you could go there and abduct him.'

Domacini sat back and let out a mirthless laugh. 'This is crazy shit, man. You keep running that tape and you'll see me back at the door at 11.30.'

'You get back at 11.33,' Rhys said.

'I had to piss as well. Come on.'

Warlow dropped his voice. 'What time did your shift end?'

'I did the seven to one shift.'

'And afterwards?'

'I went home to my uncle's place.'

'Not to Claudine's.'

'No.'

'That's a shame, then. She could have backed you up.'

'This is bullshit.'

Warlow's turn to sit forward. 'This is evidence. Are we going to find more? That's the question. At your uncle's house? At Claudine's flat? Plastic ties? A hammer?'

Domacini snarled. 'I haven't done nothing.' But his leg started to shake again.

A knock on the interview room door made Warlow squeeze his eyes shut in frustration.

'Really?' he muttered.

Rhys got up and pulled the door open. Warlow heard whispering, but he brought his gaze back to Domacini, ready to turn the screw another notch. Then Rhys was at his side, leaning in close to whisper.

'It's DS Jones, sir. He thinks you should step outside.'

'What, now?'

'Sir, he says it is important and,' he glanced up at Domacini, 'pertinent.'

Warlow's chair scraped back. He pushed up, biting back his annoyance. But outside, he found it more difficult to hide his irritation. 'This better be bloody good, Gil...' But then he caught the expression on the DS's face: stony hard and devoid of all humour. The serious, all-jokes-aside expression he kept for whenever things truly hit the fan.

'It's our rural crime colleagues, again. They had an anonymous tip-off they followed up today. They're in somewhere called Black Covert Woods.' He shook his head as if the words he was speaking were in some foreign language. Hard to accept let alone comprehend. 'It's another body, sir.'

'Male or female?' Warlow asked.

'Female, sir.'

Warlow squeezed his eyes shut. 'Any identification?'

Gil shook his head. 'It's bad. Someone tried to burn the body. Looks like it's been dumped and covered up.'

'Povey on the way?'

Gil nodded.

Warlow was already heading back to the Incident Room. Gil caught up with him.

'It might not be related,' Gil said.

'True, it might not be.'

But in his head, he was already thinking the worst and hoping, forlornly, that for once he might be wrong.

CHAPTER THIRTY-ONE

THE WOODLAND WAS NOT LARGE. A jagged strip next to the River Ystwyth about nine miles from Aberystwyth town. They went in two cars. Jess wanted to see the spot too, so she travelled with Catrin. Warlow with Rhys, leaving Gil to man the fort.

What struck Warlow immediately was that not one, but two B roads ran parallel to the woods, making access by vehicle easy. Once again, the scene evidence recovery manager had found a field for them to park their vehicles. Because the find was so recent, Warlow and the others suited up. They walked away from the river on a maintained road to a junction with a couple of gates and three trails, one with signage indicating National Cycle Route 81. But beyond this, two more tracks led off into the woods.

Two hundred yards in on the eastern track, they came across a new Apache Village and a large cordoned-off area. Warlow had already texted Povey, who was waiting for the team.

'You've brought an entourage,' she said. Crime scene

experts were always wary of too many bodies tramping all over their sites.

'This is something we all need to see,' Warlow delivered his reply in a way that announced an end to any discussion.

'Okay, well, be careful. We're only beginning on this one. The exhibits tent is over there, but I suppose you want a look at the body?'

'I do.'

The access corridor was very narrow, earmarked by waist-high tape attached to marker posts stuck into the soft ground. The area was hopelessly overgrown fern and grass and the eponymous trees on this Birchgrove section of the woodland. Out of sight of the main track, the body lay at the bottom of a slope. The perpetrator had used two black bin bags in an attempt at covering it up. But foxes or other predators had tried to remove the wrappings such that the blackened torso remained exposed to the elements.

The face was unrecognisable, the skin there, and on the neck and exposed arm, blackened by fire. The flames had scorched half of the head clean, but the other half still retained a skein of blonde hair, while the heat had contracted the flesh of her face to expose her teeth in a mocking corpse's grin.

'Is she clothed?' Warlow asked.

'From what I can see without removing the plastic bags, yes,' Povey said.

'HOP?'

'Tiernon is on his way.'

'Any sign of fire here?'

'No.'

'So, the burning took place somewhere else, and she was dumped here?' Jess asked Povey.

'That would be my guess, yes. The search advisor is already here, and we'll get going in the surrounding area as soon as possible. But we've already found some drag marks coming down off the road. My take is that they've parked up there and dragged her down. Interestingly, only the torso and head seemed to have been badly burned. The feet seem intact where the black bag has torn. And the jeans she's wearing are visible where the bags meet. Scorched but intact, too.'

'But there is no way anyone can identify her from her appearance, is there?' Catrin's observation was more a statement than a question.

'We can spare the relatives that, I think,' Povey said.

Warlow cast his eyes around at the crouching members of Povey's team, all intent on examining the difficult ground for anything that might pass as evidence. These were trained people. Fastidious. 'I can make an educated guess,' he said after a while. 'I have a terrible feeling that our victim is Mirain Hughes.'

'Who?' Povey frowned.

'She's someone linked to Alistair Lyndon,' Warlow explained. 'She's been out of circulation for a few weeks because of her mental state, but—'

'Wait,' Povey said and ran back up the slope to the tent where she nipped inside only to reappear a few seconds later, holding a plastic evidence bag.

'We found this in the drag area about ten metres from the road.' In her hand, inside the protective plastic bag, was a distorted and twisted debit card.

Warlow took it and peered at the card in a bad attempt at reading it. After several abortive attempts, he gave up. 'Rhys, you have a look. I've left my bloody glasses in the car.'

Rhys took it and read out the half-melted remains of a surname. 'U, G, H, E, S,' he read out, and then looked up.

'Oh, God,' Jess said. 'That poor woman. She'd kept her unmarried name, Mirain Hughes.'

Rhys handed back the bag.

'We'll need dental records to be certain,' Povey said, 'But I'm sure Tiernon will organise that for today. He's an arrogant sod, but he'll pull his finger out for something like this.'

'And who was it made the finding?' Warlow asked.

'The Rural Crime Team,' Povey explained. 'There are two of them. A Sergeant Thomas and a PCSO called Prosser. Both said they knew you.'

Warlow nodded. 'They do. We have, as they say, history. And none of it pleasant.'

The team retraced their steps, eager to get out of their snowsuits. Catrin and Jess headed back to the Incident Room and Rhys texted Tiernon to find out when he was due to arrive, using the pretext of possibly hanging around for his arrival. Not that Warlow had any intention of doing such a thing. Seeing a dead body was enough to dampen anyone's mood. He didn't need an added dose of Tiernon to send it plummeting further south.

Warlow found the Rural Crime Team's big four-wheel drive parked farther down one of the B roads, advising drivers headed for the woodland that access was now restricted. Both officers wore Hi Viz jackets, and both turned smiling faces towards Warlow as he approached. Tomo, the sergeant, waved down a car, but Hana Prosser walked towards Warlow with her hand outstretched.

'We meet again, sir.'

'Under the most delightful of circumstances, too.'

Hana shrugged. 'Goes with the territory, I suppose.'

She looked as fit as he remembered, hair tied back under her cap, the bulky, top-heavy uniform unable to disguise her lithe frame. He was delighted that she did not appear in any way nervous or unhappy to see him. The last time they'd properly spoken, he'd been consoling her for losing her father, in the pejorative sense, since he'd been arrested for murder. That sort of thing could easily ruin a person. He'd made damn sure that there were no comebacks for her from the Force, but still it had taken some backbone to even want to stay. Naturally, he remained unsure of what kind of reception he'd receive. He needn't have worried. It was a testament to her strength of personality.

'I see Tomo is still herding cars.'

'He has a sheepdog gene, we reckon.'

'It's good to see you, Hana,' Warlow said with genuine feeling. Nothing remotely unprofessional here. He felt about her the same way he felt about Catrin. As a mentor and, God forbid, in this white privileged day and patriarchal age, fatherly. A little bell rang somewhere in his head. Bloody hell, if Myst, or one of their legion, could read his mind now they'd be summoning the howling Twitter mob before you could say burn him at the stake for "white knighting" or even thinking such thoughts. But he ignored the bell. Ignored it because he hated even having allowed Myst and the idea of the thought police to enter his head. He was a believer in victim and oppressor; it was the bread and butter of his job. Such terms defined criminal acts. But to define the whole of society and every single interaction within it in the same way gave him brain freeze. If victimhood and identity was the new religion, then he'd remain an agnostic atheist who dealt in fact, thank you so much.

And the fact was that Hana Prosser had been dealt a lousy hand by a murdering father and Warlow had done what he could to help her survive it.

'Thank you, sir. For everything. I was going to email you to let you know that they have accepted me to the Force. I'm a fully-fledged constable from September.'

Warlow grinned. 'Fantastic. So, goodbye to Rural Crime, then?'

'For a while. I'd like to come back to it, eventually. It's where my heart is.'

'They'd be lucky to have you, too.' He nodded. But from what he knew of Hana Prosser, she'd be flying high within a few years, or he'd eat his hat.

Tomo supervised the car he'd stopped and helped it reverse to a passing place and turn around before coming back to join his colleagues. He was a big man in all senses of the word, red of face, including nose. But not from booze, as was the common misconception. Hana had put Warlow right on that the last time, citing Rosacea as the root cause of Tomo's ruddiness.

'Nasty business, this,' Tomo said. 'Any clue who she is?'

'We have a link to the first death.'

'Alistair Lyndon?' Tomo frowned.

'That's right, but we'll need formal confirmation.'

'Awful,' Hana said, looking appalled.

'The tip-off,' Warlow asked. 'Did it come to either of you?'

'No. There's a sticker on the back of the old Ford. Report anything suspicious to this number. It's also on Facebook and the Force website. The message came through yesterday.'

'What did they say?'

'That something had been seen at the bottom of a bank in these woods. They wondered if something, an animal, had been dumped.'

'Have you heard the call?'

Hana nodded. 'Male, I'd say local-ish. Sounded quite shaken by it. As if mentioning the word "animal" upset him.'

'No caller ID?'

'No. That's the odd thing. We've traced it to one of only two payphones in town. There'll be CCTV, of course.'

Warlow sighed. 'We'll get someone on to that.'

'How long are they likely to be up there?' Tomo asked. 'I don't mind helping out, but we have somewhere to be.'

Warlow understood. 'I'll get someone else to do this. Tiernon, the pathologist, isn't here yet. It could be a while.'

Another car was approaching, and Tomo hurried over to flag it down. 'Thanks,' he called over his shoulder.

'It's a bad business, sir,' Hana said.

'Very. We have someone in custody, but...' He let the sentence hang and put a brief smile in its place. 'Look after yourself, Hana.'

'You, too, sir.' Her reciprocating smile would have done a toothpaste advert proud.

By the time Warlow got back to his car, his smile had long gone. Having two people dead on your watch tended to take the shine off things. First Lyndon and now his partner.

Worse was the nagging doubt that he had no way of dispelling. If they'd moved faster, got more answers, could he have prevented Mirain's death?

Rhys got back to the Jeep, and they watched Tiernon drive in. Rhys raised a hand. Tiernon ignored him.

'Lovely chap,' Warlow said.

'Probably thinking about what he's going to have to do, sir,' Rhys said in a moment of surprising candour. 'Can't be pleasant knowing what's waiting for you.'

'No,' replied Warlow, remembering the charred remains he'd briefly seen. Still, everyone had a job to do. And his was now to tell a father that he'd lost his daughter, and a child that she'd lost her mother.

CHAPTER THIRTY-TWO

WARLOW AND RHYS arrived at Carwyn Hughes's address at Bow Street a little after midday. Rhys had texted ahead, and the man opened the door before they could knock.

'I saw you arrive,' he said. He'd not bothered to change from his gardening gear; that was obvious. His old jeans had moist stains on the knees and his forearms were dusted with dried mud.

'Thanks for seeing us.' Warlow followed him into his kitchen.

'I was about to put the kettle on.'

'Good idea,' Warlow said. 'But let Rhys do that. It might be an idea if you sat down.'

Carwyn turned from where he was filling the kettle. All movement stopped and his expression froze. He clunked the kettle down on the worktop, moved away from the sink and sat in a chair, hand clenched in front of him, his eyes glued to Warlow's. 'Sounds serious.' He tried to make it a joke, but his smile never formed fully.

Warlow sat opposite him, Rhys behind him. 'It is serious. The most serious thing there is.'

'Mirain?' Carwyn asked in a tremulous voice.

'We found a body over at Black Covert Woods. Though we aren't one hundred percent certain yet, it's only fair to tell you we believe it is your daughter.'

Carwyn's hands flattened out on the tabletop, and he sucked in air in great gulps. Warlow turned to Rhys. 'Get that kettle on,' he urged gently.

'In the woods?' Carwyn asked.

'Yes,' Warlow said. 'Someone had tried to get rid of her body. Out of desperation, I'd say.'

Carwyn hunched forward, head down, his hands now on his thighs, moving up and down the material of his jeans as if he was trying to scrub the denim off. He didn't glance up when he asked, 'How?'

'We don't know. Not yet. There'll be a post-mortem today. As soon as I have any information, I promise you'll be the first.'

The older man glanced up; his face contorted in pain. 'Joel? Does he know yet?'

'No.'

'Nor Heledd?'

'No.' Warlow had discussed this with Jess. Joel was Heledd's father, but he and Mirain had divorced, and so Carwyn, Mirain's dad, remained the next of kin.

'I'll do it,' Carwyn said. 'I need to be there when Heledd finds out. It ought to be me.'

'We can save you the pain, Carwyn.' Warlow's offer was genuine.

Carwyn shook his head. 'No. I'll do it. I'll go and see Joel once we've finished here.'

The kettle boiled. Tea was made and drunk. Warlow did his best to quiz Carwyn gently about Mirain's movements. The answer had been a reiterated and firm 'no idea'. Warlow listened as the grieving father explained, painfully, how Mirain's disappearing acts had begun in her teenage years, worsening as the illness progressed. How she ended up in cheap hotels and once an Airbnb. He explained how she'd get ideas – grandiose, the doctors called them – about finding herself, needing to be alone, her brain tricking her into imagining she was something she was not. Once, she was convinced she was a concert pianist, and they found her in a music shop playing a piano. The notes she played were nonsensical, but she believed they were a masterpiece. Twice she'd ended up being admitted for "re-balancing" after these episodes. And so, Carwyn conceded that he'd given up trying to find her this time because she'd always come down from those awful highs and then need his, and her mother's, help. But while she was flying, it had always proved pointless.

'But you always worry. You always fear she'll do something stupid or get herself into real trouble. As a father, you can't help it.'

Warlow kept probing. Both men knew that guilt over not trying harder to find her this time would haunt the both of them.

'We're going to get a Family Liaison Officer to come and speak to you, Carwyn. Stay if needed.'

'I don't want anyone.'

'It's standard practice in cases like this.'

'Is it Gina, sir?' Rhys asked.

Warlow checked his phone. 'Yes.'

'I don't need anyone.'

'You'll like Gina, Mr Hughes,' Rhys said. 'And she's good at this. She'll help with arrangements between you and us. How and when Mirain gets released for burial or cremation. All that sort of thing.'

Carwyn looked up. 'Sounds like you're a fan.'

'I am,' Rhys answered. 'A big fan.'

Carwyn nodded and turned back to the mug of tea he clutched in two big, rough hands. 'Will I see her?' He didn't look up.

Warlow was prepared. 'I don't advise it. For now, she'll be with the pathologists, and we'll need to make the identification from dental records. Confirm it with DNA, but that takes some time. The dental records are quick.'

Carwyn nodded. 'I don't want to see her if—'

'You won't have to.' He turned to a photograph on the fridge of Heledd and Mirain. 'That's how you need to remember her.'

Carwyn nodded again.

'We've talked about the last time you had communication with Mirain, but we'll need to go through all of it again. In more detail. We need to piece together where she went and what happened.'

'Yes. Okay.'

Warlow leaned in. 'This will be the smallest of consolations, but I promise we'll find out what happened to her, Carwyn.'

'You said you'd find her, and you did.'

Warlow dropped his gaze before dragging it back up. 'I wish it could have been different.'

Carwyn reached for a scruffy handkerchief from his pocket, sniffed, and dabbed his eyes. 'So do I.'

———

Jess met "Byronski" in the reception area of Aberystwyth station and thanked him for coming in.

His smile on seeing her was a tad uncertain. 'Isn't Catrin, um, Sergeant Richards seeing me?'

'She's busy at present. It's only me.'

Byron smiled. Jess had seen that kind of smile before, and she didn't like it. She didn't know the man well enough to call it sleazy, but there was a light in his eyes she didn't like. All confirmed when he said, 'I'm not complaining.'

'Good,' she replied. 'We prefer to keep a professional

distance in a murder investigation. Not muddy the waters with previous relationships.' She had the door held open for him, but on hearing the word 'murder', he'd stopped walking.

'Wait… What?'

'Have you not seen the news today?'

'No. I've been in college… What's this about murder?'

'Come on up and I'll fill you in,' Jess said.

Byron followed her, though not without some hesitation in his steps.

Although this was a voluntary conversation, Jess chose the formality of an interview room with its stark interior and the blinking ceiling camera in full view. A camera Byron looked at warily.

'Don't worry, we're not recording anything. Unless you prefer us to?'

'No. Not unless we have to.'

'We don't.'

They sat opposite one another at the table. 'I'd offer you refreshment, but that would be from a machine and it might be construed as some kind of torture if I did.'

'That bad?' Byronski took the offered joke and ran with it.

'Definitely. As I say, thanks for coming in. You missed the news, so I'll give you the gist. We've confirmed that the body found in the mineshaft is that of Alistair Lyndon.'

The pained expression that crept over Byron's face said it all. 'Oh, God. I mean, after your lot came to see me, asking about Alistair, I sort of put two and two together as a worst-case scenario, but murder?'

Jess nodded. 'We are treating his death as suspicious.'

'Shit. Oh my God. Alistair? But who… I mean… Sorry, you're hardly likely to tell me, are you?'

Jess smiled. One of her icy specials. 'No. But it is a

good question. And it's why you're here, after all. You worked with Alistair. You knew him as well as anyone.'

Byron baulked at that. 'Not that well. I mean, we weren't best buddies. We'd go out for a drink now and again. Staff do's and that. But Alistair didn't have mates, as such. You'd never hear him talk about nights out with the boys. He was too busy chasing after... Other things.'

'Such as?'

'He liked girls, I know that.'

'And how do you know that?'

'Because even when we were out as a crew, he'd be flirting, chatting up someone. Plus, he'd always have something to say about members of staff and...' Byron caught himself.

'And who? Were you going to say students?'

'It's a sixth form college. Some girls there are very attractive.'

'To you?'

Byron shrugged. 'To anyone with a pulse, I expect. Can't pretend otherwise. But you put all that to one side. You have to.'

'But not Alistair?'

'Let's just say he didn't mind expressing his opinion amongst friends.'

'Did that make you feel uncomfortable?' It genuinely intrigued Jess. Her own daughter attended a sixth form college, and she wasn't naïve enough to think that every teacher there was a monk. But she hoped they adopted a professional stance.

'Sometimes, yes.'

Him the devil and you the saint, then.

'And can you confirm the last time you saw Mr Lyndon?'

'Yes. Last Friday after work. We had a drink and he left early. Around six-ish.'

Jess made a note. This was all in the file, but it looked better that she was taking notes. 'And you can account for your movements on the Sunday after that Friday?'

Byron pondered. 'Umm… I play football on a Sunday morning. Afternoon we go to the pub. I'm usually back at my flat at five. But after that, no. I'd be on my own. Sunday night horrors, you know.'

'No, I don't.'

'The inevitability of Monday. Don't you get those?'

'Not usually.'

'Lucky you…' Suspicion suddenly clouded his brow. 'Hang on, you don't think that I had anything to do with Ali's… With what's happened?'

'These are routine enquiries, Byron.'

'Look, Ali could be a bit funny. Aloof might be the best word. And he liked the laydees,' Byron added a jocular lilt to the word, but the joke faded when he registered the unamused expression on Jess's face. 'We were work mates. That's all.'

'Anyone you can think of who might want to do him harm?'

'No. No one.'

'Did he tell you about Ava Farley?'

'Who? Oh, hang on, is that A? Yeah, he said he'd met a girl called Ava. Said she was coming on to him. But Mirain was in the mix, still. I mean, she'd gone, but he was expecting her to come back,' he frowned, 'I think.'

'Right, well, that's very useful.'

'Is that it? Can I go?' Byron stood up.

'There is one more thing.' Jess gave him her best dazzler of a smile.

Byron sat down again.

'I understand that you and Catrin Richards have some history?' She kept it light to start with. Pandering to his ego.

'You could say that. We had a bit of a wild fling in uni.'

'And you've been trying to re-establish a relationship?'

Byron made a noise like a horse snickering. 'I wouldn't call asking her for a coffee re-establishing a relationship.'

'Perhaps not.' Jess took a phone out of her pocket and typed in a code. It lit up, and she scrolled to the image that Byronski had sent to Catrin that morning. 'Not the most flattering photograph, would you say?'

He gave a hollow laugh. 'Just a bit of fun.'

Jess nodded. 'Indeed. Would you say that the woman in this photograph would be proud of this image?'

'Proud? Not proud, I suppose. But it happened. I mean, you can't change that fact.'

'It did happen. Clearly it did. But from what I can see, she looks more than a bit intoxicated.'

'You could say that. She could drink me under the table.'

Jess sighed. A soft sound, but one heavy with subdued anger. He still didn't see it. Idiots like him seldom did. 'And so, when she was drunk, you asked her permission to take this image?'

Byron looked up from the phone to Jess's calm face and straightened his shoulders. He made more noise than usual when he swallowed. 'Look, we were both pissed...'

Jess sat back and put the phone down, image upwards, letting her gaze drift up to engage with Byron. When she spoke this time, the friendly conversational tone had disappeared. Replaced with a stiff formality that had sent a chill through many a perpetrator. 'It is an offence for a person to disclose a private photograph or film of a sexual nature if the disclosure is made either without the consent of the individual who appears in the photograph, or with the intention of causing that individual distress.'

'Christ, hang on. This was only meant for Catrin.'

'But you sent it electronically. And it looks to me as if you took this without her consent.'

'Oh, come on—'

'More importantly, I can tell you that seeing this has caused that individual quite some distress.'

'For fuck's sake—'

'No. For *your* sake, you better listen to what I have to say, Mr Evans. Usually, when someone comes in here voluntarily, we still record the interview. Notice I haven't done that today.'

Byron jerked his head around. The camera on the wall had no red light lit up.

'That's deliberate on my part. To give you a break that, personally, I don't think you deserve. Revenge porn is what the law I just quoted to you is commonly known as. That's two years in jail. No more teaching jobs. Your name on the sexual offenders register for God knows how long. The target of all sorts of Wild West online vigilantes. In other words, your life in shreds.'

'Are you threatening me?' He tried to raise his voice, but his hands had started to shake. The fear there deflated the bravado of his words.

Jess's eyes rolled up. 'Not a threat, a warning. Plain and simple. Because that is my job. Now, we will be in touch again if we need to contact you about Alistair Lyndon. Shame you don't have an alibi for that Sunday night because that is when he went missing. I strongly suggest you destroy every image you have taken without DS Richards's consent, too. Personally, I don't want to see your face ever again. But you will see mine if I hear even the slightest whisper that you've been in touch with Sergeant Richards now or in the future.' She held up the phone, still displaying the image. 'Do we understand one another, Mr Evans?'

Byron glared at her, but then nodded jerkily. A second swallow sounded even louder than the first.

'I'm going to get someone to show you out. Sit here until that officer comes.' Jess got up and moved to the door, where she turned and said, 'I have a seventeen-year-old daughter. I hope to God she doesn't have any teachers like you. Oh, and Dyfed Powys Police thanks you for your cooperation.' She shut the door behind her.

Jess had taken three steps when a door next to the interview room opened and Catrin Richards walked out, her eyes shining and slightly damp, her bottom lip quivering.

'Thank you, ma'am,' she whispered. 'I won't forget that.'

Jess put a hand on her arm. 'Just promise you'll forget him.'

The two women walked down the corridor. 'I hope I'll be able to do the same for you one day,' Catrin said.

Jess passed the phone back. 'Get rid of those snaps. And no need to thank me. I can honestly say that it was an absolute pleasure.'

CHAPTER THIRTY-THREE

WARLOW AND RHYS took another long trip to Cardiff that afternoon. A three-hour journey topped off by another two hours spent with a mutilated corpse while Tiernon did his job. He x-rayed the jaws, and, within those two hours, the forensic dentists compared the dental records and confirmed that it was indeed Mirain Hughes that lay on the cold metal table. Lay unseeing while her organs were removed and weighed, samples of filth and dirt and small, still-wriggling insects taken and bagged for further investigation.

Warlow watched it all, masked up, polo mints in his mouth, with the usual numb detachment he used for such occasions. Rhys, undeterred by the sights he was seeing, once more paid close attention, genuinely interested in what was, by far, the worst aspect of the job for most people. This time, Warlow found it even harder because somewhere inside him was an unremitting belief that this was the key. That Mirain's death held the answers to what had happened to her and her partner. But he also knew with gut wrenching certainty that he'd have to dig deep to unearth that answer, and not all of it was going to be found in her cold flesh.

They did not travel back to Aberystwyth late that afternoon. Neither man fancied another three-hour slog in the car. Especially as they could be in Carmarthen in an hour and a half. Warlow made the call. Better they start afresh in the morning.

He dropped Rhys off at his house and drove on for the last fifty minutes to Nevern and his cottage. And though he yearned for a Cadi fix, Warlow did not disturb her this evening. He left her instead in Cold Blow with Molly. With a bit of luck and no morning traffic, he'd make it to the Incident Room in Aberystwyth in an hour. At some point, they'd need to issue another statement and identify another body to the hungry press. He'd need his bloody tie again and reached up to his neck, but it had been long since removed and now made a bulge in the material of his jacket pocket. He took it out and hung it back up, checking it for stains.

None. It would do.

Hungry from not having eaten properly all day, Warlow made himself some decent food. An omelette with some mushrooms and a chopped-up avocado and tomatoes with a side of sourdough toast. He felt tired from the long hours in the car. And yes, he didn't need to be in Aberystwyth to dissect the case, but his brain was in no condition for deductive reasoning. It barely coped with some inane TV. He made some tea and, in a snub to Gil, had a Hobnob with it. As good a way as any to dispel the despondency. But still, the case wouldn't go away.

Of course, they still had Domacini in custody, but though they'd done their best to link him to Lyndon, Warlow had seen nothing so far that suggested he knew Mirain.

A partner and a mother who'd taken herself off as she

had done so many times before and always come back safely. But not this time.

He thought of her father's words to him that morning.

You said you'd find her, and you did.

A poisoned chalice if ever there was one.

He thought, too, about the moment in the postmortem when Tiernon's dissection had confirmed a fractured hyoid bone as the probable cause of death.

Mirain had not died from blunt force trauma, like Lyndon.

Fractured hyoid bones were almost always the result of strangulation.

———

THE FOLLOWING MORNING, at 8am sharp, the entire team assembled in the Aberystwyth Incident Room. No jokes this morning. Everyone looked tired, except for Catrin, who looked sharp and keen. So much so that while they waited for her and Gil to update the Gallery and the Job Centre, Warlow leaned over and whispered to Jess.

'Notice something different about Catrin?'

'It's a nice blouse, isn't it?'

'Is it?' Warlow said, glancing back at the DS. 'I suppose it is. Is that what's different?'

'Well, it's one thing.'

He contemplated Jess with a wary narrowing of his eyes. 'Thing is, even if it isn't a new blouse, I wouldn't be able to tell because we don't notice things like that.'

'We?'

'Men.'

'Well, you should.'

'And by mentioning it, you've successfully shifted emphasis away from whatever is truly different.'

'That's so cynical,' Jess objected.

'Isn't it just?'

Out of earshot, Gil cleared his throat. 'Right, I think we can start, sir.'

'Rhys. You're up. Tiernon hasn't put his preliminary report up yet. The floor is yours.'

'Thank you, sir.' Rhys flipped open his notebook. 'Mirain Hughes is a thirty-three-year-old—' The shrill ringing of a desk phone interrupted his flow. A Uniform picked it up, put his hand over the mouthpiece after listening for a minute, and said, 'A Doctor Nixon?'

Rhys's eyes widened, and he glanced at Warlow. 'Sorry, sir. I should probably take this.'

Warlow waved him off and got up from his seat. 'Mirain's body was in a bad state. Tiernon thought he could smell some accelerant. Petrol maybe. But as you all saw, it hadn't been successful in destroying the body. There was a lot of dirt from the dragging, but the plastic bags provided shelter from the elements. No sign of burning in the woods. She had a fractured hyoid. They strangled her.'

'Strangled and burned somewhere else, we think?' Jess asked.

'Yes,' Warlow agreed.

'Povey hasn't posted her prelim either yet,' Catrin said. 'But I took a call from her last night.'

'On your mobile?'

'No, sir. Here. She rang at about nine, hoping to catch someone.'

'Nine?' Gil said. '*Arglwydd*, what time did you get home?'

'Before midnight,' Catrin said, as if that made all the difference. 'Craig's on nights, anyway.'

'What did Povey say?' Warlow asked.

'She sent over a photograph, sir.' Catrin went to the Gallery and pointed to an image of something unrecognisable on a white card next to a ruler.

'Pubic hair?' Jess asked.

'No, this is artificial. Nylon, she thinks. You can't tell from the image, but it's blue.'

'Just like the one on Lyndon?' Warlow leaned forward.

'Exactly like it, sir. I mean, they'll need to do more tests to confirm it a hundred percent, but—'

'It links them together,' Warlow said in a half whisper.

'And the toxicology screen came back on Alistair Lyndon,' Catrin added. 'It seems he had traces of ketamine in his system.'

'Ketamine?' Jess repeated. 'Lyndon liked Special K?'

None of these detectives needed an explanation for what "Special K", the street name for the dissociative anaesthetic known as ketamine, was. More commonly used to sedate animals and sometimes children, it remained a controlled substance that drug users craved for, the detached, out-of-body experience it gave the user.

'Are we back to these being drug-related killings now?' Gil looked troubled.

'No one has mentioned drug abuse in Lyndon's case, have they?' Warlow tried to remember if he'd seen any mention.

'No,' Catrin answered. 'And that's definite. But we'll have to wait on the tox screen for Mirain Hughes.'

Warlow rubbed the little spot of stubble he always missed when he shaved. 'And there was nothing ketamine-related to the drugs we found in Domacini's possession?'

'No,' Gil said. 'Anabolic steroids and amphetamines. The exact opposite of ketamine, in fact.'

Warlow weighed up this information. It seemed significant, but he didn't know how. At Rhys's desk, the DC ended the call and turned a smiling face towards the team.

'How was the cream, cat?' Gil asked.

'Good,' Rhys said. 'Really good.'

Catrin groaned. 'Oh, no. I can see that little sparkle of excitement in his eyes.'

Rhys ignored her. 'That was the forensic entomologist. Povey said she was going to get some samples couriered down to Dr Nixon in Swansea uni. She's had a look at some already...' He paused, willing them to ask.

'And?' Gil did the necessary.

'Perhaps I should explain a bit first.'

Catrin's eyes rotated skywards. 'Look out, he's going to go full *Blue Peter* on us.'

Rhys was already at the Gallery and, using a ballpoint pen, pointed at Mirain's body as found in Black Covert Woods. 'She was lying partly covered by burnt clothing and plastic bags, but sizeable areas of flesh were exposed. I saw maggots, we all did. It's amazing to think that flies can tell us so much, though, isn't it? I mean, with time there are beetles, too, but to start with, there are only the blue-bottles and the greenbottles.'

'Not *Blue Peter*,' Gil muttered. 'It's *Lord of the* bloody *Flies*.'

Rhys continued, 'Povey said that because it's been warm, that helps. Not many flies about in the winter. But this time of year, they're plentiful. Anyway, Dr Nixon just said there were maggots, but not much else. That means not enough information for successional analysis.'

'Whoa, Rhys,' Gil said.

The DC blinked. 'You must know all this stuff, sarge.'

'I do,' Gil said, feigning offence. 'But we need to find out if you do.'

Rhys nodded. If he noticed any of the sceptical looks Gil got from everyone else in the room, he was too caught up in his entomological analysis to notice. 'Insect successional analysis uses the fact that changes occur in the body as it decays. This changing ecosystem attracts different species. Body ooze is too acidic to start with for some flies, for example. So different species are involved at differing decomposition stages. If you have many species of insects present at a site, you can gauge how long the body has been there. But this only happens over weeks or months.'

'Remember to breathe, Rhys,' Catrin said.

'But when the body has only been in position for a few days, then only maggots of one or two species, usually Calliphoridae – blow flies – are present, usually in natural openings. Eyes, ears, mouth, etcetera.'

'Do not expand on the etcetera,' Jess said.

'So, by identifying and measuring the maggots' lengths and stages of development and considering climate, you can be fairly accurate at estimating how long the body has been there.' Rhys beamed.

'How long?' Warlow asked, cutting to the chase.

'Ah, Dr Nixon said she'd have something for us shortly. She only rang to say that she was impressed with the details of the collection and accompanying notes. That's down to Povey, sir.'

'Good. Then that's to come.' Warlow nodded and stared at the new pieces of information that had blossomed on the boards. 'I hate to make assumptions, but so far, and correct me if I am wrong, this still looks like we may have links to drug-related crimes.'

'What are you thinking?' Jess asked.

Warlow shrugged. 'The ketamine. Perhaps Lyndon got into debt or fell out with a dealer. Perhaps he was part of a drugs ring himself, selling to kids up at the college. What if they took Mirain as punishment or revenge, and then Lyndon paid the price, too?'

'Sounds brutal, sir,' Gil said.

'Brutal or not, it's all we have at the moment. If Nixon can come up with a time of death—'

'It's called the PMI, sir. The post-mortem interval.'

'Thank you, Rhys. If Nixon comes up with a PMI, then we'll have somewhere to focus on for her timeline.'

'Why hasn't your insect lady come up with a PMI for Lyndon, Rhys?' Gil asked.

'Fair point, sarge. But Lyndon was almost totally covered in stones and rubble. That would have made access difficult, even for flies.'

Warlow stared at Rhys for so long, the DC felt obliged to expound his explanation. 'Besides stones, there was dust, sir—'

'I know, Rhys. I get the point. And it's a good one. Such a stark difference in the attempts at hiding the bodies.'

'Or not,' Jess observed.

'Exactly.' Warlow sighed. 'In the meantime, while we wait for Nixon's PMI, let's chase up everything else as much as we can. Jess, will you get on to Povey and see what else she can tell us about these fibres of hers? Rhys, you wait on Nixon. Catrin, what about Mirain's phone records?'

'Almost done, sir. I need to apologise. I got distracted.' She glanced at Jess, who returned the look impassively.

Warlow chose not to comment on the exchange. Instead, he raked his eyes over the boards one last time in the hope of seeing something that might jump out. 'Don't apologise, just get it done. Gil, chase up the caller who reported Mirain's body. Wasn't there a possibility of CCTV?'

Gil raised a finger in acknowledgement.

Warlow contemplated the room, too restless to settle. 'I need to go over something here but then I think I'll head back out to Ystumtuen to check something out. I'll be back by lunchtime. It would be good if we had something to move on by then.'

CHAPTER THIRTY-FOUR

WARLOW'S PHONE buzzed just as he was sliding on his jacket. The number belonged to his youngest son, Tom. They spoke in Welsh.

'*Tom, shwd wyt ti?*'

'*Iawn, dad. Ti?*'

'Up to my armpits in blood and gore,' Tom said in response to his dad asking him how things were.

'Same old, then?'

'You and me, both. Except your clients are alive. You at work?'

'No, study day. Post Grad meeting starts at ten. Jodie's gone to work, so I have the flat to myself.'

'Jodie well?'

'Great, thanks. We saw you on the news, Dad. Jodie said you looked very smart.'

'She's a charmer, that girl.'

'But the case sounds horrible.'

'This one won't be made into a Disney film, that's for certain.'

Gil walked past and Warlow waved to him whilst he kept talking to Tom. 'Whilst you're there, Gil wanted a

word with you. Something medical. I told him you
wouldn't mind.'

'No, that's fine.'

'He's here. I'll hand him over while I find my keys.'

'You off shopping in Tesco's?'

'Revisiting a murder scene.'

'Same thing, isn't it?'

'I'll speak to you later, okay? Enjoy the academics.'

'I'm presenting, so lots of coffee for me.'

Warlow signalled again to Gil. 'It's Tom.'

Gil looked momentarily horrified. 'Oh, right, well, I
don't think I need to bother him now, I mean—'

'He's here. No time like the present.'

———

Gil stared at the phone Warlow handed to him. The urge
to hand it back and make his excuses was strong. But he'd
put all this off for too long. And once again, on getting up,
his morning pee had been pink-tinged.

Behind him, the Incident Room had swung into quiet,
determined, work-mode. No one was taking any notice of
him for once. He turned and said, 'Okay. I'll be two
minutes.'

No one responded except Rhys, who looked up and
held up a thumb in acknowledgement.

Gil pushed through the door and walked outside. The
day was shaping up to be a good one. Though there was a
stiff breeze coming east over the Irish Sea and Cardigan
Bay. But the sun warmed Gil's face as he stood in the car
park, watching seagulls wheeling in the wind. He shivered
a little as he spoke into the phone. Not the wind, more an
adrenaline anxiety.

'Hello?' Tom's voice came through loud and clear.

'Tom, this is Gil Jones.'

'Hi, Gil. Dad said you had some questions for me.'

They already knew one another, having met at Tom's mother's funeral. 'I'm so sorry. Nothing worse than some stranger asking for advice.'

'It's what I do, Gil. Besides, you're not a stranger.'

'Well, thanks for that. Your dad has caught me on the hop, though. I only mentioned the idea in passing.'

Tom didn't answer, and Gil knew he was being given space. A technique he'd used many a time himself for on-edge suspects.

'Right,' Gil said with a mental girding of the loins. 'I realise you're an ear nose and throat bloke, but your dad said you'd done surgical rotations in other things.'

'Yes, I've done my share.'

'This is definitely an opposite end of the system question, so to speak. You know, waterworks. I said I'd try to find out for a mate.'

'Well, you're in luck there because I did a six-month rotation on a urology unit a few years back.'

'Honestly?'

'Before I got the ENT rotation. Knee deep in catheters every day. I have my own collection of renal stones.'

'Really?'

Tom let out a pulse of air. 'No, not really. That was meant as an icebreaker, Gil.'

'*Arglwydd*, I thought you'd turned into one of these trophy collectors. Like serial killers.'

'Sorry.'

'Don't apologise. You're like your dad. He enjoys a bit of the old gallows humour. But I'll get to the point. Thing is, my mate has been waking up these last few days and seeing a bit of pink in his urine.'

'Right. A touch of haematuria.'

'Is that what it's called?'

'It is.' Tom paused before asking, 'Since we're having this conversation, I take it you haven't been to your GP?'

'It's not me, it's my mate.' More silence until Gil capitulated with a sigh. 'Not yet.'

'You should. That would be my advice in any case of haematuria. But it is dilute stuff, yes? Not clots of fresh blood?'

'God, no. I'd have rung for a bloody ambulance if I'd seen that.'

'Look, I'm sure you've googled this. And I also presume there are no other symptoms. No pain?'

'No.'

'Are you going more often? Any difficulty when you go?'

'No. Well, a bit, but that's normal for men, right? I mean, I'm not getting up at night or anything. Plus, I do drink a lot of tea.'

'Well, there are haematuria clinics that deal with this kind of thing quickly. Your GP might want to feel your prostate and check for a kidney infection, but it doesn't sound as if it's acute.'

'Right,' Gil's voice dropped low. He'd read up on all this stuff. Kidney infections, prostate cancer, bladder cancer. The list was a long and crappy one.

'The clinic will arrange a battery of tests and an exam by someone who knows what they're feeling for.'

Coldfinger.

'My eyes are watering already.'

'No way around that, I'm afraid.'

'No. But I feel well. Anwen, that's the missus, she's got us on a health kick. Less meat, salads for supper, that sort of thing. Says I need to lose some weight. As someone who's seen my physique, I realise that must be a difficult concept.'

Tom chuckled. 'The healthy eating sounds good. It all

helps. Once you've been to the clinic and they've done tests, I'll be happy to talk you through the results. And I have some links in South Wales. I can put you in touch with a couple of really good guys.'

'Thanks, Tom.'

'The change of diet is interesting, though. I remember seeing one woman in clinic who'd done exactly that. She'd become a vegetarian and presented with pink urine. But in her case, it was just beeturia.'

'Beet what?'

'Beeturia. Pink urine after eating beetroot. About ten percent of the population experience difficulty breaking down the pigment in beets and their urine goes pink for forty-eight hours. Stools too sometimes.'

Gil didn't answer because his voice had suddenly disconnected from his brain, which was doing backflips.

Beeturia?

'I've never really liked beetroot,' he said absently. 'Avoided it to tell the truth.'

'I see,' Tom said. His words contained a hint of where-the-hell-is-this-going-now in them.

'Until about a week ago,' Gil went on, 'when Anwen got it into her head that we should do all this. She mustered the family troops. My brother-in-law has an allotment, and he's been bringing all this stuff over and—'

'Don't tell me. You've been eating lots of beetroot,' Tom interjected.

'I have. Loads of the dark-maroon bloody stuff. In salads. Even sandwiches.'

Tom's laugh was a soft ripple. 'Then what I'd suggest is to stop eating them for a week. If your urine clears up—'

'I'm one of the ten percent.' Gil's tone had changed from anxious patient expecting the worst, to condemned man receiving the governor's pardon letter on his way to the gallows.

'It's worth a go, anyway.'

'Too bloody right it is. Beeturia... Ah, Tom, you're a marvel.'

'I haven't done anything.'

'Yes, you have. Oh, yes, you have. I owe you several pints for this.'

'Okay, but stop the beets first, and then go to the GP if it doesn't work, okay?'

'Yes, doctor. Sorry, it's mister, isn't it? I always get that wrong.'

'Tom will do fine.'

'*Diolch*, Tom. *Diolch o'r galon.*' And they were indeed heartfelt thanks.

With the call finished, Gil stood with the phone in his hand, staring up at the sky and the birds above with fresh eyes, letting the relief wash over him. Okay, he couldn't be certain, but it all fitted.

Bloody Beetroot!

'Right, this calls for drastic action,' he muttered to himself.

He walked across to his car and opened the boot, leant in, and removed something from under a blanket.

———

With Gil on his phone to Tom, Warlow made use of the time by checking through the local database and shared emails once more before heading off for Ystumtuen to see if anything jumped out. The trouble was there appeared to be a lot more threads to pull on now that Mirain's body had been found. There were links between the two victims, of course there were. They'd lived together for several months as a couple, so there were bound to be. And yet, that nagging awareness of something that had tugged at him during yesterday's post-mortem tugged again now. If only he could find the damned thing.

The Incident Room door opened, and Gil walked in. But this was a very different Gil from the man who'd walked out clutching Warlow's phone in a shaky hand. He'd done his best to hide it, but Warlow had noticed it when he'd passed over the handset. This man positively swaggered in. The Gil of old. Chest out, smiling, and clutched under his arm, a red painted tin with the words "Rover Assorted" just visible on the lid.

He took hold of it and held it up before anyone could ask. Much as a prince might if he were offering a glass slipper to a him, her, them, or miaow.

Rhys, who could smell food from three-hundred yards upwind, stood up, craning his neck to see.

'What's that, sarge?'

'Behold, I come bearing gifts. This is a retro biscuit tin found at the back of my mother-in-law's pantry when we, that is the Lady Anwen and I, emptied the house of ninety years' worth of bric-à-brac. I last saw this tin on a caravanning holiday in 1998 when it contained scones that could have penetrated bullet-proof glass if thrown with enough force. Anwen's mother would not have won Bake Off. With incredible acumen, I resisted the urge to send it to the dump, only to find now, three years later, someone willing to pay twenty smackers for it on eBay. God alone knows why, but who am I to question the vagaries of human nature and the power of nostalgia? Naturally, I have decided that if we wait another three years, it is likely to double in value.'

'Nice,' Jess said.

'Oh, but ma'am, you should know by now that I am not one for show alone. *Dyma Trysor.*'

Jess cocked an eye towards Catrin, who translated, 'he says it's a treasure, ma'am.'

Gil lifted the lid to reveal the contents. 'Here we have shortbread, plain Hobnobs, custard creams, and ginger nuts. In short, our old friends, the "Away Team".'

'What happened to the no biscuit rule?' Warlow asked.

Gil placed the box on a desk and drew himself up to reply like a fire and brimstone preacher of old. 'You see before you a man who has stood on the precipice and stared into the abyss, only to step back and realise his folly. Thanks to modern medicine, my demise, as predicted by several mornings of pink urine staring back at me from the bowl in which it had been deposited, has proven to be nothing more than an overdose of beetroot.'

Catrin laughed out loud. 'Beetroot?'

Jess shook her head. Warlow could only stare at his sergeant in disbelief while Rhys, with the perspicacity of youth, said, 'Bagsy a Hobnob.'

'Help yourselves. Meanwhile, I will visit the water closet with renewed enthusiasm now that I know I am not bleeding to death.' He left, and the door closed behind him to absolute silence in the room. Strains of a slightly out of tune, jauntily whistled version of *Whistle While You Work,* from Snow White accompanied him down the corridor.

As stage exits went, it was a bloody good one.

CHAPTER THIRTY-FIVE

CATRIN PUT her phone face down on the desk. Since Jess's chat with Byronski, there had been no more communication from him. With every passing minute, her relief grew. For the first time in days, she could concentrate fully on the task at hand, which was collating the phone records for Alistair Lyndon and now for Mirain Hughes. She'd printed it all out because somehow it was easier to look at it on paper than on a screen.

Alistair Lyndon's phone had gone dead on Sunday, the 21st of August, a little after 2pm. Up to that point he'd been active. Phone tower pings placed him near Nant Yr Arian. But at 9pm, his phone was switched off and had not been switched on since.

Mirain's records showed an unusual pattern. Not the same as Lyndon's, but not too dissimilar. According to the records, she'd used her phone to message for the last time on Saturday the 20th of August, the day before Alistair's phone died. But her phone stayed active and mobile phone tower pings placed her in the Llanbadarn Fawr area of the town until it, too, had ceased to respond two days later on the 22nd of August. What did that mean? That she was killed after Alistair?

Catrin explained all this to the team as she stood next to Gil in front of the Gallery once she'd pieced it together. She used a pen to point at the snaking timeline.

'So, Ava Farley leaves Lyndon on Sunday the 21st of August in the morning. No one sees him after that. His phone goes dead several hours later in the Ystrad Meurig area. My best guess is that his phone is at the bottom of the same quarry we found his car in.'

Jess nodded her agreement.

'Why not in the car, then?' Gil asked.

'Thrown in separately?' Jess suggested.

'That makes a kind of sick sense,' Catrin agreed.

'Great film, *Sixth Sense*.' Gil was staring at the boards too, but he was seeing something very different. 'When the kid tells his mother… What's the name of the actress again?'

'Toni Collete.'

'That's her. When Haley Joel Osment tells her about the grandmother's earring in the car. Gives me shivers every time.' He looked around at the nonplussed faces of his colleagues and shrugged. 'Just saying. Spooky. Like this bloody case.'

'And I'm saying that suggesting Lyndon's phone is in the quarry doesn't really help us with Mirain Hughes,' Jess said.

'No.' He studied the map they'd posted up to include Aberystwyth and its environs. 'You say her phone stopped responding to signals somewhere else altogether? Where was it again? Llanbadarn Fawr?' Gil leaned into the map, using his finger to find the place, tracing a line out towards the south and east of the town.

'Why does that ring a loud bell?' Jess joined him.

'That's where the college is, ma'am,' Catrin explained.

'Where DCI Warlow and I went to see Lyndon's place of work?' She couldn't bring herself to mention Byronski's name. But it earned her a quizzical look from the DI.

'The college isn't the only thing there, but…' Gil let his suggestion hang in the air.

'Significant?' Jess asked, fishing for thoughts.

'You know what the Wolf thinks of the "C" word,' Gil answered.

Referring to Warlow as the Wolf made them all nod their head. And "C" for coincidence was a very dirty word indeed amongst the team.

'So, how do we put all this together?' Gil asked. 'Are we still saying that the killer or killers abducted Mirain and held her to coerce Lyndon to pay a debt or do something for them? They run out of patience, abduct him, kill him, get rid of his car and phone, and then kill Mirain and try to burn her body.'

'But that doesn't work, or they're interrupted in that attempt, and they panic and dump her in the woods,' Catrin finished speaking with a frown. It explained the timeline, but her expression spoke for everyone in that it somehow didn't quite fit.

Jess summed it up. 'None of this works because, during those four weeks of her supposed abduction, she was posting on Facebook and messaging her daughter on WhatsApp.'

'Uh, it's even more complicated than that.' Rhys stood up at his desk and his words drew everyone's attention. 'I've been emailing Dr Nixon. She's come back to me with her preliminary analysis on the maggots.'

'Now, that's not something you hear every day,' Gil muttered.

'Maggots are amazing,' Rhys said, his eyes alive with enthusiasm. 'You can measure length and the number of spiracular slits—' The raised eyebrows of everyone around him made him hesitate. 'Breathing holes. You measure length and the number of breathing holes to estimate developmental time. The longer the length and the more breathing holes, the longer the maggots have been there and—'

'Why does it complicate matters, Rhys?' Jess nipped the explanation in the bud, not letting him stray off the point.

'Because, according to Dr Nixon, the post-mortem interval is at least three weeks plus. Mirain had been in those woods for at least that length of time. Whoever was sending those messages to Heledd Rampley, it wasn't her mother. She was already dead.'

Everyone stared. Gil was the first to clap Rhys on the shoulder. 'Hey, maggot man. Good job. Ever thought of becoming a detective?'

Jess turned away, her phone already in her hand. 'We need to speak to the Markses again.'

———

WARLOW PARKED IN THE, by now familiar, lay-by next to the copse in Ystumtuen. The discovery of Mirain Hughes's body would bring the press out in droves again. They'd already been to take establishing shots, and the area was still marked off with police tape. But he wanted another look at the Lyndon crime scene before the hyenas arrived. Seeing Warlow there would no doubt whet the press's appetites and he'd do his best to avoid that scenario if he could.

The day had opened out into a pleasant late August morning. From somewhere, the thrum of a tractor engine filled the air and a woodpecker rat-tat-tatted in the copse nearby.

Though he acknowledged the country sounds at some level, his mind was very much elsewhere. He hurried down to the stile and crossed over to ascend the hill to *Yr Het Fawr*. He opened his phone and searched for some crime scene images. Something had come up on Povey's latest report. A blood sample taken from one rock had matched Lyndon's, and he wanted to see where it had lain. He took his time orientating his position. The rock was in the lab for analysis, but they'd left markers in the ground, and he found the spot quickly enough at the bottom of a steep slope which might, in the past, have been a shaft entrance but which time, weather, and erosion had filled in. Now, nothing more than a bowl-shaped depression with steep sides remained. He found the marker and stood looking up to the rim of the higher ground above.

From his low viewpoint, he could see little except the rocks of *Yr Het Fawr* fifty yards away. Was this where Lyndon died? Had the murderer marched him up to this point and then hit him with the rock that was even now being forensically assessed? Had there been an altercation here? Had Lyndon tried to get away?

Unanswerable questions all.

Warlow clambered up to the rim and looked back to where he'd come from. The land sloped away. Warlow made out his car and the incongruent scrap yard which had been out of sight behind the slope of the land and some trees while he was down in the depression.

Intrigued again by its incongruousness in the landscape, he headed straight for it, ignoring the path he'd come up by. Forcing his way through a little grove of trees, he arrived at the edge of the field and its rusting hulks. He crossed a fence, this one devoid of barbed wire, thank God, and wandered through the junkyard. The PolSA must have included this in the search area when the brief had been a hunt for a potential weapon. Yet, as he wandered through, looking up at the enormous machines and the caravans and the chest freezers, what struck him was the opportunity this strange place presented. An ideal spot to hide something.

Or even someone.

He spent twenty minutes looking into and under spaces, not sure what he was hoping to find until he came to the caravans. One had a door missing, two had no windows, but the third had windows and a door, though that was open with a damaged top hinge. He pulled the door open further. It came with a resistant creak. Inside, the wooden fittings with a curved bench seat and a table were still intact. The rest was a complete mess with stained curtains, ripped-open cupboards and a detritus-strewn floor covering a murky carpet under the dirt.

Warlow backed out, a vague idea forming in his head like a silhouette without form or detail. He dialled Povey's number and gave her the benefit of his thoughts.

'The PolSA did include it and they have searched it,' Povey told him.

'Did any of your lot have a look at it?'

'No. Nothing got flagged up. Nothing that looked remotely like the murder weapon.'

'But that's not all we should look at, is it?'

'No, it isn't.' To her credit, though overwhelmed now with two crime scenes and all the extra work that entailed, Povey remained motivated. 'I'll get a couple of my best nit-pickers over there. See what they can find.'

'Thanks.'

'Oh, and we should have some toxicology reports on Mirain Hughes by the end of play today. We know what we're looking for, so the immunoassays are almost done.'

Warlow thanked her and headed back to the car. Now it was a matter of pulling on as many threads as they could until one came up with something solid.

CHAPTER THIRTY-SIX

PC GINA MELLINGS had never seen *Malory Towers* on the TV, but by the end of today she was going to be an expert, since she was now on episode three of series two with Heledd Rampley sitting by her side on the settee. They were at Joel Rampley's flat. He'd taken the day off work but kept going to the window to check on the small media circus loitering on the street outside.

'But what the hell is it they want?' Joel asked for the tenth time.

Gina got up from the sofa. She'd shed the heavy accoutrements of her uniform and looked slim and capable in her trousers and top. 'Don't forget the reason they're here. It's getting a snap or a quote that will sensationalise the story. As simple as that.'

'But we're trapped here. I've already had some neighbours on the phone. The chap downstairs is on a mobility scooter, and he's scared to go out. I couldn't even go to the gym last night and Hels should be in summer school—'

'I don't want to go today, Dad,' Heledd said.

'It's okay, Hels, you don't have to go.'

'Everyone will ask me about Mam, won't they?'

Joel sighed and went to his daughter, sat next to her, and put his arm around her. She snuggled into him. 'You're going to have to be very brave, Hels. Yes, people, even your friends, are going to want to talk about your mam. But it doesn't matter what they say. It doesn't matter what you read or see on the TV. You knew her better than anyone else. You know she loved you, right?'

'Can we look on the computer to see if she left any more messages, Dad?'

Joel squeezed his eyes shut. 'There won't be any more messages, Hels. There can't be.'

'What if I looked on *Tadcu's* computer?'

'It's Facebook, Hels. It's the same.'

Gina walked back over to the settee. 'It's almost teatime. What do you fancy, Heledd?'

She shrugged, her face miserable.

'What do you normally have?' Gina persisted.

Heledd shook her head. 'I don't want anything.'

'Well, today you can have anything you want, right, Dad?' Gina side-eyed Joel.

'Yep, anything.'

'Come on,' Gina said, 'let's go into the kitchen and you can show me what you'd like.'

Gina held out her hand, and a pouting Heledd took it.

They were experimenting with jam and fruit loop sandwiches when the door to the flat opened and Carwyn Hughes walked in. Heledd immediately ran to him and grabbed him around the waist.

'*Tadcu*, did you see those horrible people outside?'

'I did.'

'Did they ask you questions about Mam?'

'One of them did,' Carwyn said ominously.

'I don't like them.'

'No, neither do I.' He turned to Joel. 'You two can't stay here.'

'I need to go to work tomorrow. The boss said okay to stay off today, but...'

'Did you bring your laptop, *Tadcu*?'

Carwyn looked down at Heledd and shook his head. 'What's wrong with your dad's?'

'Nothing, but maybe Mam left a message on yours.'

Carwyn said nothing, but Gina picked up on the tears that pricked his eyes. 'That's not... She isn't...'

'Come and finish your sandwich, Heledd,' Gina called to her.

Reluctantly, Heledd let her grandfather go and walked back to the kitchen.

It was not a large second-floor flat: two bedrooms, a bathroom, and a galley kitchen off an open-plan living room, with a table and chairs as a dining area separate from the TV and settee.

Small enough for Gina to hear everything that was being said as she helped Heledd. The little girl was determined to prepare some sandwiches for her father and grandfather and did so with renewed enthusiasm now that she'd been given free rein. And though they chatted, the men's voices filtered through.

'Have the police said anymore?' Carwyn asked, his voice low and gravelly.

'No, nothing,' Joel replied. 'They don't want me to see her. They say it's not something I'd want to remember. Why would anyone do that to someone?'

Silence.

Because Joel got no answer, he pressed the point. 'Do you think she got trafficked or something? You read about women who meet the wrong bloke and... You know what she was like when she was on a high.'

'Don't say that,' Carwyn warned. 'Don't use words like that.'

'I mean her illness. The mania—'

'Yes. But other people won't. The police already asked me if she was on drugs.'

'They asked me, too. Why? Do you think drugs have something to do with all this?'

'No,' Carwyn's answer left no doubt as to his certainty. 'Whatever's happened, it isn't her fault. Remember that, Joel. It's important that Heledd knows it, too.'

'Who's saying it's her fault? I'm just saying her illness may have—'

'I know what you're trying to say, Joel, and it's an easy excuse to make.'

Gina heard the warning in Carwyn's voice and wondered if Joel heeded it. This was a grieving father. One not prepared to have his daughter's name dragged through the mud. His tone softened when he spoke next, though.

'How is she taking it, the little one?'

'Not too well,' Joel said. 'She keeps wanting to check if her mother's left any more messages.'

'She'll need time. We all do.'

A horn blasted outside as traffic was forced to negotiate the press presence. A presence that seemed to have little regard for the occupants of the street or traffic. Gina stepped out of the kitchen in time to see Carwyn walk to the window and stare down. '*Diawled*. Those buggers aren't helping, are they?'

'Tell me about it,' Joel said. 'I'm half expecting one of them to climb up a ladder.'

Heledd appeared, smiling, and carrying two plates laden with sandwiches of white sliced bread.

'This one is red jam and loops,' she held one plate up, 'and this one is apple and banana.' She took the plates over to the dining table and set them down.

Both men watched her indulgently.

'Come on, before it gets cold,' Heledd said, repeating

something she must have heard more than once from a parent or grandparent.

'I'll get the kettle on,' Gina said and added as an afterthought, 'Why don't I bring Heledd over to you tomorrow, Mr Hughes? Once Joel goes to work. It'll look like I'm taking her to her summer school, and it should put the hyenas off the scent. I'll come too. We can stay well out of the glare of all this that way.'

'Good idea,' Joel said.

Carwyn nodded, though not with as much enthusiasm as Gina had expected.

'Right, tea,' the PC said and made a beeline for the kettle.

———

Hubert Marks opened the door to Catrin and smiled broadly.

'Nice to see you again, detective. And the inspector, too,' he called over his shoulder into the interior. 'Glenda, it's the police, *cariad*. Better get those biscuits out.'

Once again, they were shown into the kitchen to sit on the wheel-back chairs. This time, only the guests had tea.

'We had our second cup at lunchtime,' Glenda explained. 'One more around six and that's our lot for the day.'

Everything in moderation.

Jess explained they were not here about Alistair Lyndon this time. But at the mention of his name, the Markses felt obliged to express their horror at what they'd learnt from the news.

'Awful. So awful. Mirain must be heartbroken.'

The officers exchanged a quick glance.

'It's Mirain we're here about,' Jess said. 'When was the last time you actually saw her?'

The Markses turn to glance at one another this time. Hubert, gurning with the effort of recall. 'We think it was a Friday because we had the bins out and I always do a last-minute run for the food recycling after breakfast. They were on the way into town, all three of them in Alistair's car. They only had the one car, and they did the school run and sometimes Mirain would go into town. They all waved at me.'

Glenda chipped in. 'It was a Friday because on the Sunday, Hubert was cutting the front lawn when Alistair came home. We hadn't seen Heledd all weekend because she was at her dad's. He used to pick her up after school on Fridays when it was his weekend. We saw Heledd on Monday of course. School holidays had started. But that Sunday, that's when Alistair told us that Mirain had gone away for a while and that he was going to get a few chores done.'

'That's what he said? His exact words?' Catrin demanded.

'Yes, gone away for a while,' Hubert confirmed. 'And then, the end of that week, Alistair told us Heledd was with her dad—'

'Did he say what chores?' Catrin persisted, interrupting Hubert in full flow.

'No. But they were in town, he said.'

'And the date?'

Glenda walked to the fridge and the little calendar hanging there. 'The date we last saw her was the 22nd of July. That's a bin day and Hubert cuts the lawns every other weekend. We keep tabs to know where we are.'

'Best to be organised,' Hubert said, showing a row of tombstone teeth. A smile that faded as a dawning awareness of what was going on gradually sunk in. 'Why are you asking about Mirain? She's not... Nothing has happened to her, has it?'

'It's all a part of the investigation, Mr Marks. You've been very helpful,' Jess said, 'but we can't give away any details.'

Glenda leapt on to that. 'Oh, no, of course not. But they said on the news it was foul play in Alistair's case. Does that mean actual murder?'

Jess's lack of denial answered the Markses question with no need for added detail.

'Did Alistair and Mirain have any regular visitors?'

'The only visitor they had was Mirain's father, Carwyn. Lovely chap. He'd take Mirain places if she didn't go to town with Alistair, since she didn't have a car. Or he'd come, and she'd take his car and he would look after Heledd.'

'Of course, we were always available for that if they were desperate,' Hubert added.

His words made Glenda's eyes widen with fresh anxiety. 'She's okay, is she, Heledd?'

Jess nodded. 'She's fine. But back to visitors. No regular callers? No new callers over the last few weeks?'

'No. Sometimes they'd have a Tesco delivery and parcels from Amazon, but that was it,' Hubert said.

'You don't think that the kill... The person who did this has been here, do you?' Glenda's voice went up an octave.

'There's no need to be alarmed, Mrs Marks.' Catrin leaned in and took hold of Glenda's hand worrying at a napkin. 'We're here because you are such good witnesses. We hoped you'd remember the last time you saw Mirain. And she was well, then?'

One more exchange of glances. Glenda looked to be on the verge of tears. 'She's such a lovely girl. Big smile. And she loves Heledd and dotes on Alistair. She waved at me. Smiled and waved.'

'And when Alistair told you she'd gone away? On the Sunday, did he seem upset?'

Hubert frowned, and as always, turned to Glenda. 'Funny you should say that because he wasn't his usual self. Not as chatty. Just wanted to get away and get on with his chores. That's one of the things we liked about him. Fastidious, always clearing up. But I told you, Glen, didn't I? Alistair got up on the wrong side of the bed this morning. I said that.'

Glenda nodded.

Jess smiled thinly. They weren't to know that Mirain had a history of manic depression. They weren't aware that she sometimes, in manic phases, took herself off on wild jaunts. But Alistair would have known. Reason enough for him to be upset.

'Though he did ask me if I had anything for the Amenity Centre,' Hubert said.

'The what?'

'Recycling. The Civic Amenity Centre. He was clearing out the sheds, he said. That's the trouble with those smaller houses. No garage. And there's nothing that cheers you up more than getting rid of stuff. We love going to the Amenity Centre, don't we, Glen?'

Catrin made a fresh note.

'When you find Mirain, give her our love, won't you?' Glenda said.

The officers finished their tea and thanked the Markses and then crossed the street to stand in front of Lyndon's house.

'Think the recycling centre is important, ma'am?' Catrin asked.

'No idea,' Jess said with an added sigh. 'But we'd better check with CID. We once had a cocaine ring operating out of the recycling centre off the Oxford Road in Manchester.

Who pays any notice to you when you're fetching and carrying bags to a dumpster?'

'You still think this might be drug related?'

'Personally, no, I don't. But the ketamine angle needs to be followed up. It's one of the few clues we have in this damned case.'

CHAPTER THIRTY-SEVEN

WARLOW SET off early for the Incident Room the next morning. He hadn't slept well in the hotel bed and even the big breakfast they'd delivered to his table, half of which he'd left, didn't help. He'd not been able to quash the nagging itch that they were missing something big in the investigation. The previous afternoon had slipped by with nothing new to add to the boards. And yes, they'd moved quickly in a few days and lulls were common and to be expected. Still, that knowledge did little to help his mood.

As he arrived on the outskirts of Aberystwyth, his phone rang. The caller ID came up as Gina Mellings.

'Morning,' Warlow said.

'Morning, sir.' The background rumble and hiss told him she, too, was driving.

'You out and about, Gina?'

'I have Heledd Rampley in the car with me, sir. We're going to her *tadcu*'s on an adventure. I'm hoping the press assume we've gone to Heledd's summer school. Her dad left for work, and I didn't want to stay in that tiny flat all day.'

'Good thinking, Bat… Person?' Warlow said.

'Batwoman is fine, sir,' Gina said.

'Thought it might be, but you never know, right?'

'You don't, sir.'

'How are they? I mean, can you talk?'

'Heledd has my earphones on and is playing Alto's Adventure on her iPad. It's okay to talk. Because her mum has been away for a while, it hasn't sunk in she isn't coming back. She keeps asking to check Facebook for messages.'

'What about her father?'

'Upset, obviously. But more upset for Heledd than for himself.'

'Understandable.'

'Mirain's dad is the worst of the three.'

'I can understand that, too.'

'But he's putting on a brave face for Heledd. They both are, to be honest. But I'm just ringing to let you know where we'll be.'

'Noted,' Warlow said. 'Blast,' the word slipped out of his mouth before he could stop it.

After a three-second pause, Gina said, 'Did you not want me to go there, sir?'

'What? No, oh God, take no notice. I've just hit a bloody tailback. That means that the team may well arrive at the office before me.'

'Is that the end of the world, sir?'

'No, but it's not my style. And worse, it's ammunition.'

———

THE TAILBACK PUT an extra twenty minutes on Warlow's journey thanks to a burst water main. But, as he walked in through the Incident Room door, his annoyance evaporated. He sensed a frisson in the air. If someone had asked him to explain it, he would not have been able to. But there was something in the way everyone looked busy. Too busy to take much notice of him as he slid in and slipped off his jacket. Even Gil, the master of the withering put-down for any latecomer, let him off the hook.

'The burst water main, was it?' Gil asked.

'Indeed,' Warlow said.

'See,' Gil turned to Rhys, 'I told you he didn't sleep in?'

Rhys's mouth dropped open. 'I never said—'

Behind Warlow, a voice said, 'Brilliant timing, DCI Warlow.'

Warlow swung around to see Jess carrying a tray of coffees and teas. 'I suggested we do a walkthrough once you arrived.'

'Sorry, Burst—'

'Water main, yes, we know.'

'How?'

Jess sent Rhys a look. 'Gina, sir. She rang and said you'd been held up.'

Warlow looked around at the team. 'Fair enough. You are detectives, after all.'

Gil bent over, and something rustled under the table. He emerged with an oblong of greaseproof paper and a plate.

'In discussion with the Lady Anwen and considering my remarkable recovery from a terminal illness—'

'Beeturia,' Catrin said.

'—she's made some Bara Brith which I have sliced and buttered. I've even brought serviettes for the *diolchgarwch*.'

'Gratitude, ma'am,' Catrin muttered to Jess.

Gil handed out the serviettes, bizarrely decorated with Christmas trees. 'All I could find in the spares drawer.'

'Now you're talking, sarge,' Rhys said as he accepted a slice of the fruit loaf.

'I was going to bring in some Caerphilly, but there's no need to go overboard, is there?'

'You eat cheese with this?' Jess asked. 'I thought they only did that in Yorkshire.'

'How does that song go?' Gil asked. 'Anything you can do…'

Everyone took a slice of buttered cake and, suitably armed with a hot brown liquid of their choice to wash it down, they pulled chairs out from under their desks and sat in front of the Gallery and Job Centre mash-up, with Catrin at the helm.

She began with Alistair Lyndon, running through the toxicology report which confirmed the ketamine in his system. According to Tiernon, the drug appeared to have been administered via an intramuscular injection into the thigh.

'It was a solitary wound. No sign of any other injection site,' Catrin added. 'If he was a Special K user, he wasn't an injector.'

'Snorter?' Jess suggested.

'Maybe. But it is odd that there were no other signs.'

'You get a bigger hit with an injection,' Jess added.

Everyone agreed it was an anomaly worth noting. Then Catrin told them about Povey's latest addition to her list: the bloodstained rock, which further analysis showed hair and flesh embedded in its surface. Given Alistair Lyndon's pattern of injuries, it looked very much as if the rock was the instrument that caused his death.

Catrin put a photograph on the board. An oblong stone, nine or ten inches long, with jagged and eroded excrescences on its surface.

'How heavy?' Gil asked.

'2.69 kilos.'

'That's what, six pounds in old money?'

'Cumbersome as weapons go,' Jess noted.

But easy enough to hold in two hands and pummel someone's head with. No one said it. No one needed to.

'Nothing new from the car?' Warlow asked.

Catrin shook her head. 'And the preliminary toxicology screen on Mirain showed nothing. That came through this morning, too.'

'She was not a user,' Rhys said.

'Nothing to suggest it. She was on medication, um, olanzapine and fluoxetine.'

'Were her prescriptions up to date?' Warlow asked.

Catrin nodded. 'She'd picked up a fresh one the week before she disappeared.' Then she told the team about the last time the Markses had seen Mirain and that, according to them, she'd been happy. But the sergeant's eyes kept straying up to Gil's wavy timeline. She directed everyone's attention to that now. 'We have Rhys's bug evidence Mirain died almost four weeks ago. That puts her time of death at or around the weekend that Alistair tells Hubert Marks she's gone.'

'What about the Facebook and WhatsApp messages to Heledd in the following days and weeks? How do we explain that?' Rhys asked.

'The only thing we can say for certain is that it wasn't Mirain that sent those messages.'

'Whoever killed her wanted everyone to think she was still alive,' Jess said.

'In order to string Lyndon along?' Gil posed the question.

'There's something nagging me about Ava Farley,' Jess said. 'She was the last person, aside from the killer, to see Alistair alive, but I need to check her statement. That's happening today.'

'You think she could have killed Mirain? Get her out of the equation?' Gil asked.

'There is motive there if she and Alistair were having an affair,' Warlow said.

Jess shook her head. 'I'm not sure I'd go that far, but

something she said doesn't add up. I'm going to speak to her again. Go over her statement.'

'Whoever sent those messages, pretending to be Mirain, must have had access to her laptop or her phone or her iPad,' Rhys said.

'No sign of any of those at the house, though.'

'That's another strange thing,' Warlow muttered. 'Mirain's things all locked away at the house she shared with Lyndon.' Another thread to pull. But as yet, he was feeling nothing. No tingle of anticipation or a hint that they were progressing.

'Lyndon was a tidiness freak, sir,' Catrin said. 'The Markses confirmed that.'

Warlow cast his mind back to the house. It's neatness, with everything squared away.

They sat, picking crumbs of Bara Brith up with their fingers and sipping the last of the beverages, each with their own thoughts. They had a lot of information, but as yet, no glue to stick it all together with. And whoever had done this was still out there. If this was some drug-related vengeance, who was to say there would not be more victims?

Warlow looked away. They were missing something. He could sense it. But there was no point voicing these thoughts. Not yet.

'There is one more thing.' Gil got up. 'One of the clerical staff took a message last night from Byron Evans, Lyndon's colleague. You've spoken to him, right, ma'am?' He looked at Jess.

'What did he want?' Jess's eyes narrowed.

Gil shrugged. 'The message said that he'd found something that might be important.'

'What does that mean?' Warlow asked.

Jess shook her head. 'Can I leave that with you, Gil? Evans is a creep.'

'Really?' Gil smiled. 'I specialise in creeps. I'll give him a ring, see what he's got.' Gil got up from his chair, but then paused, looked at his watch and then at Warlow. 'Domacini, sir. He's still here. We have him for another hour unless we charge him.'

'I hadn't forgotten. He's on my list. But let's go through everything else before I have a chat .with our friend Luca…'

———

A LITTLE BELL rang when Jess opened the door of the Dressy Fox. Ava Farley stood behind the counter next to a till. Her smile faltered for just a second as she recognised the DI. A lone customer swiped through a hanger full of tops to the left, and a larger woman, presumably the shop owner hovered near the back, checking stock from a cardboard box.

'Hi, Ava,' Jess said. 'Thanks for agreeing to chat again.'

Ava's nod was small and uncertain.

'There are a couple of things we need to clear up, and it shouldn't take more than a few minutes,' Jess explained.

'Fine. We're not busy.'

The customer walked by, muttered a quick thanks, and Ava responded with a wave and a cheery, 'Thank you.'

At the back, Tessa did not look up.

'Your statement said that Alistair Lyndon first came into the shop a few weeks ago. Can you be a bit more precise?'

Ava thought and then turned to her phone, talking as she did so. 'He came into the shop and then came back a week later and we went for a coffee. That was when I gave him my number and he texted me to thank me for being a good listener.' She scrolled through and found the right screen, which she then showed to Jess. 'That first message was on a Wednesday, the, uh, 20th of July. He came in first the week before that.'

'When you went to Lyndon's house for the meal he cooked you last weekend, was there any sign of his ex-partner?'

'No. None. I felt better about that because he must have been telling the truth. You know, there would have been something in the bathroom or in the shower. Stuff he wouldn't have used, but there was nothing at all.'

'The weekend of the 23rd of July, the weekend after you had coffee with him, were you around?'

Once again, Ava scrolled through her phone. Just like Molly, it was a multimedia record of her life events. 'Yeah, I thought so. I was at the Fix It Festival in Cardiff. I don't remember a lot about it if you want details, but there are four other girls who will tell you I was there for three days.'

'If you could give me some names, that would be great?'

'Are you checking up on me now?' Ava asked, taken aback.

'It's what we do, Ava. Checking and re-checking.'

'Then why haven't you found out who did it? Who killed him?' Tears welled in her eyes.

'Because we need to check everything. Like I'm doing now.'

Ava blinked, but the flaring anger ebbed away quickly.

'If you could write down those friends' numbers, I'd be grateful.'

Ava looked puzzled. The sort of look Jess was used to seeing on Molly's face when she was asked to do something non-technological. 'Why would I write them down?' Ava said. 'I've already sent them to your phone.'

Bloody Gen Z.

CHAPTER THIRTY-EIGHT

WARLOW SAT across from Luca Domacini and Keri Nichols, who seemed to have gained confidence over the few days since she and Warlow had met. Since she'd convinced Domacini to go the tight-lipped route of "no comment" whenever he got the chance, she knew she was on safe ground.

Well, thought Warlow, time to cause a tremor or two.

'As you can see, this is not a formal interview this morning, Mr Domacini.' Warlow looked at his watch. 'There is an hour and fifteen minutes on the custody clock. The good news is that despite your refusal to cooperate, we have, after many hours and phone calls, established that you were not in the area at the time of Alistair Lyndon's disappearance and subsequent death.'

Domacini's face split into a triumphant grin and he turned to his solicitor, who nodded her head.

'Of course, you could have saved us a lot of time if you had volunteered that information at the outset. Still, the right to silence is one we understand and respect.' Warlow composed his face into the semblance of a smile. He hoped it looked as fake as it felt. 'You will not be charged with murder.'

The solicitor pushed her chair back.

'However, there is the matter of possession of Class B drugs and actual bodily harm as the result of an attack on one of our officers.'

The solicitor sat down.

'I also need to tell you that Alistair Lyndon is not the only victim we have discovered as part of our enquiries. Another body has been found. A—'

'No comment,' the words were out of Domacini's lips before Warlow finished.

Warlow sighed. 'The thing is, Luca, we can go around the roundabout all over again. Because this is a distinct case, we can let you go and then fetch you back in. And, since you like the food and the bed so much, maybe that's what you'd like us to do.'

'No comment.'

Next to him, Keri Nichols bristled. 'I don't think that threats of further detention—'

'These are not threats, Ms Nichols. They're a valid part of the investigation into the murder of a young woman. We've established a link between your client and Mr Lyndon, and there is a clear link between the other murder victim and Mr Lyndon as well. Simple maths. Now if Mr Domacini were to tell us about his movements, starting with the weekend of the 22nd of July, so that we could eliminate him from our enquiries, it would make my life, and my team's life, a lot easier.'

Nichols glared at her client. 'No comment,' he said after a moment's hesitation, though a lot of the bravado had gone.

Warlow dropped his head. 'Shame, because I was going to speak to my younger colleague, the one you dropkicked down the stairs. I mean, he's a reasonable bloke.

Tough kid. Rugby player. A few stitches in the head are nothing to him. I was going to chat to him about taking this one on the chin and not pursuing the charge. I mean, you're a bouncer, right? An ABH conviction would scupper that for a start. So, what does that leave you with? Some personal training down at the gym? But then I guess you'd be doing that full-time if there was enough work. Ah, well.' Warlow got up and gathered his papers.

'I was at a tournament,' Domacini said. It burst out of him like a bullet from a gun. 'MMA.'

'What?' Nichols asked.

'Mixed martial arts,' Warlow explained. 'Where?'

'Birmingham. I was at a mate's flat.'

'A name and a phone number would be good,' Warlow said.

'Luca, you don't have to do this,' Nichols said.

'Definitely not,' Warlow agreed. 'Up to you, Luca.'

This time, Domacini looked up at Warlow. 'A woman, you said. The second body?'

Warlow had put a lot of thought into this tactic. Despite Domacini's testosterone-driven problems, there'd been no complaint about him from a woman. And his relationship with Claudine Barton had him as her minder. In some distorted way, Warlow guessed Domacini had a code of behaviour when it came to women. Time to test it now.

'A woman,' Warlow said, adding a slow nod for emphasis.

'Don't be fooled by this.' Nichols sent Warlow a disdainful look and kept it up as she spoke to her client. 'Let them prove you were involved. Say nothing. Do nothing.'

But this time, Domacini frowned and turned on her. 'Hang on. A woman has been killed here. It was nothing to do with me, and I can prove that. Why wouldn't I help?'

'They're manipulating you, that's why.'

But Domacini shook his head and turned back to Warlow. 'Like I say, I'm sorry about the other officer.'

'I'll have a word.'

'Red mist, man.'

'Sounds like it's your favourite colour. You need to work on that, Luca.'

'I know.' Then, much to Nichols's disgust, he wrote down the name and phone number.

———

WHEN WARLOW GOT out of the interview room, only Catrin was at her desk.

'Has he gone?' she asked.

'About to.' He plonked down the piece of paper. 'Name to check his movements at the time Mirain went missing. But it isn't him. Where is everyone?'

'DI Allanby went to see Ava Farley, and after speaking on the phone with Byron Evans, Gil and Rhys went out to see him.'

'Anything interesting?'

'He's found a locked box under a workstation that Lyndon used.'

'Does Gil have a key?'

'No. He said they'd wing it. Oh, and Povey rang. Asked you to ring her back. She's at the…' she looked down at a note in her hand, '… junk yard. She said you'd know.'

Warlow picked up his phone from the desk and walked outside to dial Povey's number. She answered after four rings.

'Are you psychic?' Were her first words.

'No, though some might say psychiatric.'

She emitted two notes of a knowing chuckle. 'Another classic, eh, Evan?'

'So, what have you got?'

'What makes you so sure we have anything?'

'I can hear it in your voice.'

Another chuckle. 'The caravan. The most intact one, with the door hanging off its hinges. Under the rubbish on the floor is a blue carpet. I've had a quick look and the fibres there match those found on Lyndon and Mirain Hughes. We're swabbing everything as we speak. It isn't much, but it is something.'

'At bloody last.'

'You think they were held here?' Povey asked.

'I do.'

'So where do we go from here?'

'I need to find out who owns that place and quick.'

―――――

GIL AND RHYS followed Byron Evans through the quiet corridors of Coleg Ceredigion at Llanbadarn to a store-room with a small desk, a lumpy-looking iMac, and a printer.

Steel shelving units lined one wall full of spare printer ink, toner cartridges, paper, art materials and whatever else departments ran out of and needed replacing. On the other side, a load of monitors, old floor standing CPU's, and the odd keyboard, lay stacked against the wall.

'This is a storage room, I take it?' Gil asked.

'Yeah. You know what it's like. I teach computer science and the trouble with computers is that they become redundant. We do recycle and this lot will go somewhere. But I also set up this old Mac. It runs on El Capitan. Hard to believe that's seven years old.'

Rhys nodded. Gil tried not to look too befuddled.

''Course, the RAM in this old one is crap, but good enough for people to come in and type notes or lectures and get them printed off. Don't need bells and whistles for that.'

'So, Alistair Lyndon used to come in here?' Rhys asked.

'Him and others. All the time. It's quiet. No kids. And I cannibalise the printer stuff. The manufacturers rig the cartridges to run out early. They're hackable.'

'Right,' Gil said with a kind of fixed smile that told Rhys he did not know what Byron Evans was talking about. 'What have you found?'

'I was making room. There.' He pointed to the left of the desk. 'Shifting that stack of old upright CPU's'.

'Computer processing units, sarge.'

'Knew that,' Gil lied.

'In between a couple of them on the floor, I found this.' Byron pointed at a grey lockbox with a Perspex lid, and the word "Lyndon" stuck onto the surface in DYMO tape. The box looked worn, its corners scuffed, the tinted Perspex lid scratched. Gil put on some gloves and lifted the box. Something rattled inside it, and he placed it on the desk. Rhys leant forward. 'I see some papers, and yes, is that a pink phone?'

'Did you find a key?' Gil turned to Evans.

'No. But there's a few in the desk drawer. Been there for years.'

Rhys pulled the drawer open. A plastic inlay had pens, pencils, some old floppy discs, and a few silver keys. He looked up at Gil.

'Worth a go,' said the sergeant.

The third one did the trick.

The key was marked with a Red Cross, hiding in plain sight. 'Open sesame,' muttered Gil, lifting the lid. He took out the contents. The papers included a letter from a solicitor confirming a divorce and a folded-up print of an OS map. But the phone interested the police officers the most.

'Lyndon's?' Gil asked Evans.

'No. I've never seen that. And Alistair… I wouldn't say he was a pink sort of bloke.'

'What about Mirain Hughes? Was she a pink sort of person?'

Byron Evans suddenly looked a little sick.

'I'll ring Gina,' Rhys said.

Gil flattened out the folded photocopy of the OS map on the desk. Someone had drawn a circle around a spot with a smudged-out illegible name. At the top of the sheet were the letters "GP". 'Do you have any A4 plastic covers?' Gil asked. 'Transparent ones?'

'Cello bags? Loads.'

'Can I have one?'

Evans disappeared and came back with the covers. Gil put the sheet inside one and then got Evans to scan the map again.

Rhys came back in, looking serious. Gil read his expression and retrieved the maps, both original photocopy and the copy of the copy. 'Thanks, Mr Evans, you've been very helpful. Can you give us a minute?'

Evans nodded and made to leave but turned at the door. 'Can you tell DI Allanby I was helpful?'

Gil raised his eyebrows. 'Why does she need to know?'

'Just tell her, please.'

When he'd gone, Rhys went to the phone. 'It is hers, sarge. Heledd told Gina the phone was pink. She also knows the passcode.'

Gil had the phone in another Cello bag. Rhys tried the power button. 'Battery's dead.'

'Charger?'

'There's one in the car, sarge.' The two officers looked at one another and Gil nodded. 'We'd better tell the Wolf.'

CHAPTER THIRTY-NINE

SOMETIMES, you had to wait. Sometimes hours, sometimes days, and not infrequently weeks for a piece of evidence to surface. For a lab inundated by work to come back to you. For the CPS to weigh up relevance or the weight of evidence before you could arrest and charge.

But today was not one of those days.

Momentum.

That was the name for it. A domino falling. Or the beat of a butterfly's wings. The snowball that triggers an avalanche. Whatever idiom melted your butter, Warlow could feel it now. And it came, innocuously, by way of Rhys ringing him from Gil's car, and telling him what Byron Evans had found hidden under that little lecturer's workstation in Coleg Ceredigion.

He'd taken the call at his desk, but now he was pacing in the corridor, heading for the entrance, needing to feel fresh air on his face. A few colleagues nodded at him as he walked past. But he didn't see them, didn't hear them. All he could hear was Rhys. He and Gil were on the move.

'You're sure it's her phone?' Warlow demanded. 'How do you know?'

'We don't. We're charging it, sir. But it is pink.'

'And how far are you from the site marked on the map?'

'Twenty minutes, sir. Dr Google says it's an old, abandoned schoolhouse.'

'Right. Let me know what you find.'

The morning sun lit up the DCI's face as he stood and sucked in the sea air. Jess was still not back, but Povey's call about the caravan and the fibre had been the game changer. Unbelievably, they still hadn't found the person who owned the junkyard, or field, or whatever the hell you wanted to call it.

He'd put Catrin onto the job, so if someone did own it, they'd find out soon enough. She'd found a number for the nearest farm, but all they had come up with was a name. And in typical Welsh fashion, it had been a first name and descriptive term. Not quite Jones the Bread, but close enough. Brian Scraps was someone from Capel Seion who dabbled. He owned a few horses, did a bit of subcontracting, and had fields dotted around the area. Some he kept for livestock, others not. One of these "not" contained the caravans and abandoned tractors. But the helpful farmer did not have a number for Brian Scraps and Catrin was now tracking him down.

'Any joy?' Warlow asked her when he got back to the Incident Room.

'I think so, sir. Real name Brian Williams and I do have an address for him. He owns several vehicles and has a property in Capel Seion, but no phone number as yet.'

'Any previous?'

'A couple of parking tickets in town, but nothing else. Certainly, no drug link.'

Warlow nodded. Nice to have that little theory confirmed. Alas, not to be.

'The address will have to do,' he said. 'I'm going out there now. See if we can track this bloke down.'

'Want company, sir?'

'I do, but you're going to be more use here.'

Catrin nodded. She was being polite. They were both well aware this trip might be a total waste of time. She handed him a torn-off sheet of paper with the address and directions. 'Back south over the river and then the A4120.'

Warlow grunted out a thanks and grabbed his jacket. 'And if anything else comes in...' He waved his phone at her.

'I will, sir. Straight away.'

———

LLEDROD WAS AN ABBREVIATED NAME THAT, when stretched out, read *Llethry Troed*, which meant at the foot of a slope; so Rhys explained as he googled the name.

'Not much imagination used there, then, Rhys,' Gil said. 'That could apply to almost every other village in Wales.'

'We're only driving through, sarge. The actual building we want is half a mile out.'

The map sent them northeast of the village and then down a narrow lane to a spot at the bottom of a hollow. That it had once been a school was clear from the sturdy wall and the wrought-iron fencing sitting on it. The gates were padlocked and over the school's name a dilapidated hand-painted sign read "Gollum's Pottery", though the wire used to secure it had rusted and given on one side, which meant it hung drunkenly at a comical angle.

'That'll be the "GP" on the map, then,' Gil said.

'Why would he have a print of a map anyway?' Rhys asked. 'Why not use the map?'

'He was a careful bloke. A touch of OCD even. OS

maps are bloody big things, and they have a life of their own once you start to unfold the buggers. And it was a photocopy, remember? He's found the bit on the map he wanted, copied it and made a spare. That's just two seconds at the photocopier.'

'Why not just download that section?'

'No search history on a photocopier, Rhys.'

The DC nodded. 'I suppose if you go to the trouble of using one, it makes sense to print a spare.'

Behind the gates, the building was losing its battle with the elements. Several windows were now glass-free and stared back at the men like empty eye sockets. They'd hammered chipboard against the front door, but this, too, looked eroded and swollen from the rain, with one side angled away from the wall.

'Your choice of a bed and breakfast venue is bloody awful, Rhys,' Gil said.

'The local history site I found said it was a private school once. But that closed late sixties and in 1970 it became some kind of art commune.'

'Is that who Gollum was?' Gil asked.

'You're not into *Lord of the Rings*, sarge?'

'I know an Orc when I see one, but it wouldn't be my chosen subject on Mastermind.'

'Gollum was the chap who wanted the ring back from... Whoever else had it. Bottom line, he thought it should be his.'

'Right. So, seventies and *Lord of the Rings* means they were hippies, then?'

'If you say so.'

'Art commune,' Gil muttered. 'I wonder if that was why Lyndon had this marked on a map. Wasn't that what he taught? Art and design?'

'Maybe there was a *Lledrod* art movement. Local history and all that.'

'Not much art here now, by the look of it.' Gil rattled the gate. The rusty padlock looked seized solid. His eyes drifted up to the wall and the spiky wrought-iron fence topping it. 'We're going to have to climb it, aren't we? Go on, you first.'

Rhys chose the gate since it had a flat top with no finials or rail spikes. It wobbled alarmingly as Rhys got over it in a half vault, landed on his toes, and dusted himself down on the other side.

'It isn't too bad, sarge,' he said.

Gil glared at him but managed, with even more alarming wobbling, to clamber over. They inspected the warped boards over the front door. A sizeable gap showed a very dusty and murky interior. Rhys got down on his haunches. 'We might get through if we crawled on our bellies, sarge.'

'I'd need prolonged emergency liposuction to get through there. Forget it. Let's have a look around the outside first.'

Gil stood back and surveyed the grounds which, like the child-sized gap to the side of the door, appeared to be a daunting prospect. The Ceredigion countryside was reclaiming the land from the old school. Bramble and nettle had encroached on all sides leaving a very narrow gap around the side of the building to the rear.

'*Iesu post*, did you bring a machete, Rhys?'

'No, sarge.'

'That's the trouble with you, no foresight.'

'There's a joke there about circumcision, sarge.'

Gil batted away some branches and muttered, 'Leave the jokes to me, Detective Constable.'

At the rear of the property, a yard area of about thirty square metres ended with more overgrown greenery. In the middle of it all stood a grey block constructed of the same stone as the school.

'I wonder what that is?' Rhys asked.

'If this was a school from way back, then my guess is a toilet block.'

'Outdoor toilets?'

'You don't know the half.' Gil peered through the brambles. 'I can't see us getting through this.'

Rhys had wandered off. 'Hang on, sarge, there's a path of some sort.'

Gil followed to find Rhys staring at a neatly cut and beaten down area of vegetation that led to the block. 'Someone has been here, that's certain,' Gil muttered. 'Go on, then, after you.'

Rhys led the way, picking at the recalcitrant fronds of blackthorn branches that caught in his trousers and shirt. He'd shed his jacket because of the heat and now, in the middle of all this greenery, instead of feeling cooler, it had warmed up considerably as the humidity rose.

'It's muggy, sarge.'

'Thunder on the way, I reckon.'

They picked their way through until they stood in front of the block in an area of concreted ground which formed a barrier against the overgrowth. The block sat at right angles to the school building, but there was no sign of a urinal. Instead, the doors of the cubicles were off, and a couple of walls taken down to make three spaces instead of six. In each space sat a curious construction of bricks arranged almost like a beehive above a rusting metal box with an open mouth. In the third space, bricks removed from the beehive just above the box left a void of two feet in diameter.

'*Beth uffern…*' Gil said.

'Kilns, sarge. I watched someone make something like this on YouTube.'

'Kilns. For pottery?'

'Gollum's pottery.'

Rhys walked across to the kiln with the wall removed, his brow lowering as he sniffed the air. 'This one smells a bit of damp burnt wood and… Something else. And there are smears on the floor here, sarge. Looks like wax or… Is that fat?'

'Someone been making candles?' Gil said, walking over. 'Don't tell me this is bloody witchy stuff. I hate bloody witchy stu—' He stopped and stared at what Rhys had seen.

'That's not wax, Rhys. That's burnt fat.'

'Someone been barbecuing out here?'

Gil stepped back, almost as if he'd been stung. His face drained of colour as he stared at the kilns. 'Don't touch it, Rhys. In fact, touch nothing.'

'What, sarge? What is it?' Rhys looked around in panic.

'*Mam fach*, this isn't a barbecue. It's a bloody crematorium.'

CHAPTER FORTY

Warlow was halfway to Brian "Scraps" address when Povey rang him.

'This is getting to be a habit,' he said as he punched the answer button and brought her voice up through the car's speakers.

'I know, I'm thinking of emigrating. There's a job going in Florida, wrestling alligators.'

Warlow snorted. 'Too cushy for you. You'd be bored to crocodile tears. What have you found?'

'Not what. It's who.'

An electric thrill of fear ran through Warlow. 'Please don't tell me it's another body, Jesus—'

'No. Not a body, though he has a body, this bloke. And what a body. I mean, he's not some kind of ethereal being.'

'What the hell are you talking about, Alison?'

'You told me earlier you were keen to find the owner of our rural scrap yard. I've just come off the phone with DS Richards and she said you were on the way to find him. Well, I am saving you a job. He's just turned up here in Ystumtuen.'

'What?' Warlow immediately checked his mirrors,

signalled, and pulled off the road and up onto the verge with his emergency blinkers on. 'Is he there with you?'

'He's standing right next to two of my techs, discussing the merits of a battered-looking David Brown tractor with no engine. I'd like to say he's a fine figure of a man, but then I'd like to say that the moon is made of Saint Agur Blue. Both would be a lie.'

'Can you put him on?'

Povey hesitated for a beat. 'That'll mean him putting his mouth near to my phone.'

'Doesn't he have a phone of his own?'

'He does, but it looks like he stole it from a museum. If it was a smart phone, it must have cheated on the test.'

'I need to speak to him. Somewhere quiet.'

'I'll take him to one of the vans. We'll probably need to fumigate it afterwards, but at least I'll be upwind of him.'

'That bad?'

'Let me put it this way. If we left him on a windowsill next to a Petri dish, I'm pretty sure we'd discover a new strain of penicillin by the morning.'

'Is that a science joke?'

'Believe me, Evan, Brian Williams is no joke. And I suggest you speak to him in Welsh. He struggles with English. I'll send you a snap and ring you back.'

Warlow waited for a call, but before that, a two-tone blip indicated an incoming message. Warlow kept his eyes on the screen as a blurry image appeared and took its time to clear. It showed a man wearing a broad-brimmed bushman's hat over a voluminous waxed coat that extended to his ankles. He'd half turned to the camera, and the coat lay open to reveal a pair of trousers, undone at the waist and held up by a too-large belt with a flapping overhanging end, over a faded checked shirt. The reason for the voluminous coat became obvious in the second side-on view, which revealed a considerable belly. Williams's face remained obscured by the hat.

Warlow tapped the wheel as he waited for Povey's return call, and when it came, it made him start. Povey's face appeared on the screen and then the camera panned around to a closeup of Williams. He'd taken off his hat to reveal wafting skeins of thin grey hair. He hadn't shaved for days, and the lazy man's stubble, combined with several missing teeth and hair, made him look as wild as the countryside that was his habitat.

'Mr Williams, *shwd I chi?*'

'*Go lew,*' Williams answered, the 'not bad' response automatic in his thick accent, the words machine gunning out. Povey was right, this would be better in Welsh and so Warlow did exactly that.

'You're a hard man to track down, Mr Williams.'

'Keep busy, you know.'

'But that's your field, correct?'

'Mine, yes. Too small for the horses, see? Okay to keep the old machinery in, though.'

'Why?'

'Why the machinery? I take bits out, see, sell them sometimes on the eBay. Or my son does. Or I clean them up and use them to fix up old machines.'

'You enjoy that?'

'Oh, yes. I have a big collection of old tractors.' His pronunciation of tractor, which was the same word and spelled the same way in both languages, changed the vowel sound of the o, from an "er" to a pronounced "awe-r".

'What happens to them when you've taken out what you want?'

'Once every twelve months, we get a man from Birmingham comes and takes all the scrap away, see?'

'We're more interested in your caravans.'

'Yes, the lady was asking about the old Sprite.'

'When was the last time you were there visiting?'

Williams scratched his chin. The finger he used was stained yellow from tobacco, the nails black with dirt, the noise like sandpaper on a wire brush. 'Must be two months. I just came to get a gear stick from the old David Brown there at the back—'

'But the Sprite, how long has that been there?'

'Not that long. Eight months, I'd say.'

Warlow reasoned that whoever held Mirain and Alistair Lyndon must have known about the caravan and this place. 'That caravan, the Sprite, can you remember where you got it from?'

Williams frowned and then nodded. 'My son and me, we have a trailer to collect machines, but this one, it came on a trailer. That place in town. Humphries and Sons. Young bloke said he was doing his in-laws a favour.'

Humphries and Sons. The garage where Joel Rampley worked.

Warlow's mind raced.

Rampley. But they'd checked his alibis. He'd been one of the first they'd checked after they'd found Mirain. He'd been cleared, hadn't he?

But from what Brian Scraps had said, Joel knew where the caravan was.

The silence lasted so long that Povey's quizzical face appeared on the screen. 'Evan, are you alright?'

Warlow blinked. 'No. But we'll need a formal statement from Mr Williams. Uniforms on their way?'

'Yep.'

'Okay. Thanks, Alison.'

He rang off abruptly.

Another link in the chain. Warlow's brain formed an image he'd seen in Carwyn Hughes's house. A family photograph of happier times. All the Hugheses, their daughter Mirain, her partner Joel, and their daughter

Heledd in front of a caravan. In his mind's eye, he saw it now. Old, curved in shape, a vintage one. The one in Williams's field.

And then he thought about Mirain's Facebook messages and WhatsApp messages and the phone that Rhys and Gil had found. Dominos all lined up, but still needing that single one to fall to set them toppling.

He put the car in gear and drove to a spot where it was safe to turn around. He needed to speak to someone urgently.

And she was only eight years old.

———

No one answered immediately when Warlow knocked on the door of Carwyn Hughes's property. At the second attempt, it did open, and he stood looking down at Heledd Rampley, dressed in leggings and trainers, a cape and a tiara.

'Hello?' she said with a disarming grin.

Behind her, PC Gina Mellings appeared, not in uniform today, but in jeans and a T-shirt. She held a phone to her ear and looked very preoccupied, but on seeing Warlow, beckoned urgently for him to come in.

Heledd stepped aside and Warlow followed Gina through into the kitchen. The back door was open. Carwyn Hughes's well-kept garden looked green and welcoming in the September sunshine. A ball, a wand, and a Mary Poppins style carpet bag lay on the lawn.

'Would you like a glass of water?' Heledd asked in Welsh.

'I would, thank you,' Warlow answered.

Heledd went back into the kitchen and Warlow heard a tap running.

'I'm on the phone with DC Harries and DS Jones, sir.

He rang me five minutes ago. He's a bit shaken. I had no idea you were coming.' Gina's voice was breathless, her expression of surprise devoid of apology. There was something else there, too. Something like horror.

'He's here, now, yes,' Gina said into the phone and handed it over. 'It's DS Jones, sir.'

Intrigued, Warlow took the phone and listened to Gil tell him what they'd found. The kilns, the burnt remains. The smell of scorched meat. 'I'd put money on this being a botched attempt at getting rid of Mirain's body.' Gil's voice sounded raw.

Warlow turned his face up to the sun and breathed in to slow his pounding heart. 'Povey needs to know—'

'Rhys is on it, sir,' Gil said.

'And you're sure that this isn't Byron Evans sending you up a long and winding garden bloody path.'

'No, I am not sure. But he's an idiot if he did. There will be a ton of forensic evidence here.'

Warlow nodded to himself. Gil was right. He'd met killers who thought they'd distract the investigation with selective information. But no one would have known about the pottery if Gil hadn't found the map. It made no sense for Evans to implicate himself.

'None of this adds up,' Warlow said.

'Hang on, sir, Rhys has something here…' The muffled shuffling of a phone being handed over again reached Warlow's ears.

'Sir, it's Rhys.'

'What have you got?'

'It's Mirain's phone, sir. As I said, Heledd's a smart kid. She knew the passcode. I've tried charging it and it's worked, sir. The WhatsApp app confirms it's Mirain's.' The DC's voice hardened. 'And there are messages dated after she died.'

'Lyndon?' Warlow rumbled out the question.

'I can't think of anyone else.'

Warlow whirled around to look at the kitchen again. At the photos of the happy families. Of the image of everyone in front of that caravan.

'Good work, Rhys. Outstanding work. Get over to Rampley's place of work and bring him in.'

'You think he's involved, sir?'

'No, but I'd rather I knew where he was.'

If Rhys was tempted to probe for further explanation, he had the sense not to.

Heledd appeared at Warlow's side with a glass of water. He looked down.

'Rhys, I must go. Get to Rampley.'

Warlow took the water over to the table and sat down.

'Heledd, can I ask you something?'

The little girl nodded, eager to please, and walked across to sit next to Warlow.

'Gina tells me you remembered your mother's passcode for her phone?'

She nodded again, a toothless smile on her face.

'That's brilliant. Sometimes I have to write numbers down. You must have a good memory.'

'Mam says I have a memory like a elephant.'

'What about her other things? She had an iPad. Can you remember the passcode for that, too?'

Heledd reeled off the numbers. '891216. That's her birthday back to front.'

'And what about Facebook? Did she have a password for that, too?'

'Mirimirain1216.' Again, reeled off without hesitation.

'Did anyone else ask you for those passwords and the passcode, Heledd?'

She tilted her head and jutted her chin out. 'Only Alistair. After Mam went away. He said that he could find her phone if he had the passcode. And he could send Mam a message if he had her Facebook password.'

Warlow kept his expression calm. He'd had enough practise from talking to people who'd done heinous things. It didn't do to let your emotions show. Not that this little girl was guilty of anything except being blisteringly honest and guileless in the face of a monstrous manipulator.

But Heledd, inches away from him, watched him for signs, and in the end, couldn't help herself as her eyes went bigger and her smile slid into a pout.

'Mam told me to keep them a secret. But Alistair said it would help find her.'

'You did nothing wrong, sweetheart,' Warlow said.

But Heledd's eyes filled with tears, and she sniffed.

Gina came forward and knelt next to her. 'It's okay, Hels. It's okay.'

'*Tadcu* said it was alright when I told him, but he didn't look alright. His face went hard, and, and I thought… I thought he was going to turn into a monster.'

Warlow caught Gina's eye, a signal for her to step in. 'Your *tadcu* wouldn't turn into a monster, would he?'

'No. But he asked me, like he did.' She pointed at Warlow. 'About Mam's phone. And when I said I'd told Alistair,' Heledd sniffed again, 'he dropped his cup of tea, and it made a big mess on the floor.'

Warlow didn't feel anything physically click, but something did. They'd got it all wrong. They'd got everything totally bloody wrong. He realised his hand was gripping the edge of the table with such force it hurt. He kept his voice as even as he could not to alarm the little girl and asked, 'Where is Carwyn?'

Heledd turned her face to Gina's. It was the DC who answered.

'He went to his allotment for a while. Said he had some things to do.'

Warlow stood up and drained his glass of water. 'That was good. Can you get me another one, Heledd?'

The little girl, keen to please, took the glass to the sink. Warlow leaned into Gina and whispered, 'Lock the door when I'm gone, front and back. Do not open it to anyone except me, understand? Where are the allotments?'

'Somewhere south of the river.'

'Text me the location.'

Confusion crumpled Gina's brows. 'What—'

But Warlow shushed her with a finger over his mouth. He stood up. 'Heledd, keep that glass for me, *cariad*. I'll be back for it in a few minutes, okay?'

She turned, glass in hand, and nodded, solemnly.

By the time she placed it on the table, Warlow was out of the front door and running for his car.

CHAPTER FORTY-ONE

IT COULD NOT HAVE BEEN MORE than four and something miles, but the ten minutes it took him to drive to the allotments was the longest he'd known in an age.

The Satnav took him to an ordinary-looking street called, ironically, Fifth Avenue. He drove past the poorly signed turnoff to a parking area that ran parallel to a cycle track and had to reverse before he could drive in. He counted four cars in the lot when he pulled up, including the Ford he'd seen parked outside Carwyn Hughes's property the first time he'd visited. A padlocked gate and a tall fence barred entry. Inside, a flotsam of small sheds and greenhouses stretched away, the hills to the east across the River Rheidol just visible through the trees lining the banks. Aberystwyth was not a big town and Warlow realised that Boulevard De Saint Brieuc and the Castle Keep were within shouting distance.

But that would not help him now.

He yanked at the padlocked gate. It clattered under his hand and stayed locked. But the movement and the noise caught the attention of someone, and a head popped up twenty yards away, trowel in hand, bandana around the forehead. Warlow waved frantically.

'Police. This is an emergency. Let me in.'

The woman, in her seventies at least, looked around just in case Warlow might have been addressing someone else.

'Police!' yelled Warlow again.

The woman walked over, negotiating the paths between the strips.

'You can't come in without a key.'

Warlow held up his lanyard. 'I need to get in. I need to find Carwyn Hughes.'

'Carwyn? He is here.'

'I know he's here. Where exactly?'

'Far end. His shed has a yellow door.'

'Good. Now can you let me in, please?'

'Good gardener, Carwyn. Nothing's happened, has it? His daughter is missing, you know.'

'Please. Open. The. Gate.'

Flustered, the woman felt in her pocket for a bunch of keys and unlocked the padlock.

'Yellow door, you say?'

'Far end, on the right.'

Warlow ran. The allotments were in strips. The path took him parallel to the cycle track and then veered right to a broader central path. Another gardener looked up from tending a vegetable patch to watch him run by. He raced past the plots and the little buildings, flicking his eyes from shed door to shed door.

Carwyn's little bit of heaven stood three from the end. Warlow didn't see the yellow door until he got to the last and, cursing, turned back. The door was positioned on the broader side of a six-by-four creosoted shed which had the sturdy look of something handmade. The plot was tidy and precise, set out in rows, no weeds, minimal mess, the vegetation healthy and verdant. But no sign of Carwyn Hughes.

'Carwyn. Carwyn?' Warlow called.

He walked towards the shed and noticed two things immediately. The door's bolt was not engaged. The padlock hung unclasped. But when he pulled, the door stayed shut. Two black bins sat on one side. One full of pulled weeds and cut vegetation ready for a three-boarded compost heap at the rear. A smaller bin for refuse sat half full of packaging, fertiliser sacks and scrunched-up plastic bags. Warlow picked out the one at the very top of the pile and teased it apart. It bore the logo of a garden centre and inside, a till receipt. Two items only.

Weedkiller and drain cleaner.

Warlow shuddered. 'No, no, no.' He turned back to the door and yanked violently at it. Someone had bolted it from the inside. 'Carwyn. Carwyn. It's Evan Warlow. Carwyn, tell me you're in there, for God's sake.'

'What do you want?' The voice was a desperate, subdued grunt.

'Open the door, Carwyn. Open the door, please.'

'No. Bugger off. You can't help—'

'Yes, I can. Listen to me. Whatever this is, think of your granddaughter. She's the only one that matters now. That stuff you've bought, it's… If you do anything silly, it'll be bad. It'll be awful. That stuff isn't instant. It eats you from the inside out. I've seen it and believe me, it isn't pretty.'

'It doesn't matter!'

'Yes, it does. We know, Carwyn. We know Alistair Lyndon killed Mirain.'

Warlow waited and listened. He could hear Carwyn Hughes breathing. Elsewhere, the only noise came from the distant hum of traffic and birds calling to each other in the trees, the rustling of the leaves and the rasp of someone hoeing the ground augmented by the rich smell of earth permeating the air.

Normality impinging upon unspeakable chaos.

Once again, Warlow spoke in Welsh.

'*Carwyn, gwranda. Ni'n gwbod am a caravan.*'

He needed to know that they'd found the caravan.

Carwyn's heavy breathing paused for a moment. Warlow took his chance. 'Talk to me, Carwyn, please, just talk to me. Heledd told us you found out Alistair had asked her for Mirain's passwords. She's bright, that one. Such a lovely kid.'

A broken sob erupted from behind the door. 'I can't face her. I can't face her when she finds out.'

'Carwyn, I know Alistair killed Mirain. Whatever happened after that—'

'I didn't kill him. I wanted to, but I didn't. But tell me who is going to believe me? No one will believe me.'

'I will.'

'You're just saying that.' A sob followed.

'Let me tell you what I know. Please?' Warlow kept his voice reasonable and even. It was a struggle.

More ratcheted breathing from behind the door, but breathing, nevertheless. Breathing was good.

'The weekend that Mirain went missing, she didn't go of her own accord, did she? Alistair had met a girl. He lied to that girl. He told her his partner had left him. He did that so she would sympathise with him. She is an innocent party to all of this. His next shiny new thing. But then Alistair took his chance. Mirain didn't go on one of her manic episodes, though Lyndon made everyone believe she did because she'd done it before. But he took her and killed her and hid her body in the caravan. Am I right, Carwyn?'

Nothing.

'Carwyn? Tell me about the caravan.'

He spoke then. A low rumble through the door. 'I sold

it for scrap and Joel borrowed a trailer to take it out to Ystumtuen. But Mirain… She was mad about it. She wanted one last photo of the bloody caravan. To remember her mother and our holidays before her mother got ill. Mirain's illness made her do those wild things, but what can you do? During one of her odd periods, when the medication wasn't working too well, she went back out to visit the bloody caravan and that bastard Alistair took her. That's how he knew where it was.'

'Was it the texts that gave him away?'

Another deep exhalation from Carwyn. 'I won't lie to you. I never liked him. He had that look on his face always. Like he knew something the rest didn't. Like he was better than us. But what could I do? Mirain… She fell for him. As a father and a grandfather, you have to shut up and put up. Heledd said they argued. But he was hands off with her. I kept an eye on that. I don't think he liked kids.'

'Was it the texts, Carwyn?' Warlow asked again.

'The Facebook messages. They were for Heledd. But I could tell something wasn't right. And the texts… They weren't like Mirain. Too short and… Something was off, that's all. And when Heledd told me Alistair had asked for the passwords, then I knew what he'd done. Those messages were nothing but burnt echoes of my girl.'

'Did you take him to the caravan?'

'Not to start with. First, I brought him here. I said I needed some help to move some bags of topsoil. But I got some Ketasetic from the stables—'

'Ketamine?'

'Maybe. I know it as Ketasetic. But it worked. I hit him once with a spade and then injected him and, after that, he was quiet. When it was dark, I took him to the caravan. Wheeled him out in a wheelbarrow to my car like the sack of shit he was. When he came to, I convinced him to tell me everything,' Carwyn's voice had dropped to a quivering whisper. 'I made him tell me what he'd done to my little girl. How he'd strangled her and tried to burn her body and how he'd dumped her in the woods like a bag of bloody rubbish when that didn't work.' The words hissed out of his mouth like bitter spit.

Warlow remembered the broken fingers at post-mortem. 'Was it you who phoned in where to find her?'

'I couldn't leave her there anymore. Out for the birds and the animals to pick at. I couldn't...' He sobbed.

'What happened to Alistair, Carwyn?'

'After I found Mirain in Black Covert, I was going to do terrible things to him. I was going to make him pay for what he'd done. But when I got to the caravan, he'd got out. I saw him run as I parked the car. He ran, and I ran after him. It was pitch black. He ran through the trees and up the hill towards *Yr Het Fawr*, but he must have fallen. I swear. I heard his scream and stumble and then a noise... A crack... I'll never forget that. He fell and hit his head. A terrible blow. He moaned only once, and then there was nothing. I took a while to find him. He must have fallen full pelt because the rock had smashed the side of his head in. He had no pulse. He was dead by the time I got to him.'

Forensics and Tiernon would know if one blow had done the job. They could confirm or refute Carwyn's story. 'So, you dragged him up to the shaft?'

'I panicked. I didn't know what else to do. I'd walked the land dozens of times, checking the overhead cables to the farms. I knew *Yr Het Fawr* was close by. I threw him in and covered him up with stones and dirt. Buried him. Which is more than he had done for my Mirain.' He faltered again at the mention of her name, and this time, the slow sobs that followed lasted a good minute.

'Carwyn, listen to me. We found the stone that killed Alistair. From what you've told me, it all fits.'

'No,' Carwyn shouted. 'They'll say it was me that struck him. They'll say it was me that tortured him.'

'Perhaps,' Warlow replied. And in truth, the decisions about all of this were not his to make. 'But you didn't kill him. And this was a man who had murdered your only daughter. It isn't an excuse for all that you did, but I bet there would be people on a jury who might wonder if they would not have done the same.'

There would be charges. False imprisonment, assault, even administering a noxious substance if the CPS felt it was in the public interest. But a good barrister would argue a strong case of extenuating circumstances if it came to trial. And there would be reasonable doubt.

'I didn't kill him,' Carwyn said again, softly.

Warlow squeezed his eyes shut. He heard the truth in the denial, as well as relief. Confessions could do that. Catharsis was a very underestimated state of grace.

'I believe you. And Heledd will believe you when she is old enough to understand. She's lost her mother, Carwyn. Don't let her lose her grandfather, too.' Warlow leaned closer to the door. 'I promise you this, I will do everything I can to make sure you don't get punished for something you didn't do. You may well go to jail, but it won't be for life.'

After a long fifteen seconds, the metallic sound of a bolt sliding back came through the wood of the door. Warlow stepped back. The door opened. Carwyn Hughes stood there, in front of a rickety chair, some tools, open fertiliser bags, and two plastic bottles. One a weedkiller, the other a drain cleaner. Both were unopened. He blinked in the light. He looked older than Warlow remembered. Stooped and broken, but intact.

He stumbled forwards, and Warlow caught him, and, for a moment, held him.

'Good man,' Warlow said. 'Good man.'

CHAPTER FORTY-TWO

THERE WERE, of course, loose ends that needed tying off.

Warlow visited Gollum's Pottery and met Povey there. It didn't take her long to confirm that the splashes and greasy stains they'd found were human remains. Warlow tried to imagine that scenario — half a body inside an oven, the smell, the crackle of flesh, the smoke — and quickly filed the imagined image away into the locked cupboard in his head where he kept such things. He'd learned never to take them out and study them unless he absolutely had to. The trouble was that the door tended to spring open at the most inopportune of times.

That Lyndon's half-arsed plan hadn't worked was obvious. Had he abandoned the idea, or had he been disturbed so that he'd panicked and gone to Black Covert Woods? That they might never know.

The team went into full throttle in an attempt at dotting as many i's as they could. Lyndon's work in the creative arts brought him into contact with artists and he would often visit art shops in the area. The Gollum's Pottery link was there for everyone to see. It remained a bit of a movement, with some older ceramic artists proudly mentioning it in their bios. It wasn't beyond anyone's imagination to believe that Lyndon had visited the place to see where the roots of a certain kind of art had begun in the area.

As for motive, they had Lyndon's ex to thank for providing them with an opinion.

'He'd always be looking for the next best thing. In a room, he'd talk to you but have one eye on finding someone more interesting, prettier, more influential.'

'Are we saying he'd got fed up with Mirain and tossed her aside?' Gil asked, a dull anger behind his eyes as they sat in the Incident Room late that evening, the Rover's biscuit box open and almost empty.

'He wanted a new life, a new girlfriend. Another bright and shiny thing,' Jess said. 'Until the lustre faded, and he'd start looking again, no doubt.'

'Ava Farley has no idea how lucky she is to be rid of him,' Catrin said.

No one argued with that one.

There was some light relief. Someone had left a plastic bag for Rhys and a card, signed only with a big X after the words "thank you". Everyone waited for Rhys to open the parcel, which he simply stared nervously at.

'Well, come on,' Gil urged. 'Might be something edible.'

The bag had been rolled around its contents in a cylindrical shape.

'I doubt it. It doesn't weigh enough.' Catrin hefted the gift.

Gil sat up. 'Could be those pastille chocolates they make to look like coins?'

Still oddly hesitant, Rhys unwrapped the parcel.

They weren't chocolates. Inside was a long black plastic cylinder with a ribbed handle at one end.

Gil snorted. 'Hah, thank God someone has a sense of humour.'

'A plastic truncheon,' Jess said. 'Nice.'

But Catrin had her arms folded and her eyes on Rhys, who had gone bright red. 'What's the matter with you? You look troubled. Do you know who this is from?'

He wouldn't tell them. Of course, he wouldn't. Instead, he doubled down. 'One of my many admirers who wishes to remain anonymous but grateful.' He threw the light-weight toy at Catrin, who caught it. 'But to be honest. I'm disappointed. I was hoping for the chocolates.'

'As if,' Catrin said, catching the toy and hitting herself gently on the head with it.

The moment passed, and they settled back to tying loose ends, Rhys turning away and squeezing his eyes shut with a vast sigh of relief.

———

LATER, in the car on the way home, Catrin revisited the topic.

'So, how are you going to explain the gift to Gina?'

'What gift?'

'The truncheon.'

Rhys shook his head. 'What's there to explain? It's a kid's toy. I'll give it to one of my nephews. He'll love that.' He would too. 'I probably wouldn't even bring it up. It's silly.'

'Are there some things that happen at work that you don't share with Gina, then?

'Some things, yeah. Some of the truly awful things. I mean, she's in the business but, I don't know. I suppose I'm a filter. We all are, right? We deal with this stuff so that ordinary people don't have to. Not that Gina is ordinary. And neither is Craig—' Rhys caught himself, surprised at his own insight. 'Are we still talking about the truncheon here?'

'Sort of,' Catrin said. 'You're right. It's not important, it's just embarrassing, right?'

'I suppose. But let's say someone sent you a pair of toy handcuffs—'

Catrin raised her eyebrows and looked across at him. Something, a vague panic, fluttered over her expression. 'What did you say?'

Rhys frowned, surprised by her reaction. 'You know. Some people have a weird sense of humour. And truncheons and handcuffs can have... Connotations.'

Catrin had her eyes in front, her mouth thin, nodding.

Rhys blinked, his mind racing. 'Has someone sent you some handcuffs?'

'Once. A long time ago.'

'My guess is you didn't enjoy it much.'

'No. I didn't.'

The mutual laughter that accompanied this was uncomfortable. The silence that followed even more so.

'Tell you what, let's talk about something else.'

'Like what?' Catrin asked.

'Like, does your pee go red when you eat beetroot?'

This time, the sergeant's laughter was deep and genuine.

————

BY THE FOLLOWING WEEKEND, much of the dust in the case had settled, and the team had said goodbye to Aberystwyth. On a bright Saturday morning, Gil opened the door of his house in Llandeilo to find Evan Warlow standing there. They spoke in Welsh.

'Evan, this is a surprise. Come in.'

'No, I'm not coming in, Gil. Not now anyway.'

Gil frowned. Behind him, from somewhere in the house, came the noise of children shouting and faux screams. Gil looked around, pretending to be annoyed. 'The aliens have landed. It's like bloody *Independence Day* in there.'

Warlow nodded. 'I spoke to Anwen this morning.'

'Oh?' Gil's surprise was genuine.

Warlow pointed to the Jeep parked on the road and the black Labrador staring out of the back window. 'Cadi and I are going up to Talley Woods. I thought you'd like to come along.'

'Oh, I've got the troops, though.'

'They like dogs?'

'They love dogs—'

'But they can never eat a whole one. A classic.'

Gil grinned at the joke, but then frowned again. 'But you're miles out of your patch here.'

'I had something I needed to do up this way, so I rang your house and the Lady Anwen answered.'

'Yeah, you need to be careful about that. If you really want to speak to me, ring three times, stop and then ring again. A secret code.'

'Does that work?'

'Not at all.'

A girl of no more than five appeared at Gil's knee. '*Tadcu, Tadcu*, Meinir is calling me a Bobhead.'

'Probably not Bobhead, but close. Tell her I will be in to throw her into the goldfish pond in a minute.'

The little girl, satisfied by the implied punishment, giggled and turned to run back in, only to stop after three strides and turn back. 'But you don't have a goldfish pond.'

'I'm going to dig one. Mwah ha ha.'

Delighted by this, the little girl went back to running, already announcing the punishment to her sister.

'Look, I remember our chat in Aberystwyth. I'm delighted that beeturia is curable,' Warlow said.

'By not eating beetroot.'

'Exactly. But the other stuff. The ticker, the weight, that's a bugger.'

Gil nodded. 'I see. An intervention.'

Warlow shrugged. 'You're on your own in there. Anwen and your daughters have gone wedding outfit shopping.'

'Or, as I like to call it, throwing money into a deep pit while wearing a fascinator.'

'Consider this a rescue mission, then.'

'Talley Woods, eh? Haven't been there for a long time. It's an uphill walk.'

'And then a downhill walk. I've checked the weather. Come on, grab the girls.'

'Why not? Though they might take a bit of persuading.'

'Tell them there's a visit to Frank's ice cream parlour as a reward. I'm paying.'

Gil, eyebrows raised, nodded. 'You had me at I'm paying. Ten minutes. We'll follow you up.'

'Alright, I'll see you there. I'll bring the oxygen.'

Gil raised a hand and closed the door. It might have been a wave he gave Warlow, it might have been something far more insulting. Either way, it made the DCI smile as he turned away and headed for his car and the dog waiting patiently for him.

ACKNOWLEDGMENTS

As with all writing endeavours, the existence of this novel depends upon me, the author, and a small army of 'others' who turn an idea into a reality. My wife, Eleri, who gives me the space to indulge my imagination and picks out my stupid mistakes. Others who help with making the book what it is like Sian Phillips, Tim Barber and of course, proofers and ARC readers. Thank you all for your help. Special mention goes to Ela the dog who drags me away from the writing cave and the computer for walks, rain or shine. Actually, she's a bit of a princess so the rain is a no-no. Good dog!

But my biggest thanks goes to you, lovely reader, for being there and actually reading this. It's great to have you along and I do appreciate you spending your time in joining me on this roller-caster ride with Evan and the rest of the team.

CAN YOU HELP?

With that in mind, and if you enjoyed it, I do have a favour to ask. Could you spare a moment to **leave a review or a rating**? A few words will do, but it's really the only way to help others like you discover the books. Probably the best way to help authors you like. Just visit the book's page on Amazon and leave a few words.

FREE BOOK FOR YOU

Visit my website and join up to the Rhys Dylan VIP Reader's Club and get a FREE novella, *The Wolf Hunts Alone*, by visiting:

www.rhysdylan.com

You will also be the first to hear about new releases via the few but fun emails I'll send you. This includes a no spam promise from me and you can unsubscribe at any time.

AUTHOR'S NOTE

Burnt Echo transports the team to the north-west corner of the patch. An area, like all of Wales, rich in history. The Romans really did mine silver and lead here and there are mineshafts all over the landscape. Be careful where you tread! But this case also exposes members of the team to the hidden dangers lurking in their own private lives as much as the criminals they're forced to deal with. And sometimes, those personal demons can be just as troublesome. Luckily, with a little help from their friends, everyone comes through. That's what working in a team is all about.

A band of brothers. Or, as Gil might say, and in order to keep everyone's gender cap straight (as if), a band of bothers. Oh, and if you haven't made it to the red kite feeding station at Bwlch Nant Yr Arian, put it on your bucket list. It is a sight to see.

And once again, who'd have thought that such a wonderful place as West Wales could harbour such heinous crimes. Of course, most of the time, the worst you're going to come across is a stray sheep on the road, or a bull in a field (my advice, go around).

Those of you who've read *The Wolf Hunts Alone* will know exactly what I mean. And who knows what and who Warlow is going to come up against next! So once again, thank you for sparing your precious time on this new endeavour. I hope I'll get the chance to show you more of this part of the world and that it'll give you the urge to visit.

Not everyone here is a murderer. Not everyone… Cue tense music!

All the best, and see you all soon, Rhys.

READY FOR MORE?
DCI Evan Warlow and the team are back in…

A Body of Water

When a delivery driver stumbles across the dead body of a recluse in a remote area within a stone's throw of the Llyn Brianne dam, his first thoughts are that the elderly man has had a heart attack.

But the knife sticking out of the corpse's chest tells a different story.

Why would anyone target such a defenceless victim? That's the first problem DCI Evan Warlow has to solve when he and his team arrive to investigate. But soon, some missing walkers, a secretive cult, and the unwelcome presence of paranormal-hunting podcasters all add to the team's woes. But the killer is abroad and has already ended one innocent life. If Warlow can't peel away the layers to get to the rotten heart of the case and quickly, more deaths are sure to follow.

Tick-Tock — June 2023

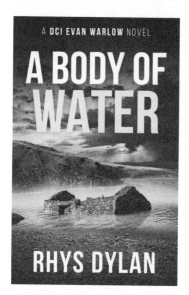

Made in the USA
Monee, IL
24 June 2023